PENGUIN BOOKS

A MOTHER'S BURDEN

H.Y. Poon is a civil servant living in Singapore. In a few decades of service, he has worked in an eclectic mix of areas such as manpower policy formulation, finance, investment promotion, enterprise development, and biodiversity conservation.

A Mother's Burden

H.Y. Poon

PENGUIN BOOKS

An imprint of Penguin Random House

PENGUIN BOOKS

USA | Canada | UK | Ireland | Australia
New Zealand | India | South Africa | China | Southeast Asia

Penguin Books is part of the Penguin Random House group of companies
whose addresses can be found at global.penguinrandomhouse.com

Published by Penguin Random House SEA Pvt. Ltd
9, Changi South Street 3, Level 08-01,
Singapore 486361

First published in Penguin Books by Penguin Random House SEA 2023

10 9 8 7 6 5 4 3 2 1

This is a work of fiction. Names, characters, places and incidents
are either the product of the author's imagination or are used fictitiously,
and any resemblance to any actual person, living or dead, events or
locales is entirely coincidental.

ISBN 9789815127164

Typeset in Adobe Caslon Pro by MAP Systems, Bangalore, India

www.penguin.sg

Contents

Chapter One

China, Song Dynasty, 1041 AD

The pursuit of justice—a noble cause or peasant entertainment? Hard to tell at times. While the spectators standing outside the county courtroom in Renli clearly craved entertainment, they were not getting much of it. Indeed, the herd had halved after a long day of uneventful cases.

The court was down to its last case of the day. There was, however, a delay as the litigants were locked in a raucous tug of war. The one trying to haul the group to the front was a young man in black-and-white mourning attire tailored with luxurious silk. Resisting him were two monks—one who was advanced in age and the other, not long out of his teens—in coarse, grey robes. All the huffing, puffing, and raised voices achieved little. The match was even, with a stalemate the result.

Was this a struggle of poor against rich? A conflict between the material and spiritual? A touch of the supernatural, perhaps? To the audience, the little scene at the side held promise for a juicy showdown. One could almost feel the crowd willing the three to get on with it.

'What is going on?' The deep voice of the presiding magistrate resonated from the opposite end of the room. Magistrate Liu Ye was seated, ramrod-straight, on a raised platform, close to the rear of this confined box of a room, which was not more than thirty paces across and twenty deep. His words parted the watching crowd, unveiling to him the trio. They called off their tussling match to face the magistrate.

'Ah, Young Master Ouyang,' the magistrate said as soon as he recognized the scion of the city's largest merchant family. 'Are you bringing a complaint? I hope our wait would not be long.'

'Your Honour, I do have a problem in need of resolution,' said Ouyang, stepping forward and dragging the elderly monk by his sleeve. The young monk followed as if tethered to his elder by a short and invisible cord.

All three knelt. The two bald monks were huddled together with the young merchant to their left. The elderly monk, with his snow-white beard and wrinkled forehead, settled down without a word, his face serene. In contrast, the junior monk could hardly suppress the trembling of his body as he used the old monk as a shield from the portly Ouyang. They went through the protocol of prostrating themselves in front of the judgement seat before straightening up, still on their knees.

While this was going on, Zhou Junxian, seated behind the magistrate to his right, leaned forward to whisper into the official's ear. A grandfatherly man with silvery hair and a matching goatee, Zhou was experienced in the art of dispensing counsel to higher authority. He advised Magistrate Liu on official matters big and small, out of a familiarity bred over nearly two decades of service to the same man.

At the same time, the magistrate's young personal attendant, Liu Yong, stepped up with a teapot in hand to pour hot tea into the porcelain cup next to the magistrate. He then took two steps back to return to his usual seat just behind his master's left shoulder. A young lad, Yong took care of everything considered too menial for anyone else, tasks like grinding ink sticks, arranging stationery, cleaning the spittoon pot, and, yes, serving tea.

'Before we start, Young Master Ouyang, please accept my deepest condolences on your father's demise,' the magistrate said in a softer tone. 'From the reluctance of the religious men, I suppose you are the complaining party? What is so serious and urgent that requires settlement at this time of bereavement?'

'My heart receives Your Honour's kindness,' Ouyang replied with practised courtesy. 'The matter I'm bringing before you has much to do with my father's passing. These wretched monks took advantage of our family at this difficult time to swindle us out of our money and wrong my father.'

The onlookers stirred afresh, sensing that their patience might be rewarded after all.

'Oh? Please proceed.'

Ouyang cleared his throat. 'My father, on his deathbed, made me promise to arrange for the famed Shuanglin Monastery on the Southern Hill to perform the funeral rites to elevate his status in heaven. Alas, these two did not do a proper job. Last night, my father told me in a dream that he was still locked in purgatory torment. Sir, I beseech you to grant my family justice.'

As Ouyang clasped his left hand over his right fist in front of him to round off his petition, Magistrate Liu could not help but notice the constellation of precious stones embedded in the gold and jade rings on his fingers. He thought this opulent show of wealth was rather unbecoming at a time of profound familial loss, but he supposed modesty had its limits in the face of overflowing affluence.

'Let us hear the details,' said the magistrate.

'Thank you, Sir. Once my father passed on, I was overwhelmed by the numerous tasks and arrangements I had to attend to, being the eldest son. By the time the dust settled, it was a mere three days before the burial. The next day, before sunrise, I made my way up the Southern Hill with a servant. At the gates of the monastery, a middle-aged caretaker received us. He said visitors were forbidden in the morning, though he would convey my request. When he came back, he informed us the monastery would send two of their monks to our house later in the day. I offered a donation three times that of a typical service.'

'Quite generous of you.'

'I was worried the monks might not turn up. The caretaker had insisted on half to be paid up front, which suited me fine. These two showed up quite late in the night though.'

'What did the rites involve?'

'Late at night, after the visitors had left, the old one would go through cycles of chanting while walking around the coffin. This went on for two nights. The young one maintained a spiritual vigil at our front gate to keep out evil spirits.'

'Go on.'

'The horrible dream I mentioned came the night before the burial. When the monks came to me the day after the funeral, asking to be paid, I refused. In fact, I demanded a full refund.'

'Including the deposit? They were not well pleased, I'm sure.'

'How they complained! They refused to budge at first. Only when I proposed to petition this court did they offer to waive the final payment to settle the issue.'

'Seems more than reasonable. What is the problem then?'

'Well, I said no. I want nothing less than a full refund and spiritual restitution for my father.'

His face passive, the magistrate nodded to acknowledge Ouyang's testimony before addressing the monks. 'Now for your side of the story.'

The older monk pressed both palms together in front of his chest in a prayer posture and let out a loud sigh. 'I will not take up your precious time to dispute his account of events. But this dream—it could have been the work of demons. Or perhaps the sins were too great for heaven to be moved by the most earnest of prayers. He could see we had not once let up on our efforts for two whole nights.'

'Was there any guarantee of the spiritual results?'

'No, we made no such promise,' answered the elder monk without hesitation. 'We agreed on two nights of rites, and we delivered.'

The magistrate hunched forward, facing the merchant. 'As a businessman, surely you understand the logic of commercial dealings.'

Ouyang shuffled a few inches on his knees towards the judgement seat. 'Shouldn't this be more than a business agreement? Does the monastery not owe some moral obligation to watch over the souls of people?' Some in the watching crowd sniggered, unimpressed by the merchant's desperate bid to swing the argument his way.

The magistrate leaned back, stroking his jet-black goatee. 'I hear both of you. I cannot say this case is especially complicated. The buyer has received the services bargained for. He is not satisfied with the spiritual result, though that was not promised in the first place.'

As the official delivered the opening lines of the pronouncement, he caught a movement to his left. Liu Yong had moved forward again to top up his teacup, which was already quite full, before rotating the cup half a turn clockwise.

There it was, clear as day. *At this late hour? For this straightforward case?* These thoughts raced through the magistrate's mind. Yet, he knew Yong would not take such a course of action lightly.

'Having said that,' he continued, nary missing a beat, 'the religious aspect of this case does introduce complications. The court will adjourn as I consider this issue more carefully.'

Magistrate Liu stood up, the knee-height platform creating the impression of a towering figure despite his medium build. As he executed a sharp right pivot and headed for the side exit, the stiff, horizontal flaps jutting out from the sides of his black hat bobbed about in response to the sudden movement. His plain, dark-green official robe, which flowed all the way down to his ankles, interrupted only by a satin belt around his waist, swept the ground. A few staff members followed him out, leaving the bystanders to quiz one another on what had happened.

The chatter from the courtroom receded from behind the magistrate as he glided down the corridor and into the backroom. 'Where is he?' he said while settling down on his designated chair. 'He signalled for the recess, did he not?'

Adviser Zhou took charge and dispatched a constable to fetch Yong. A hush descended on the room, the only sound being the rhythmic drumming of the magistrate's fingers on the tea table beside him.

The constable returned a moment later to report that Yong was conversing with the litigants.

'What about?' asked Zhou.

'I can't tell. He was talking to the old monk and pouring him tea.'

'What? Tell him to come in here. Now!'

The magistrate held up his right hand, putting an end to the tapping. 'Wait. Let him be. He knows what he is doing. Most of the time anyway.'

Thus, they waited wordlessly, the magistrate staring ahead while everyone else avoided his gaze.

A few uncomfortable moments later, the thumping of hastened footsteps on wooden floorboards signalled the approach of someone in a hurry. Sure enough, Yong's tall, lanky frame shot through the door, stopping abruptly in front of his two superiors. He had some explaining to do but Zhou, face flushed, beat him to it.

'What were you thinking, making us wait for you?'

'I'm sorry, I—'

'This abrupt recess is embarrassing for the magistrate!'

Yong took a few deep breaths to regain his composure. 'Sir, Mr Zhou, my deepest apologies. There was something I needed to check.'

'Well?' said the magistrate, still as steady as ever.

'Frauds, Sir,' Yong said. 'They're frauds.'

Chapter Two

'Frauds?' said Zhou. 'Who?'

'The monks, Mr Zhou.'

'No, no. There was no promise of results, remember? Just because a buyer does not have his expectations met in a commercial transaction does not mean he has been duped.'

'Mr Zhou is right,' said the magistrate, still seated. 'The most you can accuse the monks of is profiting from people's superstitions. That is not in itself fraudulent. Even if the monks had no intention of delivering the spiritual outcome, it would not matter. A claim based on superstition is unverifiable and therefore unenforceable.'

'I understand, Sir. But what if the monks are not who they say they are?'

The magistrate lifted his eyebrows. 'That would be different. Impersonation for financial gain is a crime and, unlike superstitious beliefs, actually verifiable.'

Zhou took a step towards Yong, his forehead creased. 'This is a serious allegation. To test your theory, we would need to haul the monks to the monastery to verify their identities. If you are wrong, they and their esteemed monastery would have good reasons to feel aggrieved when it is apparent Ouyang's case is weak.'

'I'm not speculating. I know they are not from the monastery.'

'Extracted a confession over tea and chit-chat, did you?'

'Sort of. After engaging the old monk in small talk to soften him up, I asked him whether Elder Monk Zhi Yuan was well. He took a sip of tea before answering the Elder Monk was indeed well.'

'You know an elder monk from the monastery?'

'Oh no, Mr Zhou. I made the name up.'

Zhou stared at Yong for a brief moment, then pulled a grin as his gaze softened. 'Little rascal. You and your bag of tricks.'

The magistrate let out a hearty laugh. 'What aroused your suspicion?'

'Their behaviour throughout was odd. The reluctance to come to court, for one. How about the sudden swing from not ceding an inch to forgoing half the agreed price? I also found the role of the junior monk suggestive. Rather than warding off evil spirits at the front gate, perhaps he was on the lookout for real monks from Shuanglin or law enforcement personnel.'

'Fair points,' said the magistrate.

'Then, there was the timing. Why did it take till late into the night before the monks turned up for the job? Quite likely, their accomplice, the monastery caretaker, waited until the end of his workday to get in touch with them. This suggested the monks did not reside in the monastery.'

Smiling, the magistrate rose from his seat. 'Well, your little trick has made my job a lot easier. Does away with the need for further investigation.' He started to lead the way back to the courtroom. 'Elder Monk Zhi Yuan, did you say?'

'Yes, Sir,' replied Yong, scurrying after his master.

'All right. Let us finish this.'

Yong surveyed the three litigants, who were back on their knees. Ouyang fidgeted as he had done before the break. Either his kneecaps were feeling the pressure of supporting his heft, or he was uncomfortable with how the trial was unfolding. The monks kept their heads down and palms together in a serene prayer posture, seemingly oblivious to the surrounding noise.

The magistrate picked up the oblong wood block in front of him and slammed it on his table a few times to demand silence. Taking his time to lean back, he supported his elbows on the arms of the chair and rested his clasped hands on his belly.

'There is nothing unusual about people striving to improve their lot in life,' said the magistrate. 'In fact, it is an everyday occurrence in human affairs. What society deems unfair and crass is the rich throwing money around to buy such upgrades in lieu of hard work and earned merit. We see it around us all too frequently—kickbacks to grease the wheels of commerce, gratuities to ensure honoured seats in public places, and donations to pad up personal reputations. It is all about using gold and silver to hoard every conceivable advantage. Today, we heard that this procurement of advantages does not cease when one crosses over to the netherworld.'

At resumption, there was already a shadow over Ouyang's face. With the magistrate's fresh remarks, all he could do was to stare at the ground, shoulders slumped.

The official continued. 'I note the generosity of the religious figures before me in forgoing half the agreed payment. A reasonable observer would conclude they have acted with decency.'

While the old monk betrayed no emotion, his junior curved the right edge of his mouth into a faint smile.

'What is most regrettable,' said the magistrate, 'is the dragging of the good name of Shuanglin through the mud. We must put that right. I am sure the monastery would wish to facilitate an amicable ending to this sorry episode.' Many amongst the audience nodded in agreement. 'I therefore propose a constable escort both monks and Young Master Ouyang back up to the monastery. Proper rites can then be administered to appease the soul of Old Master Ouyang.'

'Your Honour,' said the elder monk with admirable composure, 'we should not trouble the Ouyang family any further. We can administer the rites at their residence for as long as is required.'

The young monk nodded with no lack of enthusiasm. Ouyang himself looked at the magistrate with a pleading expression that suggested he was not keen on a repeat trek up the hill.

The magistrate leaned towards the monk. 'This, I insist. I will write a letter addressed to the Abbot. You can hand the letter to him.' With eyes that reached into the souls of men, he stared at the elderly monk whose lips were quivering.

'But, hang on, what am I saying?' the magistrate said in mock exasperation. 'How could you pick out the Abbot when you do not know there is no Elder Monk Zhi Yuan at Shuanglin?'

At this, the mouth of the older monk hung open while the young one started shaking. Once over the initial shock, both prostrated themselves. 'Mercy, Your Honour, mercy! Our crime deserves ten thousand deaths!'

'Owning up at last,' said the magistrate, the last word accompanied by a forceful meeting of the wooden block and table. 'Impersonating Shuanglin monks to prey on a bereaved family. How many victims, I wonder, have fallen for your ruse? Mercy? You and your accomplice on the hill will receive none from me. Men, lock them up.'

Two constables swung into action to drag the monks away. Many of the onlookers nodded their approval, impressed that the magistrate had with little apparent effort extracted a confession from the monks. A chorus of praise and applause broke out, a fitting conclusion to a long day in court. Ouyang's repeated kowtows to thank the official were both vigorous and heartfelt.

The magistrate brought his oblong block down on the table to signal the end of the day for the court. The anticipated clack was, however, drowned out by a resounding clang of the brass gong at the gates of the magistrate's compound. Everyone's attention shifted to the direction of the gates, for the striking of the gong meant only one thing: Someone had an urgent case to bring to the court.

As it turned out, it was a dozen or so people, dressed in simple garments associated with farmers, ambling towards the courtroom. Another group of townspeople trailed behind, drawn by the extraordinary sight of three farmers in the front group hauling and steadying a flat wheelbarrow on which lay a lifeless body. The sackcloth over the body had slipped off at both ends, revealing the feet and head of an adolescent male.

Three women followed behind the wheelbarrow. The one in the middle, slumped and propped up by the other two, did not look far different from one who had lost her mind—dishevelled hair, dusty clothes, and puffy eyes that had had the last bit of moisture drained from them.

The murmuring court audience parted to let the procession through.

Magistrate Liu slammed down his trusty block a few times to restore order. 'What is this about?'

From the group of farmers, a wiry man with dark, leathery skin advanced two steps. 'My name is Lin Yifeng, head of Donghu village. This pitiful boy lying here is from our village. We found him dead at his home more than two hours ago.'

'What happened?'

'Your Honour, this woman,' the village headman said as he jabbed his finger at the middle of the female trio, at the one still in obvious distress. 'She killed her son.'

Chapter Three

Magistrate Liu came down from the platform and made his way to the wheelbarrow in front of the group. He pulled down the sackcloth and placed his left hand on the boy's neck. 'No pulse, and warmth has left the body.'

Next, the magistrate checked the body for wounds. There were some scratch marks on the hands. On the arms and legs were striped bruises, some fresher than others. Around each ankle ran a ring of redness where some surface skin had been scraped off.

The magistrate draped the blanket back over the body and returned to the judgement seat. The audience quietened down, eager to consume the next act of this bonus drama. On the magistrate's order, a constable dragged the accused woman forward and knelt her down in front of the platform.

'What is your name?' asked the magistrate.

The woman was hunched so far forward she was almost in a crouching position. No recognizable word emerged from her lips, just a rasping, suppressed wail that indicated her strength and voice had long been spent.

The village headman took another step forward. 'If I may, her name is Li Yingxiu, a widow who lives with Xiaodong, her only child, in our village.'

'Can you tell us what happened?'

'I will try. Most of us had gone back to our houses after spring worship at the village temple. As usual, Yingxiu and her son did not join us. We were resting when those of us near to Yingxiu's house heard a loud "pop". This was followed by Yingxiu shouting and Xiaodong screaming. Truth be told, the cries did not bother us as we are quite used to it.'

'This happened often?'

'Yes, Sir. The boy was slow up here,' said Lin, tapping his right temple with his forefinger. 'Sometimes, he threw violent tantrums for no reason. She had to be strict to stop him from getting out of hand.'

'What happened next?'

'Xiaodong stopped screaming, and there was a moment of calm. Then, out of nowhere, we heard Yingxiu's scream, like the howling of an animal. Something was not right, so I hurried over to take a look. So did a few other villagers. Yingxiu was sitting on the floor, wailing, with a broken stick by her side. The boy was lying still amidst spilled food and pieces of smashed crockery.'

The headman looked back at a few men in the group. 'One of the men went over, put his fingers on the boy's neck and told us he had a weak pulse. There were fresh striped bruises on the boy's legs and arms that probably came from the stick next to Yingxiu.'

'Did you ask Mdm Li what had happened?'

'We tried but she just kept crying. At that point, we thought we could still save the boy, so we brought him to the physician in town.' The headman then pointed to one of the women who had propped up Yingxiu. 'My wife and another neighbour accompanied her. The physician could do nothing but confirm the boy was gone. After that, the only thing we could do was to bring him and the mother to you.'

'Did she say anything of note on her way here?'

The headman looked to his wife, who glanced left and right before speaking up. 'She has been this way since we left her house, switching between wailing and sobbing. The only thing she said was "Xiaodong, it's Mother's fault." Said it a few times, she did.'

The magistrate turned back to the headman. 'Are you saying Mdm Li beat the boy to death?'

'Well, there was no one else in the house,' said the headman who paused and glanced in the direction of his villagers. 'There's something else.' He beckoned another woman, the other half of the double-act that had held Yingxiu up, to come to the front. 'This is Xue, a friend of Yingxiu. She can tell you more about what Yingxiu had said to her.'

Xue, who seemed to be in her mid-twenties, hesitated. She shuffled two steps forward while clinging on to her long ponytail with both hands. She then knelt and transferred her gaze to the floor.

'Xue,' said the magistrate, 'are you close to Mdm Li?'

With her head still hung low, Xue began to speak in a voice that had the onlookers at the back craning their necks and cupping their ears. 'Not very, because I have my chores while Yingxiu is always busy with her hand-craft work and taking care of Xiaodong ... ' Emotion welled up in her voice at the mention of the boy's name. 'Sir, I beg your pardon. I've never been in such a place.'

'It is quite all right. I know it is not easy for you. Go on when you are ready.'

'Xue,' prodded an old woman behind her, 'tell the magistrate what the woman said about what she wanted to do.'

Xue shifted the weight on her knees. 'Yingxiu has had a hard life. She works all day and has not experienced a good night's sleep in years. Look at her head of grey hair. You would not guess she is only in her thirties. With Xiaodong's condition and her own health deteriorating, she worried a lot and did not mean what she said. Please have mercy, Sir.'

'I will take into consideration her circumstances and state of mind. If she told you something important, you should let us know.'

Xue put her right hand over her mouth as if to stop the words from coming out. Lowering her hand and looking up at the magistrate, she finally spoke. 'Yingxiu is always worried about how Xiaodong would be cared for when she is no longer around. Her husband died four years ago, and she has no relative to turn to. She told me perhaps the only way out was for Xiaodong to leave this world before her.'

'Tell them what she said to you last month,' said the same old woman behind her.

'Mother, stay out of this,' said Xue as she shot a glance behind her, then turned back to the magistrate. 'Last month, when Xiaodong was again down with a bout of high fever, she confided in me that she sometimes thought of …'

The magistrate, and everyone else, waited.

'She … she said she thought of ending it all for Xiaodong and herself. When I chided her, she asked me what I would do in her position. Sir, I'm ashamed I could not answer her this time.' Xue buried her face in her hands and sobbed.

The magistrate waited a moment for her to collect herself. 'You mean she had mentioned this to you before, that she wanted to kill her son and herself?'

It took some time before Xue lifted her head. 'She mentioned this to me twice before, once about four months ago and on another occasion more than a year ago. Each time, she had been under great stress and had come around after I talked to her. But this time, she was especially distressed.'

'What was different this time?'

Xue hung her head again and closed her eyes.

'What is it, Xue? What was different with Mdm Li this time?'

Slowly, Xue opened her eyes. 'Yingxiu has been ill for weeks. She went to consult a physician, who said … who said she had at most a year to live.'

The crowd chattered anew, drawing its own conclusion.

'She is a kind person, and would never do anything to harm Xiaodong,' Xue added, a little too late.

Xue's mother knelt beside her. 'Your Honour, I have another matter to report.'

'Mother!' said Xue, reaching out to grab her mother's forearm.

The old woman brushed Xue's hand aside. 'Two weeks ago, Yingxiu asked for rat poison from Xue. I told this silly girl, "Don't you realize what she wants the poison for?" We could have been accomplices for murder.'

'Yingxiu said the rats in her house were driving her crazy,' said Xue. 'Anyway, I did not give her any.'

'What did she say to that?'

'She was unhappy at first. Then … then she said she would find her own.'

The magistrate directed his next question at the accused. 'These people are saying you killed your own child, a most serious charge. Do you have anything to say?'

Still no response beyond sobbing.

The magistrate leaned back. 'This case is most troubling. We will hold Mdm Li in custody and question her again when she is ready to talk. Meanwhile, I will retain the villagers for further questioning. Men, escort Mdm Li to her cell. Court is dismissed.'

The wooden block was slammed down on the magistrate's table to finally bring the session to a close.

Two constables picked up the limp Yingxiu from the floor and began to drag her out through the side door as they would an inanimate sack of rice. As she was about to be hoisted through the exit, Yingxiu snapped her head up and opened her eyes wide. 'I killed him!' she said in a hoarse voice that was nevertheless loud enough to catch the attention of all who were in and around the courtroom. 'I killed my son!'

Chapter Four

Despite Yingxiu's outburst on her way out of the courtroom, the magistrate did not pull her back, which was just as well. Zhou, who had followed her and the constables to her jail cell, reported that she had withdrawn into her shell right away.

Magistrate Liu parcelled out the work to be done. Together with Zhou, he would interview the villagers. He assigned the task of examining the scene of the incident to Yong, who caught hold of Constable Niu to accompany him to the village. The headman instructed a young man from the village to lead them there.

As Yong was marching across the front courtyard with his little squad, he caught sight of Liu Zhong, the magistrate's only son, emerging from the family residence and also making his way out of the compound. Zhong walked at a pace with a hunched profile, much like a deer trying to avoid the attention of predators. He slowed down once he joined up with Yong, behind Niu and the young villager.

'Where are you off to in such a hurry?' Zhong said as he cast a furtive glance back over his shoulder. 'Quite a bit of excitement back there.'

'Off to investigate a crime scene,' said Yong. 'You're in a rush yourself, Young Master. Quite clever of you to make your move amidst some disorder.'

'Don't know what you're talking about,' said Zhong with a wink as they emerged from the compound and turned right on to the busy street. 'I'm going to a friend's house. To study, of course.'

'A bit hard to do that without books on you, don't you think? What's wrong with studying at home?'

The pair of youngsters attracted curious stares from a few passers-by. The young gentleman with smooth complexion in fine attire, a member of the esteemed social class of scholars, was being chided by his equally young servant with worn clothes and a tan from more than his fair share of outdoor work.

'Cooped up at home all week,' said Zhong. 'Nothing but studying. I'll have you know that I dreamt of studying last night. It's either going out or going crazy.'

Yong slowed down to let Niu and the young villager walk out of earshot. 'You could have at least made an effort to disguise your intent. Nicely cleaned up, neatly combed hair, your best robe and cap, new shoes. You even smell like a girl. From the metallic clapping of the coins in your pocket, I'd say you sweet-talked your mother again into financing your little evening excursion.'

Zhong landed a playful jab on Yong's shoulder. 'What can I say? Nothing escapes you, my good brother.'

'I've told you many times not to call me that. Your mother will kill me if she heard. You would be wise to come home early, or you'd cop an earful from Old Master again.'

'A nag, you are. I cannot decide if you're more like Mother or Father. Hey, I'm going this way,' said Zhong as they neared a right turn into a side street.

'Oh, that friend. Now I know there'd be little studying done.'

'Good music, food, and wine never did any harm to anyone.'

'Waste of time.'

'I knew you'd say that. Anyway, got to run. Have fun, good brother.'

'I said don't ... ' Yong could not finish his sentence before Zhong scooted off. He could only smile as he stood and watched Zhong complete his getaway. Since the two had grown up together as playmates, there was some basis for Zhong to address Yong as a brother. However, Yong would never allow that line to be blurred. Though he had adopted his master's family name after being taken in as a nameless toddler, he was keenly aware he was only a servant.

He ran to catch up with Niu and their escort. A brisk walk would take them to the village in about an hour. They needed to hurry if they were to complete their assignment before darkness set in.

Along the way, Yong tried to glean information from the young villager. It was a sorry tale of a woman who, on her own, had cared for a child with severe mental disabilities. To get by, Yingxiu sewed odds and ends to sell to merchants in the city. Twice every week, on the same days, she brought Xiaodong along with her to the city in the afternoon to deliver completed assignments and to take on new ones. In fact, she had gone to town for her errand this day, right before the tragic incident.

Such was the compactness of Renli that the three young men left the busyness of town behind within half an hour. The landscape of small buildings packed close to neighbouring units morphed into greenery until, another quarter of an hour later, all they had before them was a lonely dirt road flanked by untamed vegetation and smatterings of farmland.

'It's always me,' said Niu from out of the blue, wearing a sullen look. An unlit lantern swung about in his left hand while a filled cloth bag was clasped under his right armpit. 'I'm missing my dinner because of you. Listen, my stomach is growling.'

Yong had to admit that, in the quietness of the early evening, the rumbling from Niu's gut was quite noticeable. 'Look at it this way. Amongst the constables, we trust you the most. You should be proud of it.'

'So what? Doing more, doing less, all of us constables are paid the same pittance.' This was true, exacerbated by the magistrate's absolute ban on collecting bribes and informal fees from the people. 'I do so much more work and follow you and the bosses around. Going back to my parents' farm is starting to sound quite attractive.'

'You get to have more fun than the others. Besides,' Yong said, prodding Niu's round belly with his forefinger, 'you have put on weight again. Cow in name and cow in size. Some exercise will do you some good. Don't worry, they'll save your dinner.'

'They'd better,' came a growl to synchronize with another stomach rumble.

'The village is in front, to the right,' said the young villager, perhaps to encourage Niu. He pointed to a side path a hundred paces ahead, concealed in part by thick vegetation.

Once they turned into the side path, the few houses nearest the village entrance came into view. The escorting young man pointed out that the village was not large, made up of seventeen houses sitting on a narrow strip of land, hemmed in by a flooded paddy field on one side and a wooded parcel of land on the other.

Outside the first house at the village entrance, a hunched old man sat by the door. He barely moved as the three of them approached, though he acknowledged the intrusion of the two strangers by tilting his head to face them.

'Don't mind him,' said the young man. 'He spends most of the day sitting in front of the house while the rest of his family go about their business. Since his house sits at the only entrance to the village, we call him Old Gatekeeper.'

Yingxiu's residence stood diagonally opposite the old man's house, its back about twenty paces from the edge of the woods. Right in front of the closed door, a young woman sat on a short stool. As Yong's party approached, she stood and pushed the stool aside.

'The headman's daughter,' said the young villager to Niu. 'He told her to make sure nobody goes into the house.'

The young woman greeted them with a nod. While the young man explained his errand to her, Yong pulled open both panels of the door.

Five paces from the door opening stood an old wooden table. Yong noticed the rats lying motionless. One was on the table next to a half-empty bowl of porridge, the second, on the floor in a puddle of spilled porridge next to the table, and the last one, a few feet away at the foot of the cooking stove near the far corner of the house. Flies danced around, unconcerned with the new visitors.

Yong stepped into the house, his movements all of a sudden deliberate and his mood sombre. Niu and the young man followed him in while the young lady remained outside.

'Try not to wander around,' Yong said to Niu and the young man. 'And please, do not disturb anything.'

Chapter Five

Odours of dust and mould, mingled with the stench of stale food and urine, made for a nauseating mix.

'Did you see these rats when you were here?' Yong said to the young man, who shook his head.

On the table, besides the dead rat and the half bowl of plain rice porridge, were two pairs of chopsticks, an empty bowl and a spoon, all lying about in a haphazard sort of way. A solitary stool stood two paces from one side of the table. On the adjacent edge, a short bench lay on its side. Next to the toppled bench, one of the dead rats lay sprawled belly-up in the porridge puddle, together with a smashed clay pot, a wooden ladle, an overturned bowl, and a spoon.

Just three paces from the table lay the broken stick the villagers had talked about and a thin piece of wood. Yong picked up the wooden specimen which approximated a rectangular shape. Both flat sides were etched with arcs of indents that looked like teeth marks.

'The piece of wood you're holding,' said the young villager. 'It was right beside the boy.'

'He had a fit?'

'He was not moving when I arrived. Wouldn't surprise me. I've heard it happened quite often.'

The only two windows, the one that Yong had seen from outside the house and the other at the back, were left open. Evening light angled in from the back window, illuminating dust particles suspended in the air. Near the back, flax rope of about one-and-half arm's length tied to one of the legs of the only bed in the house caught Yong's eyes. But first things first. To start constructing a picture of what had happened, he had to sweep the ground for signs of movements before they got trampled over.

The house was typical of any in a rural village in that the dirt floor, without covering, was little different in composition from the ground outside—just compacted earth with a roof over it. A trail of shoeprints from the door leading to the table and similar ones near to the porridge pool could be made out quite easily. These prints only served to confirm the villagers' reports of how they came in to attend to the situation. No fresh insight there.

'Stay here,' said Yong, firmness in his voice. The young villager stared back with eyebrows raised. But since the adult in uniform made no move to challenge Yong's authority, the young man did as instructed.

Yong combed the ground between the table and the cooking stove, treading with caution. He walked around like he was following a set route, all the while eyeing the ground. 'Interesting.'

Niu stepped forward. 'Prints?'

'It's the invisible that's of interest. The shoeprints and footprints around this place seem to belong to a woman and a child, as you would expect. But check out these other patches. Someone has done some sweeping over of the ground.'

'So, the lady has done some sweeping. How's that interesting?'

'The sweeping is not like that of general house-cleaning which would have covered whole areas. These patches are not much larger than the size of a human foot. Nor is the sweeping random. It follows a trail, or a few connected trails.' Yong lowered his voice as Niu came closer. 'Someone wanted to hide traces of his or her movement.'

Squatting down, Yong waddled around as his eyes scanned the ground. It was not long before he stopped and picked up some particles and brought them to his eye level. 'Odd.'

'Something else?'

'Different.' Yong fingered the orange bits in his hand. 'Quite unlike the dull brown of the ground. Not obvious to the eye, mind you, but there are bits in a few spots.'

Yong stood to face the young villager. 'Did any of the villagers who were here walk around the house? Here, for example, near the cooking stove?'

'Not as far as I can remember.'

'You sure?'

'Yeah. The older men and women had taken charge of the situation. A couple of us stood back, so I could observe all that went on.'

Yong took two steps towards the front window. Through this opening, he could see the village entrance to the left and a few other houses to the right. Old Gatekeeper was still in the same place, looking in his direction. Inside, to the right of the window, stood a small wooden table. Like a blanket, a thick layer of dust covered the junk sitting on it.

'Does Mdm Li always leave her windows open?'

'When she's in the house, I suppose, if the weather is not too cold. Like the rest of us, she keeps them shut when she goes out.'

'You said she went to town this afternoon.'

'Yeah.'

'Did she close the windows when she went out?'

'Guess so. Like I said, that is what we do.'

'What's this?' Yong muttered under his breath as he scrutinized the contents on and under the table.

Just then, a baby's cry pierced the silence. Yong swivelled around to check out the source of the disturbance at the entrance to the house. A baby squirmed and bellowed while clasped to his mother's hip by a combination of her left arm and a length of cloth slung across her body. A couple of other villagers had also come by, though they were sensible enough not to step into the house. Niu started to make his way to the entrance.

'Hang on, Niu,' said Yong, who then spoke to the young villager. 'Would you mind closing the door and staying outside to make sure no one comes in? I don't want anyone peeking in through the windows either.'

'You sure you don't need me here?'

'We'll let you know if we need to trouble you again.'

The young man hesitated but eventually complied. When the door swung shut, Yong beckoned Niu over to the table loaded with junk—chipped jars and broken pots of various sizes. 'Do you see this?'

'What should I be looking at?'

'These vessels on the table. You can make out dust lines hugging close to the bases, exposing small slivers of cleaner table surface that should have been tucked underneath. It was as though someone had nudged and displaced them slightly. But there are also these finger imprints on the surfaces and at the edges of the vessels.'

'Where?'

'Here and here,' said Yong as he pointed to the marked spots. 'You need to look carefully to spot them.'

'What does that mean?'

'It means instead of nudging the jars and pots, someone had picked them up and put them back down, just not at exactly the original positions. It is quite impossible to touch these things without leaving any traces given the coat of dust.' Yong lifted up every item and every lid but found nothing of interest.

Yong walked across the room to another small table, on top of which sat a covered squarish bamboo box. The same coats of dust, dust lines and finger imprints. Opening up the box and finding only a few trinkets, he replaced the lid.

He checked the cooking area for more signs of disturbance. This place he found to be relatively free of dust, which was not surprising given its daily use, so no tell-tale dust lines could be seen. Other than a bed, chest, and cupboard on the other side of the house, there was no other furniture to search through. He opened up the chest and then the cupboard. Again, nothing stood out. Backing up two steps, he lifted his gaze and blew a soft, drawn-out whistle.

Resting on top of the cupboard were no ordinary household items. One was a white ceramic urn with a blue painting of a dragon floating on patches of cloud. The other, placed a few inches next to the urn, was a wooden tablet with words in black, resting upright on a matching rectangular base.

As Yong stared at the cupboard top, Niu in turn stared at him.

'You're not going to do it, are you?' said Niu.

'As a matter of fact, I am.' Yong picked up the standing stool and toppled bench, the only pieces of moveable furniture tall enough to help someone reach the top of the cupboard.

'Those are the man's ashes and altar tablet, for goodness' sake.'

Ignoring Niu's remarks, Yong proceeded to examine the sitting surfaces of the stool and bench. 'Look what we have here. The same orange bits of soil on a few spots of this bench seat.'

'Don't see them.'

'Pay attention, will you? A few bits pressed into the grooves. He would have tried to brush the soil off but did not do a thorough enough job. He stepped on this, Niu. No two ways about it.'

Yong placed the bench at the front of the cupboard and climbed up. When he stood straight, he could take in a full view of the top surface as his chin had cleared this level with room to spare. He could tell this had not been the case for the person whose movements he was now tracing. At the edge of the top surface, to his left and right, shoulder-width apart, were prints of the person's hands. He—if the person was a man—had to hold on to the edge to lift himself up on tiptoe.

The words on the tablet informed Yong that the name of Yingxiu's late husband was Sun Jie. The tablet itself sat on a piece of folded cloth that was so dusty and discoloured it probably had not seen water for ages. Yong was not surprised to find dust lines next to the outer edges of the cloth and urn. He picked up the plaque and unfolded the cloth package but found nothing within. With both hands, he lifted up the urn to see what was underneath. Still nothing. He was tempted to uncover the lid to check inside, but decided against it. That would be a step too far, a gross disrespect to the dead.

Niu pressed his palms together, shook them and mouthed an inaudible prayer, seeking forgiveness for disturbing the spirits. Yong returned the altar to its original state and got down from the stool. After clapping dust off his hands, he restored the bench to its upright position by the table.

He moved on to the bed. As he neared the corner of the bed with the flax rope, the smell of urine that had been hanging in the room hit him with greater intensity. He squatted down and fingered the rope. Next to it were a few stones and a soiled rattle drum—a small, two-sided drum mounted on a stick like a lollipop, with two stringed beads that would strike the drum when the toy was flipped from side to side.

Niu walked over. 'What is the flax rope for?'

'To keep the boy tied up here, I suppose. There were bruises around the boy's ankles.'

The stench seemed to originate from two sources: a darkened patch on the floor and another one on the bed mat. Placed beside the wet patch on the floor were a bucket, a third filled with water, and a piece of damp cloth draped over the rim. Another taller bucket sat next to the first one, whose purpose was to soak some clothes in water. Pulling up the dripping clothes, Yong detected the same disagreeable odour of urine.

The fast-dimming light outside the back window reminded Yong of the late hour. About twenty paces ahead, the trees of the woods swayed in the breeze, silhouettes standing over a natural fence of thick ground vegetation.

As he approached the window, a tiny trace of orange soil near the bottom left corner of the window sill caught his attention. After pinching the soil sample, he went to the door and pushed it open to find five villagers and a baby watching him. 'Niu, keep everybody here.'

Once outside the back window, he looked around for shoeprints, though the ground was too hard to yield anything distinct. Of greater interest was a trail of the orange soil, too sparse to notice if he was not hunting for it, leading to the edge of the woods. Here, a row of wild shrubs separated the village from the wooded expanse.

The faint trail of orange soil led to a hedge that yielded sideways in opposite directions, a sign that someone had parted it. On the ground were a few clumps of the orange stuff. They were about the size of the digit of his forefinger, the most sizeable he had seen thus far. Picking up one of the clumps, he squeezed it with his fingers to find it still moist and malleable.

He parted the thorny hedge, taking care to avoid getting scratched, and stepped in through the opening. After battling through waist-high bushes that seemed determined to claw him back, he emerged into a clearing, seven frustrating steps later. The ground felt soft and moist though not muddy. Its colour was a lighter shade of yellow, not the orange that was now familiar to Yong. Ahead, more patches of unwelcoming thorny shrubs surrounded the clearing.

Stooping down, Yong found shoeprints he could not make out clearly for the ground was still too firm. He would have to move further into the woods to search for orange soil that was soft enough to cling on to a man's shoes.

He looked up but could not see far. Darkness had caught up with him, the scant evening light filtered by the considerable green canopy. Even with a lit lantern, it would be a challenge to pick up meaningful observations. Worse, half-blind trampling could disturb precious clues. The call of forest insects seemed to invite him to venture further. *Not now*, Yong decided. He would do it first thing next morning.

He came out of the woods to find the group still gathered by the house entrance. 'Can someone come into the village through the woods?' asked Yong.

'Nobody does that,' answered the headman's daughter. 'It's full of thorny shrubs and the ground uneven and soft. Worse after the rain last week.'

Yong re-entered the house with Niu, who closed the door. 'What was he searching for?' Yong whispered to no one in particular.

Stepping over to the bed and pulling the bed mat aside, he exposed the outlines of a rectangular cover cut out of the bed platform. Niu, having lit the lantern, came closer to add illumination. Yong dug his fingertips into the thin groove surrounding the cover to lift it up, revealing a compartment storing a few coins, a thin stack of loose papers and a roughly-stitched booklet. He flipped through the papers and booklet.

'Anything?' said Niu.

'Nothing unusual. Scribblings of numbers, names, and addresses.'

Yong set the papers, booklet, and cover back to their original places and returned to the cooking space. On an old and small table were stacked empty bowls, chopsticks, spoons, a jar of oil, small jars of condiments, and a partially-covered wooden bucket with a few cups' worth of uncooked rice. Samples of these would be brought back for examination.

By now, there was no natural light left. Yong decided it was time to tidy up and seal off the place. Niu whipped out long strips of paper with official court writings and insignias to paste across the outward faces of the windows after closing them to deter tampering. Once they got out of the house, Niu rounded up the house-sealing procedure by pasting two paper strips across the panels of the closed door.

As they were leaving the village, Yong saw that Old Gatekeeper had vacated his post. The house was dark and quiet, indicating he had turned in for the night. Yong had wanted to talk to him. No matter. There would be time for that the next day.

Chapter Six

By the time Yong and Niu reached their home base, the magistrate's compound had settled into a moonlit stillness. Apart from dozing night sentries, the constables and servants had retired back to their silent quarters. Only the few patches of illumination emanating from the main residence building hinted at activity.

Yong rushed over to the study to find the magistrate at his desk with Zhou seated facing him.

'There you are,' said the magistrate to Yong, who went over to stand next to Zhou. 'We were going through our findings from interviewing the villagers. Not much new information there. Something strange about the woman and child, though. They lived among the community but did not seem part of it.'

'That's right,' said Zhou. 'Everyone was required to attend the festival at the village temple this afternoon, yet no one thought to include them.'

'Everyone was there?' said Yong.

'Everyone who was able to, except Mdm Li and her son.'

Yong nodded. 'How is Mdm Li?'

'The same,' said the magistrate. 'I reckon we will not be getting anything out of her tonight.'

'The coroner identified poisoning as the cause of death,' said Zhou. 'No broken bones, and the bruises on the body are not severe enough to have killed the boy. Seems she poisoned her son but could not bear to take her own life. What did you find out?'

Yong started by telling them what he saw around the dining table and the bed at Yingxiu's house. 'I think while Mdm Li was preparing the evening meal with Xiaodong tied to the bed, the boy wet himself, messing up the floor and bed mat. At some point, Mdm Li discovered this, after she had served the cooked food into two bowls.'

'And that,' said Zhou, 'caused Mdm Li to lose her temper and mete out punishment.'

'Not yet. The soiled clothes soaking in the pail of water shows she had cleaned him up and changed his clothes. Then she let him eat his dinner while she cleaned up.'

'And the boy acted up while eating his dinner and swept things off the table?' asked the magistrate.

'Yes, the bowl and the clay pot. The breaking of the pot explains the "pop" sound the headman and other villagers heard before the shouting. That was one mishap too many for Mdm Li, and she snapped. At some point during the beating, the boy went into a fit. She grabbed a thin wedge of wood and lodged it in his mouth to prevent him from biting his tongue.'

The magistrate nodded. 'This would account for the period of silence mentioned by Mr Lin.'

'That's right. After some time, the boy stopped moving. Her distress turned to shock when she could not detect any sign of life. She panicked and screamed, attracting the attention of her neighbours. We heard from the villagers what happened after that.'

'So, the poison was delivered through the food,' said the magistrate.

'That is likely the case. But I don't think Mdm Li did it.'

'Why do you say that?'

'I found traces left by a person other than the villagers who went to help. There was an intruder who sneaked into the house when no one was in.'

The older men lifted their eyebrows in unison.

'What traces?' asked the magistrate.

'Someone had taken the effort to sweep the ground in patches not much larger than a man's foot. It looked like he was trying to cover his tracks.' Yong told them about the orange soil on the floor and the dust marks that suggested a careful search of the house.

Niu entered the study, interrupting the discussion. 'Sorry for barging in, Sir. Yong told me I should come with the results of the poison tests as soon as possible.'

'And so, you should. What did you find out?'

'Yong told me to prepare some samples to feed the rats the kitchen caught this day. A few samples were taken from the porridge, water and condiments. Others I made by mixing some water into the empty bowls and with the uncooked rice. The little critters that ate the food from the table and floor went belly-up after about a quarter of an hour. All the others are still alive and doing rather well.'

'Thank you, Niu. That will be all,' said the magistrate as he waved his hand to dismiss Niu.

'Confirms there was poison in the porridge, that's all,' said Yong. 'We still can't be sure how it found its way into the food.'

'Indeed,' said Zhou, 'if the poison had been introduced by someone other than Mdm Li, the most feasible way to do so would be to taint the raw food ingredients or utensils. With these options crossed out, we are back to the simpler and less fanciful explanation that she tipped poison into the pot while cooking. Remember she admitted to killing her son with the only thing she said in court.'

'She was probably not in the right frame of mind,' said Yong. 'Maybe she thought she had killed her son with the beating. If she had planned to take the life of her son and then of her own, why bother with the trip to town?'

'To source for poison?'

'Perhaps. One could also argue that taking the effort to cook was to partake of a final meal. But why make the effort to clean up the boy, the bed and the area around it? It does not make sense.'

'How do you explain the lack of poisonous traces?'

'This someone was never likely to administer the poison through the crockery. There were a few bowls and spoons. He would not know which ones Mdm Li would use. Lacing all of them with poison for assurance would leave behind traces for people like us to find. Doping the water and ingredients would have been problematic for the same reason. No, he would want to do it in a way that made us think Mdm Li did it herself.'

'How would you do it if you were him?'

'I would apply the poison to the pot or the ladle. There was only one of each, so they would have to be used in the cooking. But since Mdm Li had used these to cook, we would not be able to test if these were indeed the conduits.'

'This sounds rather convenient.'

Yong felt a tinge of irritation bubbling up from his stomach. While Zhou might be doing his job in challenging his findings, Yong felt the last remark insinuated that he was stretching the facts to help the widow.

Zhou pushed on. 'In any case, your theory of an intruder as the perpetrator might fit if he had been there just before Mdm Li reached home this afternoon. What if he was merely a visitor who had gone into the house way before that?'

'Not likely. Traces of the orange soil on the window sill indicated someone had climbed in through the window, out of sight from the rest of the village. There were also clumps of matching mud behind the house, at the edge of the woods abutting the village. The person had, after emerging from the woods, scraped off the stuff sticking to his shoes before breaking into the house. The clumps were large enough to still be soft and wet to the touch, left behind for not more than half a day.'

'Someone could have gone into the house after the villagers took mother and child to town.'

'Again, not likely. After the villagers left for town, the headman's daughter kept watch at the closed front door while the windows remained open. There was an old man sitting outside his house opposite her place, about thirty paces away. Through the front window, he would have noticed any intruder.'

'Did the old man confirm what you said?'

'I did not get a chance to talk to him. When we were done, he had already retired for the night.'

Zhou aimed a stern look at Yong. 'A mistake. You could have asked Niu to talk to the old man.'

Yong said nothing. He knew Zhou was right.

'Too absorbed in your work, as usual,' said the magistrate. 'When do you think this intruder was in the house?'

'The windows were likely closed while Mdm Li went away for her errand this afternoon. That would have been the most opportune time, perhaps the only time, for this intruder to open up the window at the back and slip into the house unnoticed.'

The magistrate got up from his chair and took a few slow steps to the window. He stroked his goatee as he looked out. 'This man could be connected with the boy's death. Then again, he might be a common burglar unrelated to the tragedy.' Zhou, who had also stood up, nodded his agreement.

'I uncovered a storage compartment in the bed, under the bed mat. It was not hard to find. This man had made such a painstaking effort to search through the house that he would not have missed the compartment. I found some money there. Not much but it is still money. He was looking for something else.'

The magistrate turned around to face Yong. 'Did you check out the woods?'

'Yes, I went in and saw some shoeprints. Not clear enough to be useful, though. It was getting dark and visibility was low, so I turned back.'

'Unfortunate,' said Zhou. 'Did anyone see you go into the woods?'

'A few villagers.'

'I hope you instructed them not to go in there. We would not want them trampling around.'

'I did not see a need to. The headman's daughter said nobody goes in there as it is thorny and uncomfortable, as I found out myself. It was dark when we left. I don't think anyone would go in there tonight.'

'Another mistake. Someone might get curious.'

'They would be more curious if I had warned them off, don't you think?'

As soon as the last word left his mouth, Yong knew he had crossed the line separating a senior adviser and a servant boy.

Still, the only sign of Zhou's displeasure was the pause before his next words. 'You left it to chance, and should have known better.'

'Mr Zhou has a valid point,' said the magistrate, pausing for a moment. 'Nothing we can do about it now. Go back first thing tomorrow morning to comb through the place.'

Yong nodded to acknowledge the rebuke and instruction.

'What else can you say about this mystery person?' asked the magistrate.

'From the size of the prints in the woods, I would say they belong to a man. He was not tall, about a head shorter than me.' Yong talked about the urn and tablet. 'With the bench to stand on, the handprints on top of the cupboard told me he still needed to pull himself up to access the urn and tablet.'

The magistrate nodded. 'Anything else?'

'That is all for now.'

'This intrusion does throw more uncertainty on the case against Mdm Li. Mr Zhou, please remind the guards to allow her a proper rest tonight. We will try to talk to her tomorrow morning. Yong, I know you are eager to speak to Mdm Li too but leave that to us while you go back to the village. It has been a long day. Get some rest, both of you.'

Chapter Seven

For the umpteenth time that night, the naked flame of the oil lamp on the square table flickered, tugged by the slipstream of Yong's darting movements. He was shuttling between the table and stuffed bookshelves that occupied much of the usable space in the library. He retrieved stacks of official documents from the shelves to check them against the limited illumination of the oil lamp and reorganized them before filing them away in their proper places. It was mind-numbing work that found its way by default to the magistrate's personal attendant.

On a typical night, almost nothing would stir at this hour. This night, though, the magistrate was still up in his study three rooms away.

'I thought I heard something.'

Startled, Yong looked up to see Magistrate Liu standing at the door, draped in a casual grey nightrobe.

'Why are you still up so late in the night?' said the magistrate.

'Sorry to disturb you, Sir. I am arranging your journals to get ready for Justice Hou's visit.'

'Right. The visit from the Censorate is important, though we still have a few days to prepare for it. More important not to tire yourself out.'

'Still quite a lot to be done, I'm afraid, and the investigations today ate up time.'

The magistrate stood in silence. Yong was unsure how to respond except to stop what he was doing.

'Come with me,' the official said, turning to walk back to his study.

Yong set aside the documents he was working on, blew out the lamp, and headed to the study room. When he got there, his master was settling down behind his desk.

The magistrate looked up at Yong as the young man stood in front of him. 'Do you remember what day it is today?'

Yong knew, but said nothing. The magistrate uncapped his teacup with his left hand and, with his right, raised the cup to his lips. Yong started to move towards the teapot on the round table in the middle of the room.

'No need. A bit of cold tea would not do me harm.' The cup took its time to come back down to rest on the desk. 'On this day, fourteen years ago, we brought you into our household. You remember, don't you?'

Yong nodded.

'I have never talked to you about it,' said the magistrate with an almost imperceptible smile. 'You would not recall since you were just a toddler. That night, I was getting back with Mr Zhou from an assignment. Around this time, in fact. It was a chilly night, and you were sitting at our gate, balled up and shivering. Your face was deathly pale and your hands stone-cold to the touch.'

'Mr Zhou told me I would have died if you had not brought me into the house.'

'Quite so. From the tattered rags and layers of grime on your little body, we figured you had been roaming the streets. One of the maids later said she had seen you a few times following this old man around, begging for food. Something had probably happened to the old man, leaving you on your own.'

Yong remembered little of the events that night and of his life before. The old man, too, formed only hazy impressions in his mind. He had no idea how they were related and what had happened to him. Another servant told him the old man had seemed like a loner, which was to say he was likely not part of the Beggars' Sect, a human network spanning numerous towns and cities with its own hierarchy, rules, and code. Under this banner, beggars organized themselves for strength and protection.

In any case, the Liu household had moved out of the city of Lübu two years after he was picked up, on to the magistrate's next posting. Yong had not been old enough to find out more about his background. One thing he did remember was the feeling of hunger—the horrible pangs often mingled with the cold of night, dreadful during winter.

The magistrate shifted his gaze from Yong to the desk. He slid his right hand along the desk and fingered the rim of the saucer holding the cup before looking back up at Yong. 'Taking you in was the best decision I have ever made.'

Magistrate Liu was a fair and kind master, though sparing when it came to praise. There was something different this night, a lightness of mood that revealed a side of him usually veiled.

'It has been quite a remarkable journey,' the magistrate continued. 'From the time you started working as my assistant, you had shown yourself to be a bright child, learning quickly. Mr Zhou and I were shocked when, one day, you offered your views on a case. Spot on too. I wonder how many times you held your tongue while you watched us bumbling around.'

'No, not at all. I was too young to detect any errors until … I beg your pardon, Sir.'

The magistrate burst out laughing. 'That is what I like most about you. A bit too quick with your words and deeds sometimes, but always frank and honest. I remember it well, our first breakthrough case three years ago in Biaoxin. It was indeed an error, well spotted.'

'I only helped a little.'

'A little? Before you, resolution of cases had been slow, to put it mildly.'

'Everybody knows you are a righteous official who would not resort to coercion or underhanded means to resolve cases.'

The magistrate nodded to acknowledge the point. It was true that he had held fast to his principles, sometimes at the expense of career progression. He eschewed the methods of some of his peers such as beatings and torture to extract quick confessions. These officials would reason they were convinced of the guilt of the accused and just needed confirmation. Magistrate Liu preferred to trust hard evidence and logical deduction. He would rather the wheels of justice turned more slowly if it meant the truth had a better chance of surfacing.

Since his appointment as a county magistrate after passing the gruelling Imperial examinations, his career had meandered through a series of unremarkable three-year assignments. While promotion meant postings closer to the Capital and to the Imperial Court itself, assignments in his eighteen-year career had been nearer to borders than the centre. That changed in Biaoxin when he resolved a few significant cases with Yong's help. The next move to his current perch was closer to the centre of power, a step up and a better opportunity.

'Perhaps Old Heaven saw I needed help. Your powers of observation and deduction—they are extraordinary. You possess rare gifts.'

'Whatever I know, I learned from you and Mr Zhou.'

'Yes, Mr Zhou, a capable and loyal man who has been with me for almost two decades. We have been through a lot together. All these years, he has never grumbled about the difficult outposts allotted to me. He could have left for a job with better prospects and I would not have blamed him.'

The magistrate rested his elbows on the arms of his chair. 'I know he appreciates your contributions. He told me so on a number of occasions. You are like a grand-nephew to him. But as your importance to us grows, he might feel a bit left behind, though he may not consciously think of it that way. While he has been hard on you lately, I know him well enough to understand he means no malice.'

'I spoke out of turn this evening. He was right to be angry with me.'

'That will pass. He is not someone to hold grudges. I want you to know I agreed with you that there was no need to instruct the villagers to keep out of the woods. Doing so could well have stoked the curiosity of a few, as you said. Telling you to go back first thing in the morning was also superfluous. Knowing you, it would have been your plan. My reprimand this evening was a reminder that you must always accord Mr Zhou due respect. Once your teacher, always your teacher.'

'Yes, Sir. I will remember.'

'Chin up, lad. This is a teaching, not a tongue-lashing. In fact, you did well today for both cases. The episode with the monks was a nice touch, no doubt burnishing my reputation amongst the people,' said the magistrate with a chuckle.

'Just doing my job.'

'Just doing your job? The people beyond this compound know you as a mere servant. You do not receive enough credit for what you do.'

'Far be it from me to claim credit. In any case, I'm happy for others to let their guard down when dealing with me.'

'As the monks had done, to their detriment.'

Yong let out a smile.

'With your talents, Yong, you deserve a larger canvas.'

'It is my honour to serve you.'

'Have you not thought of making a name for yourself?'

'No, Sir. I mean, of course I've thought about it. But as Mr Zhou has taught, when drinking water, consider its source. To the Liu family, I owe my life. I will never serve another family.'

'Never say never. There are righteous officials with larger platforms than mine on which to demonstrate your abilities. And after me, the way my son is going, your prospect with the Liu family is not likely to brighten.' The magistrate let out a sigh. 'Both Zhong and you are of about the same age, but the levels of maturity are as far apart as heaven and earth. He is always finding ways to run away from studying. In this he is ingenious.'

Yong hesitated before speaking. 'Old Master, please forgive me for saying this, for it is not my place to comment on family matters. Young Master does try. It is just that studying is hard work. I would not be able to do a fraction of what he has done.'

'Of course, it is hard work. I studied for twenty-five years before passing the final Imperial examinations. Nothing worth doing is easy. However hard, it is the surest path to serving the country. That is all I ask of him.'

'Maybe he just needs time.'

The magistrate shook his head. 'This is a time of need for the country. With external tribes harassing us and rebel groups rising up around the country, we are expending more and more resources on the military to deal with these disturbances. Yet, so many of my fellow officials think only of themselves.'

Yong said nothing.

'I have said too much,' said the magistrate. 'You know where he has gone to, do you not?'

'He did not tell me.'

'Which is not the same as saying you do not know. For all your smarts and trickery, young man, you can never bring yourself to lie to me.'

The official stopped talking, letting silence take over the room. The reason for this soon became clear. In the stillness of the night, Yong could pick up the drawn-out groaning of creaking wooden floor boards from the main hall.

The official stood up. 'That must be him I hear.' He rounded his desk, headed out of the room and turned left towards the source of the sound.

Since Yong had no wish to stay around for the impending storm, he initiated his escape. His problem was that he had to pass through the main hall. Worse, when he was about to step out of the study, he spotted the magistrate's wife emerging from her room on his right. Elegant in her evening dress and still wearing unblemished make-up, hair perfectly in place, she was almost scampering down the corridor, heading in the same direction as her husband.

Yong, having halted in his tracks, retreated a step while fumbling a greeting to allow Madam to go past. In return, without breaking step or uttering a word, Madam angled her head to shoot him a stony glance that turned him cold, before facing forward again. After she flashed past, her long dress flowing, Yong followed behind, keeping a safe distance.

'You stay where you are!' The magistrate's voice rang loud and clear from around the corner.

Madam quickened her pace. When Yong reached the hall, he saw the magistrate, with his hands behind his back, staring at a sheepish Zhong, who lowered his gaze to the floor. Madam, fresh on the scene, stood behind the magistrate, off his left shoulder, her eyes alternating between her son and husband. An oil lamp was flickering on top of a table near them, ruffled by movements in the room. It was a small lamp that did not provide much light, but enough to illuminate the looks on the faces of the Liu family—one of guilt, another of anger and the last of deep concern. All three seemed stuck in a state of suspension, almost like they were presenting Yong with an opening to slip away.

Yong grabbed the chance, trying hard not to break into an unseemly run, and darted off once he was out of the house. He had hoped not to be entangled in the family affair, though he sensed that whatever else that was going to happen this night, he was already mired in it.

Chapter Eight

When Yong reached the village, the early morning sun had almost emerged in full from the distant hills, casting its slanting rays on the farmers dotting the fields. Old Gatekeeper had yet to take up his customary observation post.

Yong headed straight to the spot at the woods' edge with the broken twigs and compressed vegetation. He entered through the breach and overcame the first patch of waist-high shrubs with some effort to stand at the same clearing he had explored the day before. There, he laid eyes on the shoeprints again. They now stood out in the morning daylight streaming into the woods. Two sets of them pointed in opposite directions—incoming and outgoing. However, they were still not distinct enough for him to discern details.

He lifted his eyes to survey the land before him. By his estimation, the shrubs covered about a third of the ground. Trees with straight and sturdy trunks stood at attention, spaced ten to twenty paces from one another. He continued on, following the double trail.

About twenty paces into the clearing, he came to a point where the incoming and outgoing trails split into two different paths. He decided to follow the incoming trail. As he did so, he felt himself going down a gentle slope. Though he had to bash through two more large patches of shrubs, he felt his pulse quickening with anticipation as he walked along.

He could sense the ground softening and see the shoeprints getting more distinct.

Ploughing through another expanse of thick shrub, he saw in front of him that the ground was the shade of orange he was seeking. He was deliberate as he stepped into the clearing, careful not to stomp on traces left by the earlier visitor. As he felt his foot sinking into the earth, he lowered his gaze and found his prize. 'There you are, you beauty.'

Right there, resting unmolested, were imprints of shoes sculpted half an inch into a patch of beautiful orange soil. The ground was soft enough for meaningful indents to be made but with sufficient firmness to preserve details. The indentations made by the right foot were even. In comparison, the left foot made shallower impressions in the mid-section, indicating a significant arch. In the soft ground, short lines jutted out from the front of the left shoeprints, as though the man was drawing lines as he pulled his left leg forward.

The ground softened further as he pressed on, still following a downward gradient, until he reached what he perceived to be a trough in the landscape. Here, he found himself treading through soggy mud. Relief came as he climbed up on sloping ground that firmed up as he progressed, only to be met with bothersome shrubs again. He went through three of these green patches before he emerged on to a dirt road, out of the woods. This was a side road that, in less than a hundred paces, joined up to the main axis road leading to town.

Turning around to view the path he had taken through the woods, Yong came to understand how the man could have made the mistake of wading into the muddy trap. From this vantage point, the chosen path appeared to be the shortest route to the village. Little did the man know the downslope led to a basin where moisture gathered and the ground softened into a mud pool. He had likely wised up and picked a sturdier route on the way back.

Yong walked on the dirt path along the edge of the woods to locate the man's exit point, which was a mere thirty paces or so away. Determined to trace the man's steps as far as he could, Yong ventured into the woods again. By following the trail of footsteps and signs of disturbed vegetation, he was able to find his way back to the fork where the trails separated and, from there, back to Yingxiu's backyard. After he scraped off the mud from his shoes with a twig, he went round the house to the front.

Standing right in front of Yingxiu's house, with his hands behind his back, was Lin, the village headman. He stayed where he was and kept his eyes on Yong as the young man came towards him.

'One of the villagers told me you went to the back of the house but I could not find you there,' said Lin. 'You're the young man who came here last evening with the constable, aren't you?'

'Yes, Mr Lin. My name is Liu Yong. My apologies. I should have come to you first. I was eager to continue with the investigations.'

'Where's the constable?'

'I came by myself.'

'Well, I guess there's not much more investigation to be done after her confession.'

Yong did not let the slight bother him. He was here to seek the truth, not affirmation.

'How is Yingxiu?' said the headman.

'She stayed up most of the night. When I left this morning, she was asleep.'

The headman nodded to signal the end of his cursory inquiry on his villager's well-being. 'Did you find anything useful?'

'Not much,' said Yong, not wanting to give anything away. 'I wanted to look around to see what I can find.'

'Well, go ahead. I will go back to my work.' Lin started to walk off.

'Mr Lin, there is something I need to speak to you about.'

Lin swivelled back, impatience starting to show on his furrowed brow. 'What about?'

'I heard the village temple event was a dedication ceremony where everybody had to be around.'

'That's right.'

'When did it start and end?'

'The ceremony itself started an hour after noon. Ended about three hours later.'

Yong noted this timing overlapped with Yingxiu's trip to town. 'Did all the villagers attend?'

'As I said to your superiors last evening, all except the old and immobile.'

And except Yingxiu and Xiaodong, thought Yong. 'No one who was supposed to attend skipped the event?'

'No, I took attendance.'

'Did anyone leave early or step out for a while?'

'Not during the ceremony, for sure. We do not allow that.'

'One other question. Do you know of anybody around here who walks with a limp?'

'A limp?'

'Yes, sort of like dragging his left foot as he walks.'

'None that I know of. Why do you ask?'

'I thought I came across someone like that last evening, that's all. Thank you, Mr Lin.'

Lin turned and walked off in the direction of the fields through a path in between two houses. Old Gatekeeper was now sitting at his usual station, tilting his face up with eyes closed, soaking up the warm rays of the early morning sun. Yong opened the door to Yingxiu's house, breaking the paper seals in the process. He opened both the front and back windows, also tearing the seals. Without disturbing anything in the house, he walked out and headed towards Old Gatekeeper, who was now staring straight at him.

'You're the young man who came last evening,' the old man said with a broad smile and sprightly voice before Yong reached him. His skin was wrinkled and tanned from years of working in the fields, with small dark spots dotting his face. Up close, Yong could now confirm what he had assessed from a distance the day before—that Old Gatekeeper was way too short and hunched to reach the top of Yingxiu's cupboard.

'Yes, sir. I'm Liu Yong from the magistrate's office. I did not have the time to chat with you yesterday. If it is all right with you, I would like to ask you a few questions.'

The smile on the old man's face receded. 'About Yingxiu? Awful thing it was.' He shook his head and sighed. 'Go ahead and ask. Time is what I have plenty of.'

'You're always out here in the day?'

'In the late morning when everybody goes out to work in the field and in the afternoon, after my short midday nap.'

'The whole afternoon? That's a long time to spend out here.'

'I'm used to it. Sometimes old friends will drop by to talk, play a bit of chess, or kids will come by and play. I'd watch over them while their mothers are working. Time passes quickly that way.'

'And yesterday?'

'The same. Everyone had gone to the temple straight after midday. My son and his family went too. When they left, it was just my wife and I.'

'Did you leave this spot at all the whole afternoon yesterday?'

'For short spurts, I suppose. I like to sit here and enjoy the breeze, except during winter. It gets stuffy in the house, you see.'

'Were you out here when Mdm Li and her son went to town yesterday?'

'Sure. They left a bit later than noon and returned about four hours later. As always, she greeted me on their way out and back. Hardworking woman. She makes the trip the same days every week, including winter.'

'Were the windows to her house open while they were away in town?'

'No,' said the old man in a tone that suggested the question was a strange one. 'She always closes her windows when she goes out. Same for everyone around here. Not that there's anything to steal, mind you. More to keep out birds and small animals.'

'Did any stranger come into the village or Mdm Li's house in the afternoon?'

'You mean besides you and the constable?' Old Gatekeeper cracked a smile that exposed a sizeable gap where a few front teeth should have been. 'I saw you poking around.'

'What did you see me doing?'

'You were at the window, looking around. Walked about, like the other two chaps. A few other things too, like clambering up to the cupboard.'

Yong looked back in the direction of Yingxiu's house. From where Old Gatekeeper sat, the cupboard was on the far side of Yingxiu's house. He was now sure the old man was sharp enough to see whatever was going on in the house if the windows were open.

'Did anyone go into Mdm Li's house while she and Xiaodong were away in the afternoon?'

'No. The door and windows were closed, remember?'

'After Mr Lin and the villagers took Mdm Li and her son to town, did you notice anyone else entering the house? You were out here then, weren't you?'

'Oh yeah, I sat out here to watch what was happening. My son went over to help. After they left for town, no one went into the house. The headman made his daughter guard the door, you know.'

From this vantage point, the backyard and the intruder's portal at the wood's edge were blocked well by the house.

'Tragedy, it was,' said the old man. 'She did not look like the bad sort.'

Yong nodded. 'Thank you, sir. By the way, before I go, can I ask if there is someone in the village or around here who walks with a limp? Drags his left foot?'

'A limp, you say? No, not in the village and nearby. Maybe some old bones like me who walk slowly. No limp.'

Chapter Nine

At two hours to noon, Yong reached home base, breathing hard and with his back soaked in perspiration. He hoped he was not too late. Once in the compound, he headed straight for the courthouse. He figured the magistrate and Zhou would be there since the court was supposed to be in session in the morning. He had yet to cross the front courtyard when the tall and slender Lian, one of the kitchen maids, called out his name while running to him.

'Where have you been? Madam has been asking for you. Are you in trouble with her again?'

'I don't know. I think so.'

'I've told you not to provoke her. You had better go call on her right now.'

'Waste of time. I've got more important things to do.'

'Are you out of your mind? You know she has eyes and ears everywhere in the compound,' said Lian in a lowered voice though no one else was in sight. 'If she finds out you delayed going to her, there will be hell to pay.'

Yong blew out his cheeks as he weighed the options.

'Well?' said Lian.

'Oh, all right,' said Yong with an air of resignation. 'I'll go see her.'

'Now. At once.'

'All right, all right. Got it.'

'I don't know what you've done, but you'd better not treat this lightly.'

'Not any more lightly than if I were dealing with the Empress herself.'

'I'm serious. Just do what she wants you to do and say what she wants to hear. Don't talk back. This is not one of your work discussions with Old Master and Mr Zhou, do you understand me?'

'Yes, ma'am.'

'I've got to go back to my work now. Remember, be smart about it,' said Lian with a frown that curved her thin brows before she turned to head back to the kitchen.

'Say what she wants to hear,' Yong muttered to himself as he watched Lian walk away. *Let's get it over and done with*, he thought. Before his resolve could soften, he hurried over to the residence building. After he breezed through the front hall, he glanced into the magistrate's study as he passed and found it empty. As he was wondering how to approach Madam, her personal maid came out of her room.

'Hey, Feng, I heard Madam wants to talk to me. Can you please help me check if she is available now?'

'Wait here,' she said and went back into Madam's room.

Feng was taking too much time. Yong realized the wait was Madam's way of projecting her authority over him. What was more annoying was that her way of intimidating him was working. When it came to his encounters with Madam, which were almost always unpleasant, he would sometimes be reduced to an embarrassing bundle of nerves.

Feng emerged after some time and proceeded to brush past him without a glance in his direction.

Yong caught up with the maid. 'Feng, wait. I need your help. I have an urgent task to attend to. Can you please ask Madam again if she would like to see me now?'

'Right,' said Feng with a pout, 'please wait here while this humble servant girl checks if Madam is ready for the big man with the big job.' Before Yong could hold Feng back, she was off to Madam's chambers. If he had been in any doubt, Yong was now certain he was in serious trouble.

Feng appeared once more and declared with a mocking smile, 'Madam is ready for you now, *sir*.'

Not wanting to hand Feng the opportunity to gloat, Yong walked straight past her and right into the reception area in Madam's chambers.

Madam was sitting at the table dressed in a pearl-white robe, face all made up and a tight hair bun pierced through with a long silver needle. Her left side was facing him, and she was looking straight ahead at nothing in particular.

'Good morning, Madam,' said Yong with a subservient bow.

Madam did not turn or shift to face Yong. 'Feng told me you were too busy to wait.'

'Not at all, Madam. My time is nothing. I wanted to make sure I'm not holding Madam back from anything important.' *Tell her what she wants to hear.*

'Where have you been? I have been searching high and low for you.'

'I was on an errand given to me by Mr Zhou.' Yong figured he should leave the magistrate out of this tangle lest she accused him of hiding behind his master's authority.

She turned to face Yong. 'Look at you. If I had not known better, I would have mistaken you for a lowly member of the wretched Beggars' Sect.'

Yong bowed and kept his eyes on the ground. 'I'm sorry, Madam. I should have tidied up before coming to you.'

'Typical of the magistrate to let a servant gallivant around town while confining his son to this prison.'

Yong kept quiet, for answering back would draw more fire. The conversation had taken an uncomfortable turn for him, causing his heart rate to pick up.

'What did you say to Old Master last night?' There was a calm menace in Madam's voice.

Yong had rehearsed this part of the conversation a few times before he went to bed the previous night. Yet, he still felt his stomach knotting up. Thinking about how he might mess up the explanation only made it worse. *Calm down and breathe*, he told himself.

'Well?'

'It was nothing, Madam.' He had planned to say much more but the prepared speech had gone right out of the window. Willing himself to shut off everything, he focused his eyes on a particular spot on the floor tile in front of him, and drew slow breaths. The desired effect started to kick in. He felt his heart slowing down.

'Nothing? Do not lie to me.'

'I wouldn't dare, Madam.'

'Don't think I'm unaware. I overheard the mention of Zhong's name and Old Master raising his voice. Are you going to deny it?'

'Old Master did talk about Young Master.'

'Now you're owning up. What did you discuss that aroused the anger of Old Master? Be straight with me.'

'He asked if I knew where Young Master had gone to.'

'And you squealed on Zhong?'

'No, Madam. I told Old Master that I did not know.'

'You expect me to believe that? I'm sure you knew where Zhong went. Both of you spoke at length when you were going out yesterday. The silly boy, ever trusting, must have told you. And you, eager to please your master, told on Zhong.'

Yong never failed to be impressed by Madam's ability to call on informers all over the household. One thing he was thankful for—Madam's torrent of questions and accusations helped him shift his attention from his anxiety, towards the issues at hand.

'No, Madam, he did not tell me where he went. You can ask him.'

'You think I did not? Of course, the silly boy protected you. He is too soft-hearted when it comes to you.'

'It is the truth. Much of the conversation was about my past.'

'Your past?'

'Old Master reminded me he brought me into the household exactly fourteen years ago.'

For a moment, Madam fixed her gaze on the servant without saying anything. Now reminded of the date, the anniversary was too much of a coincidence for her to swat away as a convenient excuse. But Yong also knew she was not one to relent once she got going.

And so, it continued. 'Let me remind you that without us, you would be out on the streets begging for food. Don't you forget that, and don't you dare entertain any ideas above your station.'

'If not for Old Master and Madam, I would not be here today. This I will never forget.'

She looked away, but not before Yong detected a softening of her glare. For a fleeting moment, Yong saw in her eyes a hint of the affection she had shown him when he was a child. That glimpse tugged at his heart, for it reminded him that, in times past, she had been kind to him.

Both mistress and servant were locked in silence, each in her and his own thoughts.

'I'm sorry, Madam,' said Yong, not knowing what he was apologizing for.

Finally, Madam said in a soft voice, 'Get out.'

With a heavy heart, Yong walked out of Madam's chambers and then the residence building. When he reached the courtroom, he found it deserted save for a servant who was clearing up. Apparently, Magistrate Liu had postponed the session this morning. As he made his way to the magistrate's working chambers behind the courtroom, he bumped into Niu.

'Where have you been?' Niu said, the third time in quick succession someone had fired this question at Yong without real interest in the answer. 'The magistrate and Mr Zhou have just gone to talk to Mdm Li. Come!'

The guard at the jail house let them in and waved them through. A constable stood guard at the open gate of Yingxiu's cell. Through the gaps between the vertical wooden beams of the cell, they saw the magistrate, still in his official garb, seated on a stool and Zhou standing on his right. Both of them faced Yingxiu, who sat on the floor cushioned by straw. Though she hung her head low, she appeared calm. Zhou caught sight of Yong and signalled for him to join them.

'Mdm Li,' the magistrate said with a soft voice as Yong took up position on his left, 'I hope you feel better after some rest and food.' There was no response from the woman. 'As I mentioned in court, the charge against you is a grave one. I need your help to figure out what happened. Do you understand what I am saying?'

Her hair draped over her face, Yingxiu started to shake. She balled up her hands, clutching straw, like she was steeling herself for an arduous task. 'Death is too kind a punishment for what I've done,' she said in a voice hoarse and haunting.

Yong glanced at his elders whose faces betrayed nothing.

'Tell us what you did,' said the magistrate.

The accused woman raised her head. Yong was taken aback by her appearance. Her face was drained of colour. The eyes were bloodshot and the bags beneath them heavy and dark. She looked like she had aged ten years in one night.

'Your Honour, I killed him. My son.'

'How? What did you do?'

'I was angry and lost it, Sir. I hit him. Hard. Too hard ...'

'Xue's mother testified that you tried to procure rat poison, implying that you poisoned your son.'

Yingxiu stared at the magistrate. 'Poison?'

'You did not hear what the villagers said in court?'

'I ... I cannot remember.'

'You recall what happened at your house, do you not?'

'Yes. But after that ... I don't know.' Yingxiu continued staring at the magistrate, stupefied. Yong did not think her face could turn any paler, yet it did.

'Did you poison your son?'

'No, no,' Yingxiu said, shaking her head with vigour. She lowered her gaze to the ground as realization seemed to hit her. 'Poison, Sir?'

'The coroner confirmed it.'

'I don't understand. How did it happen? Who poisoned Xiaodong?'

The magistrate nodded as if to acknowledge that Yingxiu's reactions confirmed what he had concluded. It was almost inconceivable for the widow to poison her son, leave subtle clues pointing to another perpetrator, confess twice to beating the boy to death, and then deny the poisoning in such a convincing manner.

'We have reasons to believe someone went into your house while you were away in town yesterday and lined your cooking ware with poison. You have to help me figure out what happened to Xiaodong so that we can find the person responsible. That is the surest way to absolve you of this crime.'

Yingxiu's parched and cracked lips quivered as she took some time to process the news. 'Why?' she said. 'Why would anyone want to harm my innocent boy?'

Chapter Ten

On Zhou's instructions, Niu fetched Yingxiu a cup of water. The magistrate gave her time to drink and compose herself before resuming. 'Tell us what happened after you got home.'

'Sir, where is my son's body?'

Zhou was the one who answered. 'We are making arrangements for a proper burial tomorrow. Not to worry, we will bring you to the funeral.'

With some difficulty, the widow got up on her knees. 'Your Honour, I beg you to let me see him before the funeral.' She started to kowtow to the magistrate, who leaned forward to hold her up before she could strike her forehead on the ground.

'Please get up. I will arrange for you to see him by the end of today.'

'Thank you,' Yingxiu wobbled on her knees and collapsed back down on to the floor. 'My apologies, Your Honour, I …'

The magistrate held out a palm. 'It is quite all right. Please remain seated.'

The widow took a moment to collect her thoughts before speaking again. 'We went to town and completed our chores as normal. We were both tired. When we reached home, I decided we should eat and retire earlier. While I cooked, I would tie him to the bed with a rope. There were a few times he had come over and burned himself.'

'I understand. So, you started to cook.'

'Yes. When the porridge was ready, I poured it into two bowls on the table to let it cool down. I was going to untie Xiaodong when I saw the patch of urine he left on the floor. When I discovered this, he was sitting on the bed and messed it up as well.' She paused to catch her breath. 'I untied him, wiped him clean and changed his clothes. Once done, I sent him over to the table to eat while I cleaned up.'

'What happened next?'

'As I was cleaning up, Xiaodong burst out shouting, and swept his bowl and the pot to the floor.' Yingxiu paused again, this time with her eyes widened, yet blank.

The men waited in silence for her to continue.

'I was incensed and … and punished him. The anger got to me. I lost it.' Her eyes began to well up again. 'Then he started to shake. His whole body. I grabbed a piece of wood to insert into his mouth to keep him from biting his tongue. He tossed around, making strange groaning noises. I did not know what else to do. After a while, he let out a loud, terrible groan and stopped moving. All I could do was to open my mouth and scream.'

'Mdm Li, do you have enemies? Is there anyone who might want to harm you or your son?'

'No, Sir. We kept to ourselves and never offended anyone.'

'Have you received visitors into your house in recent days?'

'Only Xue, about a week ago.'

'My assistant will tell you more about this person who we think went into your house.'

Yong took over. 'Mdm Li, I looked inside and around your house. I think a man bashed through the woods and climbed into your house through the back window. I believe he walks with a limp. He is shorter than I am, perhaps up to my chin level. Do you know of such a man?'

Without hesitation, she shook her head.

'I also uncovered the hidden compartment under your bed mat. How much money did you keep in there?'

'We have very little—nine small coins.'

'Have you shifted things around in your house recently, even just lifting them up?'

'Shift around?'

'Yes, like the pile of stuff at the corner next to the cooking stove, the box on the small wooden table, and your husband's altar tablet and urn.'

'No, I have not touched those things for a long while.'

'I believe this man did a thorough search of your house but did not take any of the coins. Do you know what he was looking for?'

'I don't understand. I am a poor widow with nothing of value. Has there been a mistake?'

'Before yesterday, the last day you left the house would have been three or four days ago, am I right?'

'Yes. I go to town on the first and fifth day of the week. It has been the same for years.'

'In between those trips, did you leave your house unattended for more than half an hour?'

'No. Besides the trips to town, we seldom leave the house for long.'

'If I'm right, the only time this intruder could have gone into your house would have been while you were out early yesterday afternoon.'

The flurry of questions and revelations left Yingxiu staring ahead for a while. 'Your Honour, this does not make sense at all. It is ... confusing.'

'We understand.'

'I only have one other question. When can I go home?'

'While I believe you did not kill your son, we still need to investigate his death thoroughly. For now, you should remain in this compound as my guest. When you are ready, we will bring you back to your house for a while as part of the investigations. You can then collect some belongings. That is, when you are ready.'

The widow straightened her back and clenched her fists again. She looked up at the magistrate with a renewed sense of determination in her eyes. 'I'm ready.'

Chapter Eleven

A procession of six men, that included two uniformed constables armed with sabres and another man pulling a rickshaw, making its way towards a quiet village, was always likely to attract attention. At the entrance of the village, a number of villagers had gathered from the fields and houses to greet the incoming delegation.

As the visitors drew nearer, a few villagers recognized the stately man at the front as Magistrate Liu Ye even though he had changed out of his official robes into more comfortable plain clothes and a round cap. Zhou and Yong followed behind, flanked by two constables, Niu and Wei. An added curiosity was the rickshaw itself, its wooden frame covered in cloth, shielding a mystery passenger.

By the time the delegation reached the village entrance, the headman was standing at the front of an impromptu welcome party. Old Gatekeeper remained at his usual post, taking in the spectacle.

After an exchange of pleasantries between magistrate and headman, the visiting delegation and welcome party merged into one and shuffled to Yingxiu's house. As the rickshaw came to a halt, Zhou pulled aside the covering cloth at the front, setting off a burst of excited chatter amongst the home crowd.

The two constables helped Yingxiu out of the rickshaw. Yingxiu trembled as she stepped out, partly due to lack of strength, but also from the weight of stares of the onlookers—most of judgement and others of pity.

Yong tore off the sealing papers that he had pasted on the door in the morning and pulled the door open. The magistrate and Zhou waited for the owner of the house to enter, but she hesitated at the door. Eventually, she stepped in, and the men on official duty followed her in.

Zhou ordered Constable Wei to guard the entrance before closing the door behind him. While Niu escorted Yingxiu to sit at the dining table, Yong opened up the windows to let light in and proceeded to orientate his superiors to the locations where he had unearthed clues.

Once Yong was done, the magistrate sat down at the table to face Yingxiu. His gaze shifted up and landed on the urn at the top of the cupboard. 'Tell me about your husband.'

Yingxiu took a few slow breaths, her vacant eyes fixed on the table before her. 'My husband Sun Jie came from a merchant family in Jingshan, about three days' journey from here. His mother passed away when he was young. His father recognized his potential for books when he was ten years old. From then on, he focused on nothing but studying while his elder brothers from his father's other wives helped run the family business. My father-in-law had hoped Jie would pass the examinations, take up an official position and bring honour to the family. Every aspect of his life was well taken care of. Even after we got married, we never had to worry about a thing.'

'When and why did you move here?'

'The favour bestowed upon Jie bred resentment in his brothers. When my father-in-law passed away a year after our marriage, everything changed. The family threatened to cut off his stipend. Jie decided to take the sum of money his father had left him and move to a place where we could settle down to focus on his studies. About fifteen years ago, we moved here.

We were able to get by on our savings and the small income I made from sewing work. He earned some money by helping people in the village and town write and read letters.'

'Then Xiaodong came along.'

Yingxiu raised her head at the mention of her son. 'Xiaodong was born thirteen years ago. Thirteen years, and he was never able to take care of himself.'

'It must have been hard for you and Mr Sun.'

'It was. He had to concentrate on his studies, so I tried my best to tend to Xiaodong and the chores by myself.'

'We heard from the villagers Mr Sun had gone to the Capital.'

'Six years ago, he managed to do well in the provincial examinations and qualified to attempt the metropolitan examinations at the Capital. It was quite a few months before he left. He had to first establish contact with a distant relative, a Mr Guo, who was living there.'

'He stayed with this relative?'

'Yes, he did. It wasn't easy, though. This Mr Guo was quite the calculative sort. Even before Jie left home, he had been asking for money. When Jie replied and agreed to his demands, he wrote back to ask for more. I was wary but Jie said it was right for Mr Guo to be compensated for his troubles. Jie departed for the Capital about five years ago. He left us some money, so we were able to cope for two years or so without too much difficulty. We thought he'd be back by then.'

'Did he remain in contact with you?'

'There were a few letters.'

'What did he say in those letters?'

'Mostly about how he was settling in and getting on in his studies. In one letter, he mentioned money was running out, that he might have to work to support himself. He did not say so but I guessed Mr Guo was still taking money from him. What he had with him would not have run out so soon otherwise.'

'Tell me what happened to your husband.'

'For months, I did not hear from him. At first, I thought he was too busy to write as it was around the time of the examinations. It was not easy to get someone to deliver the letters. Then one day ...'

Yingxiu looked down again, biting her lower lip and fighting back tears. 'One afternoon, four years ago, someone showed up at our door with this urn and some letters. I knew right away what it meant—my husband was dead. The letter was from Mr Guo, saying Jie had died in a plague. He attached another note written by Jie that said he was very sick and near death. It also said he had given instructions for Mr Guo to cremate his body and send his ashes back to me.'

'We would like to take a look at those letters and others from Mr Sun and Mr Guo later. Did you hear from Mr Guo again, or did you contact him to find out more about what happened?'

'I wrote to him twice but did not hear back from him. I thought about visiting Mr Guo to find out more about what happened to Jie, but it was impossible. People told me it is a fifteen-day journey on mule cart, which we cannot afford, let alone lodgings along the way.'

'They said in court that your health is fast deteriorating. Is it true?'

'I'm only thirty-five years old, yet my body feels like that of an old woman. My bones throb with this dull ache all through the winter months. Two months ago, I consulted a physician to treat this fever that refused to go away. He told me my health had collapsed to a point where I would have at most a year to live.'

'They also said you talked about wanting Xiaodong to die before you, that you mentioned killing Xiaodong and yourself.'

'I had uttered useless words in moments of hopelessness,' said Yingxiu with her eyes shut. 'Despair enveloped me when I thought of what would happen when I'm gone.' She paused, then looked up. 'But not by my own hand. Never. I would not do it. If there was a chance, however small, to give Xiaodong a decent life, I would hold on to it.'

'Mdm Li,' said Yong. 'Besides money, did Mr Sun keep anything valuable on him when he left home?'

'There was a piece of jade his father had passed to him as an heirloom. It was almost the size of half a palm, and he always carried it with him. He treasured it and said he would never sell it. It was the only thing left to remind him of his father.'

'Do you know what happened to it?'

'Mr Guo said in the last letter that he sold it to pay for the funeral and other expenses. In my subsequent letters to Mr Guo, I asked about the jade. But like I said, he did not reply. Young sir, are you saying this piece of jade had something to do with my husband's death?'

'I'm just considering all the possibilities.'

'Would you mind showing us the letters from Mr Sun and this Mr Guo?' said Zhou.

Without answering, Yingxiu made her way to the bed, pulled aside the bed mat, opened up the storage compartment and fished out a handful of papers. 'Here they are,' said Yingxiu as she picked out three sheets from the thin stack and sat back down. 'These three we received during the early part of Jie's stay at the Capital.'

'Where are the two from Mr Guo and your husband that came with the ashes?' asked Zhou as he took the letters from Yingxiu's hands and proceeded to browse through them.

'The one from Mr Guo is gone. For days after the news of my husband's death, I was in a deep rut, depressed. Every night, I would sit here and cry while holding on to these two letters. One night, I dozed off from exhaustion and Mr Guo's letter caught fire from the oil lamp. It was almost all burned, unsalvageable. Jie's letter was singed but largely intact, thankfully.'

'So where is this final letter from Mr Sun?'

'That is precious to us, the last reminder of Jie. At the same time, I felt depressed whenever I looked at it, so I kept it in a safe place, under the altar tablet. Let me get it for you.'

'Was it wrapped up in a piece of cloth?' Yong said as Yingxiu got up.

'Yes, it is.'

'Mdm Li, I checked on top of the cupboard yesterday, under the urn and tablet. Constable Niu here is my witness. The letter was not there. It is gone.'

Chapter Twelve

Having gone up to the cupboard to verify Sun Jie's letter from his deathbed was indeed missing, Yingxiu returned to her seat, dazed. 'It was there,' she said, more to herself than to the men around her.

The magistrate took the letters that were in Zhou's hands, placed them side by side and pored over them while Yong peered over his shoulder.

'Not much in these,' said the magistrate. 'Since the bed compartment is not hard to find, we must assume the intruder had seen these three letters yet did not take them. What was the man after that was not in these letters but in the one that is missing?'

'Perhaps it was the way it was written or the handwriting,' said Zhou. 'Have you ever compared the missing letter with others from your husband?'

'I've never thought to do that. It seemed the same to me.'

'Try to recall, Mdm Li,' said Zhou. 'Are you sure the handwriting was that of Mr Sun?'

Yingxiu narrowed her eyes, almost closing them. When she opened her eyes again, she fixed them on the table. 'I remember ... it seemed like his handwriting. It never occurred to me it was not written by him.'

The magistrate lifted his eyes from Sun Jie's earlier letters to Mdm Li. 'These made no mention of Mr Guo.'

Yong said to the widow, 'The two final letters—the one from Mr Guo that was burned up and the other from Mr Sun that has been taken. Can you tell us whether they mentioned details on Mr Guo, like where he lived?'

'There was of course Mr Guo's name itself, if you consider that important, because he signed off with his full name. I don't recall there being an address. Jie's last letter referred to Mr Guo by his surname, not his full name. Nothing else, I think.'

'What about those from Mr Guo before Mr Sun left home?' asked Yong. 'They should contain more details on Mr Guo and his whereabouts?'

'I guess so, though my husband had taken them with him.'

'But what if you needed to contact him? Did he not leave any address behind?'

'He did. Before his departure, he wrote down Mr Guo's name and address in the notebook we kept in the bed compartment.'

Yong raised his thick eyebrows. 'He wrote Mr Guo's name in the notebook?'

'That's right.' As Yingxiu collected the notebook from the compartment and opened it up, Yong waited for her to confirm what he already knew.

'Strange. I thought it was here,' mumbled Yingxiu as she flipped through the pages, then twice more.

'I did not see Mr Guo's name when I checked the booklet yesterday,' said Yong. 'Let me see that again.' He took the booklet from Yingxiu's hands and examined the booklet more closely this time. 'Someone tore a page off. He did a clean job of it too. There is nothing left of it even at the stitching. Mdm Li, was the page supposed to be here?'

'Yes, it was right here.'

'Look, Sir,' said Yong to the magistrate and Zhou. 'These two pages faced either side of the page that was torn away. The smudges on these two remaining pages do not correspond to the positions of the writings on the facing pages.'

The magistrate examined the two pages. 'The remaining smudges here would have been made by writings on the missing page. Mdm Li, do you remember the contents of that page?'

Yingxiu rested her elbows on the table and propped up her head with her hands as she stared at the booklet. 'There were some notes on the merchants I dealt with. On Mr Guo, there was his full name, Guo Wutian. It is easy to remember—*wu tian* or five farms. His address was there too but it has been a number of years. I can't remember the details. I recall there was something about water, the word "water". I'd have to think about the other words, Sir. So sorry I can't be of better use.'

'Don't be too hard on yourself. It has been quite a few years. We have maps of the Capital that we can go through with you to jog your memory.'

'Have you told anyone else about Mr Guo and your husband's whereabouts?' asked Zhou. 'The girl Xue perhaps?'

'I've told Xue about Jie staying with his relative. I might have mentioned Mr Guo's surname a few years ago as a passing remark. I don't think she remembers. I've never told her or anyone else about Mr Guo's address.'

Zhou nodded. 'I think it is fair to say nobody would expect Mdm Li to share this information with anyone else, especially since Mr Sun has been dead for a number of years. And hence ...'

'Hence,' said the magistrate, 'removing Mdm Li and Xiaodong while disposing of the relevant letters would ensure it never comes to light.'

'Indeed, Sir.'

Yong chimed in. 'The intruder knew what to look for. He searched through every nook and corner because he could not find the letter that had been burnt up. Now, with the connection to Guo, the odds are good that the man either came from the

Capital or was engaged by someone from there. Since there is a chance that he is not from Renli, we can conduct a search. With this limp, he would stick out.'

'He could be anywhere in and around Renli,' said Zhou. 'The search will be harder still if a local resident is sheltering him and helping him escape.'

'True, but this is our best chance of finding him. We must hurry. If he has not left by now, he would be leaving soon.'

The magistrate got up from his seat. 'No more delays. We have to return to town right this moment.'

Chapter Thirteen

Yong's young legs rushed him back, ahead of the delegation, to relay instructions and organize the men, but it seemed a losing battle against time. The mystery man could have escaped right after laying the murderous trap. It would have been the prudent course of action. Yong was hoping he would stay to verify his kills.

It was late afternoon before Yong could mobilize all the constables and young male servants. He dispatched three pairs to man the three main city exits. Another five pairs were to comb through assigned segments of the city, with himself stationed at the centre. His instructions to the teams were to be discreet to avoid scaring off the suspect.

Three hours into their fruitless mission, darkness set in and the men were drained and complaining. Yong called off the search for the day, leaving men to watch the city exits through the night.

After a quick report to his superiors and slurping down his porridge dinner, he hurried off to the female servants' quarters. Standing outside the large dormitory room, he was about to call for his friend when one of the other maids saw him as she was coming out.

'Your little sis is not here,' said the maid.

'That's late.' Yong might as well have been speaking to the wall as the maid brushed past him. Figuring he could come back later, he turned around to leave when he saw Lian walking to him, her face glum and unsmiling.

'Looking for me?' said Lian as she handed over a small bundle wrapped in thin cloth. 'I only managed to pack a few plain *mantou* buns for you. All we could spare today. The men were hungry after the work you put them through.'

Yong noticed her hands were pale and wrinkled, signs of extended soaking in hot water. 'They made you stay back to do the dishes? For stepping out of the kitchen this morning?' There was anger and a measure of guilt in his voice, but he knew there was nothing he could do about it. Owing to his closeness to Magistrate Liu and Zhou, he exercised considerable influence over parts of the setup to do with official matters. Internal household functions like the kitchen, however, came under the supervision of Madam. The domestic servants, well aware of Madam's attitude towards Yong, viewed him with a mixture of indifference and disdain. They considered someone like Lian who dared to be friendly to Yong as a turncoat and treated her accordingly.

'It's not the first time. Looking out for a little rascal like you is not doing me much good.'

'Sorry, my fault. You should not have. I could have handled it myself.'

'Yeah, right. You were going to leave her waiting and fuming, if I recall. Heard she really chewed you up this time.'

'Nah, just Feng exaggerating as usual. I'm fine. Think more for yourself the next time.'

'Speak for yourself. You'd better not hang out with those people for too long. You know the bosses don't like it.'

'Just Mr Zhou, though he seems happy enough when I gather what he wants to know.'

'Aren't you exhausted after a whole day of walking around?'

'Shattered, to be honest. But I have to do this.'

'Silly, that's what you are. Don't give them reasons to dress you down.'

'We'll see. Thanks again. Got to go.' With that, Yong zipped off, out of the compound and into the night streets for a rendezvous his superiors frowned upon.

At this time of the night, the streets were deserted save for a few stragglers heading home and the night watchmen making their rounds with gongs and hammers, announcing the time at regular intervals. The beggars, who roamed the city during the day to eke out an existence, had returned to their habitual gathering places to spend the night.

Yong stepped into the narrow alley between two high walls, slowing down while his eyes adjusted to the darkness. About eighty paces into the alley, a left turn brought him to another path, which led to a tiny abandoned house. From a distance away, Yong could hear faint but lively chatter emerging from the house, suggesting a fruitful day for the occupying beggars.

As soon as Yong appeared outside the entrance, he was greeted with warmth by one of the beggars surrounding a half-hearted fire. In his mid-twenties and scruffier than the typical street-dweller, Bing also went by the nickname of Black Cat. The leaders of the Beggars' Sect whom Yong had met or heard of went with animal nicknames, perhaps alluding to some actual or aspirational prowess. It was true that Bing, his frame lithe and eyes bright, was always alert to danger.

'Hello there, Yong. Haven't seen you for a few days. Been busy?'

Yong placed the offering of buns into the grateful hands of one of Bing's underlings. 'Quite. Sorry, this is all I could bring.'

'We have enough for tonight, my friend. Come, sit down.'

Yong scanned the faces of the beggars belonging to Bing's circle of brothers, his direct reports who in turn oversaw their own cliques. He was familiar with the group, having interacted with them for months since he first arrived at Renli. They were a diverse rabble—old and young, different sizes, varying levels of intelligence—all sworn to a code to protect one another. They had taken some time to place their trust in him, for beggars and officers of the court were as accommodating to each other as fire and water. Yong's own beginnings on the streets helped bridge the gap.

'Guess you're working on the case of the woman who killed her own son,' said Bing.

Yong always appreciated Bing's readiness to cut to the chase. No niceties were necessary or useful with beggars. 'You've heard about it?'

'The whole town's talking about it.'

'What do people say?'

'Some paint her as a beast for murdering her own flesh and blood. Others pity her. Split half and half, just about.'

'What say you?'

'Me? I care only about my own stomach,' said Bing while patting his belly, drawing laughter from his men. 'And, of course, doing right by my brothers.' The beggars let out a chorus of approval. 'What brings you here?'

Yong waited for the men to quieten down. 'I'm looking for a man with a limp, drags his left leg while walking, a head shorter than me.'

'Sounds like Old Beard!' said Bing, pointing to the old, bearded beggar sitting across to his right, inducing more laughter.

'He'd be taller than Old Beard. This man is from out of town, most likely from the north.'

'Does he have something to do with the woman's case?'

'We have to keep this quiet for now but yes, he has something to do with it.' Since Yong needed help from these men, he would need to let them know he trusted them without letting on too much.

'You're saying the killer is someone else.'

Yong's pause was deliberate. 'Let's just say he's crucial to the investigation.'

Bing stared at Yong with eyes that reflected the fire dancing before him. Yong could imagine what he was thinking—that this woman, defenceless against the buffeting of the courts of law and public opinion, could be wrongly accused.

'Any reward?'

'Not at this point. To be honest, I don't think there would be. We're talking about a penniless woman and a boy the whole village would rather wish away. Nobody cares what happened to the boy and what will become of the mother.' Yong was appealing to the side of Bing, and that of the Beggars' Sect, that fought for justice and the downtrodden.

'Yet you do.'

Yong said nothing. He did not have to add Yingxiu and the boy were like them—the beggars and Yong himself—unnoticed by the rest of society. Someone had to stand up for them.

'A search like this would have to cover the entire city,' said Bing, 'not only my section. I reckon you'd want me to talk to the other heads.'

Yong nodded. He could approach the other four section leaders, but he was closest to Bing, who could convey the message more quickly and effectively.

'You know,' said Bing, 'Big Dog is aware we have been doing things to help the court.' A hush came upon the group of beggars. Yong noticed that mention of the top leader in Renli always brought about this effect amongst these men. Many stories of the man himself were about how he punished Sect members and the violence he meted out to enemies. A man who traded in the currency of fear.

Bing continued. 'He has not said much but I can see he's simmering. Everyone here knows you don't want Big

Dog angry.' The beggars nodded in unison. 'He hates you people. Thinks all of you are scum and corrupt to the bone.'

'Not this magistrate.'

'So far, that is. We trust you, not him. And if he isn't corrupt, odds are the next one will be.'

'All the more reason we should support the one who is clean.'

For a while, only the soft crackling of the fire filled the air as Yong and Bing locked eyes. The rest looked down or away.

'All right,' said Bing, 'we'll help. If we find him or anything useful, we'll let you know.'

Chapter Fourteen

'Nothing again,' said Constable Wei as he and Yong stepped out of an eating house after another futile round of poking around.

Through his murmurings, Wei had made it plain he considered himself unfortunate to be paired with Yong for the search as there was urgency aplenty and no breaks. Wei's complaints worried Yong, who could imagine his colleagues in other parts of the city sipping tea with their feet up now and then. In the process, they would introduce gaps in the dragnet. Well, maybe all except Niu, who followed instructions to the letter even if he complained while doing so.

The morning had started the same way it ended the day before—with searching, interviewing, and some murmuring. Yong had kicked the men out of bed before light and had been relentless since.

This was getting too much for Wei. 'Good time for a break, Yong?'

Yong too was frustrated but for the lack of a result rather than rest. They were now in their fourth hour of fruitless combing. Yet, there was still more than a third of their sector to go through.

Yong stopped, glanced at Wei with an air of resignation and turned back into the eating house, drawing a smile of relief from the constable. As they settled down at an unoccupied table, and Wei started to rattle off his order of tea and accompanying dishes fit for a midday meal, Yong sat there, unsmiling. It had been a slog, more so for him as he had stayed up late to ensure the unbroken rotation of men guarding the city exits overnight. He worried that sloppiness would set in as the men tired. The longer the search went on without success, the higher the likelihood that the man had either slipped past them or escaped the city earlier.

As he sat there thinking through the possibilities, Wei was already tucking into the dishes just laid out on the table. 'You going to eat?'

Just as Yong was picking up a pair of chopsticks, one of the court scribes stumbled in, drawing in quick breaths while steadying himself. He was on temporary search party duty covering a sector north of the city.

'There you are,' said the scribe to Yong, out of breath. 'A guest at an inn fits the description. He's not there any more but the inn helper there remembers him.'

'How far away?'

'A little less than half an hour away, if we walk fast.'

Yong walked very fast indeed, setting a punishing pace for the scribe who cursed his luck for unearthing the find.

When they arrived at the Qianxi Inn, Yong could see the suspect's choice of his resting base was not a random one. The inn itself was nondescript but large enough to hold many passing guests, too many for any one of them to invite scrutiny. It was situated at the edge of the city, close to a major road for travellers, allowing it to profit from Renli's position as a stopover point along a moderately busy route of commerce. This location was also convenient for a quick and inconspicuous exit out of the city, a convenience that the man had taken full advantage of.

The hapless scribe had not been able to tell Yong anything useful due to the rush. Yong was thus eager to speak to the innkeeper and the workers there. He was at least glad that the constable paired with the scribe was Niu, who could be trusted to secure the place to wait for his arrival.

Once Yong got in, Niu spotted him, walked over and hailed someone at the far corner of the eating area. A man at that corner, with a cloth cap flapping down the back of his head and a cleaning rag draped over his left shoulder, looked up. He was clearing a table and put up his hand to indicate he would go over to Niu after his little task.

'That's Ming, the inn assistant,' said Niu. 'He's the only one here who remembers anything much of the man.'

Ming came over soon enough. 'Yes, Mr Constable. How can I help?'

'This here is Liu Yong from the magistrate's office. Tell him about this man we were discussing.'

The short and thin inn assistant ran the rule over the boy in front of him as he spoke. 'Well, as I was saying to Mr Constable, there was this man with a limp who lodged here for three nights. He came in five days ago in the afternoon. I—'

'Which hour?'

'Late, about four hours after noon.' Ming did not sound too pleased with being interrupted. 'As I was going to say, I told Mr Constable I noticed his limp right away. He walked like this,' said Ming while imitating a walk with left foot dragging. 'I offered to carry his cloth bundle for him, but he brushed me off. Quite rude he was. He declined to even tell us his surname. Just paid up and went straight to his room.'

'What did he do while he was here? Do you know where he went?'

'He kept pretty much to himself. Nothing unusual. Fancied a bottle of wine with his lunch and dinner. He'd go out in the mornings and came back early afternoon, every day. Except two days ago, when he came back later.' This was the day of the incident.

'Where did he go?'

'Don't know. He looked worn out that day. Well, at least more tired than on previous days.'

'At what time did he get back?'

Ming scratched his head. 'About five hours after noon, I think.'

'I need you to be sure.'

'Yes, quite certain. The boss usually takes out his books to record transactions at that time. It was the lull between busy periods. So, as the man came in, I asked him if he would like some tea and snacks. He mumbled something and ducked into his room. Just ignored me.'

'Anything unusual about him then?'

'Unusual? Oh, yeah, his shoes were dirty. Quite a bit of mud on them.'

Yong shot a glance at Niu, whose immediate reaction was a slight shake of his head, his way of saying he had not told the inn assistant anything.

'What?' said Ming. 'Did I say something wrong?'

'No, no. What colour was the mud?'

'Sort of yellow, somewhat reddish. Why? Is that important?'

'Then what did he do?'

'He stayed in his room only for a short while. I was busy at the back and did not see him come down. The boss said he paid up and left. Went up the street. Probably heading out of the city.'

'Has the room been taken up since he left?'

'Almost immediately. We're in high season for visitors. In case you're wondering, I cleaned up the room after his departure. He did not leave anything behind.'

As expected, and disappointing. 'What did this man look like?'

'About my height, stocky, droopy eyes, grey stubble, streaks of silver in his hair. Quite ordinary, apart from the limp.'

As Ming was talking, Yong constructed the possible chain of events in his head. The killer had gone to Yingxiu's house, laid his deadly trap, then what? Given the late hour of his return to the inn, he had likely hung around at a convenient spot in town to take in any news of whether his mission had been successful.

'Would that be all?' asked Ming, impatient with the pause.

'Do you think you'd be able to recognize him if you saw him again?'

'I should think so.'

A thought came to Yong as he glanced at the sizeable midday clientele seated at the tables. 'There must be many guests passing through this place every day.'

'There are. Lots of guests this time of the year.'

'What made you notice this man we're talking about? Can't be just the limp, can it?'

Ming let on an impish grin and scratched his head. 'I do remember a few people who come by, that's true. The boss calls me a busybody sometimes, but I must say this gentleman caught my attention.'

'How so?'

'The way I've told it, you'd think he was a mute. But it did not start off this way. The first morning he came down for breakfast, he did chat some, but he did not like me asking about his accent.'

'His accent?'

'Yeah. I said I was from up north too and could recognize his accent though I've lost mine after so many years. He called me a busybody and hardly breathed a word after that. Strange man.'

'Northern. Near the border, perhaps?'

'Nah, that's where I'm from. His was different. Closer to the Capital.'

Chapter Fifteen

'All signs point to the Capital,' said Magistrate Liu, looking out of the window in his study while his two closest aides stood behind him. 'The question is: Why? A poor and defenceless woman and her disabled son. What would move someone to commit murder from so far away?'

A lengthy silence ensued before the magistrate turned around and said, 'Mr Zhou, what is your recommendation for our next course of action?'

'There is only one thing we can do. We refer the case to officials in the Capital. The few possible areas Mdm Li identified could be leads for the local authorities to investigate.'

'She remembered only that the street address had the words "water" or "river" in it. Given the few rivers running through the city, it was no surprise the spots were all over the place. Not much help, I'm afraid.'

'Sir,' said Yong, 'chances are, the locals would drop the case. There is still a lot to do, and the outcome is uncertain. Since this case involves a poor widow; they have nothing to gain from it.'

Zhou aimed a sharp look at Yong. 'You are casting aspersions on fellow officials we know nothing about. It is not our business to worry about how other officials do their jobs. They will handle the case the way they see fit. Remember we do not have the jurisdiction to conduct investigations over there.'

'That is true,' said the magistrate. 'We will write to the local magistrate to ask him to take up the matter. But you know,

Mr Zhou, I have not been to the Capital for a few years. After the visit of Justice Hou is out of the way, I will make a trip there to call on the local magistrate and, perhaps, check on the progress of the case. Who knows, I may be able to provide some assistance, with or without his knowledge. Let him take the credit.'

Zhou nodded, not quite succeeding in suppressing a frown.

The magistrate smiled at his adviser. 'You do not agree with my decision.'

'Sir, any intervention on our part at the Capital would constitute a major breach of protocol.'

'And hence it would be more of a social visit. You have been encouraging me to cultivate relationships with ranking officials at the centre, have you not?'

'Something you found distasteful.'

The magistrate laughed. 'Perhaps I have, for once, developed a taste for such duties.'

'We need to be careful.'

'I know, Mr Zhou. I will exercise the greatest of care.'

Zhou nodded once more.

'Sir, if I may suggest,' said Yong, 'this man with a limp left just two days ago. Perhaps we could still catch up with him on the road.'

'A two-day head start is too much to make up for,' said Zhou. 'In any case, it is out of the question for the magistrate to leave town when the Chief Censor is due to arrive in less than ten days. Justice Hou is one of the highest-ranking officials in all the Kingdom.'

'I'm thinking of going after the man myself with a constable coming along. Even if I can't catch up with him on the way there, I can still go ahead of Old Master to lay the groundwork.'

'But you are a young lad who has never been to the Capital.'

'Niu has. He went with you and Young Master on the visit last year. He can come with me.'

'Seems like you have it all figured out. But it still does not make sense. You are talking about finding a lone person among five hundred thousand in the largest city under the heavens. You have grossly underestimated the magnitude and complexity of the task. Truly ignorant of the height of the heavens and the depth of the earth.'

Half a million. Yong had heard the number from Zhou and Zhong before, but always reckoned it was an exaggeration. 'As you said, we have some leads from Mdm Li.'

'People move. Just the last few years, there have been a few fires forcing many people to relocate. This man may not live at the same address any more.'

'I could seek help.'

'You mean the street gangs? Preposterous. Why would the beggars there help someone they do not know? In any case, there is a better chance of this lawless rabble giving you trouble than lending a hand.'

Yong had no answer to that. It was true he did not know anybody there. To establish a reliable link with the Beggars' Sect at Renli took three months, a length of time he did not have in the Capital. It was also true the Sect comprised elements good, bad, righteous, and downright criminal. Whether the bunch so far away would be of any assistance to him would be no more than a coin toss.

'Listen, Yong,' said Zhou in a more measured tone, 'we are better off with you and Niu helping out here for the Justice's visit. Be sensible.'

The magistrate could not help but smile at the youthful brashness of his attendant. 'Mr Zhou is right. It would have been useful if you could go before me, but I have to weigh that against the work we need to do here.'

Yong understood what the two elder men were trying to say. Censorate officials checking on local operations in the Kingdom was not unusual, but a visit from the Chief Censor himself was rare. While this particular visit was ostensibly part of a routine tour of the region, Yong could guess, as he was sure his superiors could, why the Chief Censor might have some specific interest in Renli.

The Censorate investigated suspicions of corruption or other egregious misconduct amongst officials, and took miscreants to task. The Chief Censor would want to make sure the dramatic upturn in Magistrate Liu's efficiency in resolving cases did not stem from corruption and abuse of power. While the magistrate's conscience was clear, having Yong around would be of great help in explaining how they worked.

The magistrate had also spoken often of his admiration for Justice Hou, one of the most senior representations of the ideal Imperial official—loyal, righteous, wise, and dedicated. It was understandable that the magistrate would want his closest assistants to meet the great man.

'The game is not lost,' said the magistrate. 'I will write a letter to the local magistrate and send it out with the next mail run. After that, there is time to work out our next steps.'

Chapter Sixteen

The next day, after his midday meal, Yong headed straight for the rear of the magistrate's compound. With his head down and Xiaodong's case running in his mind, he did not notice the magistrate's son coming up to him.

'Hey, Yong,' Zhong called out as he neared. 'Looked for you at the quarters yesterday, but they told me you were out most of the day. What's up?'

'Out for the search. I've told you before it is not appropriate for the young master to visit the servants' quarters. Tell someone to summon me.'

'It's all right. I've a lot of time on my hands.'

'For how long this time?'

Zhong held up two fingers.

'Two weeks?'

'Guess again.'

'Woah! Two months in the cage? A heavy hand from Old Master this time. Can't say you don't deserve it.'

'Thanks a lot for your words of consolation. To think I came to check on you. I heard Mother gave you a proper roasting.'

'Don't believe everything you hear.'

'Well, I'm sure she did not show you her kindest side. Hey, I'm sorry. I told her you did not tell on me.'

'How could you be so sure I did not?'

'I dare you!' Zhong wrapped his left arm around Yong's shoulders and landed a playful jab on his belly.

'Don't worry, I'm used to it,' said Yong, turning solemn. 'Well, got to go.'

'Where to?'

'To check on Mdm Li.'

'Ah, yes, still on the big case. Explains your bitter gourd face.'

Yong sighed. 'You wouldn't understand.'

'What's wrong?'

'We're letting her down, that is what's wrong.'

'I thought Father and you lot are helping her.'

'Help? If Old Master is serious about handing the case over to the locals, the investigation will be dead in the water before it can get going. I've been wanting to talk to her to clarify a few things. Then again, I'm not looking forward to facing her. You know what I mean?'

'Don't fret. Things have a way of working out. Listen, I ...' Zhong paused and placed his hand on Yong's shoulder.

'What? Spit it out. I don't have all day.'

'Nothing,' said Zhong with an assuring pat on his servant's back. 'I'll talk to you another time. You go ahead. I'll see you later.' With that, Zhong spun around and made his way back to the residence.

Alone again, Yong took a deep breath and headed to the guest lodge, which sat at a quiet corner of the compound. It was a small house with four rooms, each with its own door and windows facing out. The usual occupants, few and far between, were officials from out of town, and there were none at the moment. Since the magistrate was of the mind to keep Yingxiu's release from prison under wraps, this was the perfect place to house her on a temporary basis.

Locating the guest was simple enough as the door and windows to her room were the only ones in the building left open. While Yong stood outside, debating with himself whether this was an appropriate time to intrude into the private space of the grieving mother, Yingxiu appeared at the door. Yong was startled in a pleasant way. Yingxiu's appearance was completely different from the day before. She was all cleaned up and dressed in fresh clothes, the circles around her eyes a much lighter hue. She wore a thin smile when she saw Yong, though the sorrow in her eyes was still apparent.

'Good day, young sir. I thought I heard someone coming. Are you looking for me?'

'Sorry for bothering you. I wanted to see how you are doing.'

'I'm much better, thank you.' Yingxiu's smile widened a touch. 'Oh, please forgive me for my lack of manners. Why don't you come in and sit down?'

As Yong walked in and took a seat at the round table, Yingxiu poured him a cup of warm tea and also sat down. 'Magistrate and Mrs Liu have been very kind. Madam in particular has been spending quite a lot of time with me, bless her. In fact, she was just here. She told me the magistrate and his men will try their best—sorry, your best—to help me.'

Yong nodded and looked down to hide his embarrassment.

Yingxiu continued. 'Thanks to the magistrate and to you, young sir, I'm holding on to hope that the truth will come to light, that the cloud will lift from Xiaodong's death.'

Yong's embarrassment deepened. 'Please call me Yong. I'm just a servant boy.'

'The brave one. A nice name, and apt. Your parents had it right.'

'I don't have parents. Magistrate Liu gave it to me.'

It was Yingxiu's turn to be embarrassed. 'I'm so sorry. I did not mean to remind you.'

'It's all right. I don't remember them at all. My parents, I mean.'

'Young sir—'

'Yong.'

'Yong, you're too modest. I have seen what you can do. What is more important, I can see you have the heart to help.'

'We will try, but I must say this is a difficult case involving an unfamiliar place far from here. We have to accept that the possibility of finding out what really happened is small, very small.'

'I understand,' said Yingxiu, though her softer tone conveyed disappointment.

Both Yong and Yingxiu sank into a moment of awkward silence. The thought came to Yong that it would have been better for him to stay away from her. While the hope she harboured might have been false, it at least lifted her spirits.

Yingxiu finally spoke. 'I'm grateful to Mr Zhou for arranging a proper funeral for Xiaodong. Do you know what my greatest wish was when Xiaodong was still around?'

Yong did not answer.

'My greatest wish,' said Yingxiu, 'was for Xiaodong to die before me. Can you imagine that coming from a mother? The thought of leaving him behind in this world, knowing there would be no one to take care of him, thinking how cruel the world would be to him, was too much for me to bear. And yet ...'

The widow brought her right sleeve up to dab her eyes before tears trickled down. 'And yet, when it happened, my heart was filled with an overwhelming sense of loss and injustice. My poor Xiaodong had nothing, nothing at all, except for two things: a pure heart, and a mother who loves him. He did not deserve to die in that way, and I will not, if I can help it, allow this evil deed to go unpunished.'

She rubbed her left elbow. 'This morning, I woke up with the same pain in my bones I have endured for months. But somehow, it felt less agonizing than before. If not for Xiaodong's last tantrum, I would have been dead too. I thought to myself,

"Why? What is the point of all this?" I would be gone in a matter of months anyway.'

Yingxiu locked her eyes on Yong. 'Then I realized something. More than that, I *knew*. Heaven has kept me alive a while longer for a purpose—to help bring my son's killer to justice. This is my burden to bear. I beg of you, Yong, help me.'

His head still hung low; Yong closed his eyes for a moment before looking up. 'I'll try, Mdm Li. I will do my utmost. First, I need to ask you a few questions.'

Yong made his way back to the court building, his heart still heavy from the conversation with Yingxiu. As he was still pondering over how he could fulfil his promise to the widow, he saw Niu running towards him, shouting and gesticulating.

'The magistrate wants to see you. Now!'

Chapter Seventeen

The sight that greeted Yong when he arrived at the magistrate's study was unusual. Three people sat at the round table with Magistrate Liu. The presence of Zhou indicated a discussion on official matters. Madam and Zhong never participated in official business, yet there they were, seated on the left and right of the magistrate. Nobody was talking, the only sound being the clicking of porcelain as the magistrate uncovered the lid of his cup, only to place it back when he saw his young attendant.

As Yong greeted everyone, he got a better view of Zhong's face. His young master's passive expression offered no clue on the issue at hand. The magistrate and Zhou were as inscrutable. The only emotion on display was Madam's irritation, stirred up by the wait for the servant boy. She was about to voice her displeasure when the head of the household spoke. 'Did you come from speaking to Mdm Li?'

'Yes, Sir.' Yong stood facing the magistrate, the table between them.

With the opening salvo stripped from her, Madam made do with a sideway glare at the young man. Yong wondered if his troubles with Madam had been carried over to this conference.

The magistrate nodded. 'Good. I have ordered a notice to be put up on the public board. It will say that, on the weight of evidence against her and her own admission of guilt, she will be retained in prison to await sentencing.'

A nod from Yong, who thought the arrangement made sense. Let the people think she had been found guilty, which would not be a surprise since the whole town seemed to have determined her guilt. This would buy them some time to conduct investigations without alerting the perpetrator.

'There is another matter to discuss with you,' said the magistrate, using the singular form of the pronoun while looking at Yong, which was strange given the other people in the room.

The official took his time to bring up his cup and sip from it before putting it down again. 'I have decided that you should go ahead of me to the Capital as soon as possible.'

From the expression of the others in the room, Yong could see that the announcement was not news to them. The sudden change in thinking, however, so rare with the magistrate, surprised him.

The official continued. 'As you suggested, Niu will go with you.'

Yong nodded and was about to speak, but his old master was not done yet.

'Another thing,' said the magistrate. 'I have also decided Zhong will go along.'

Yong had not expected that at all, as Zhong had never been involved in official work. Another thought went through his mind. Of course, Yong had wanted to give chase while the scent was fresh. But as he pondered over the problem, he was almost relieved the magistrate turned down his initial request made in haste. Since being adopted by the Lius, he had never ventured far from his master.

'I'm not sure, Sir. I'm not sure I can handle it. The Capital is distant and unfamiliar to me.'

'Zhong has been there and so has Niu. Both Zhong and you are old enough to do this. Many men your age are married, some with children. It is about time Zhong took up some adult responsibilities.'

Yong felt like kicking himself for not seeing this coming. What Zhong had said or tried to say, and what Madam had mentioned to Yingxiu, came into focus at once. Yong now recalled that Zhong had spoken of the Capital in awe, like some paradise on earth. It was now clear to Yong that Zhong had seen the investigation as a golden opportunity to escape his stay-home sentence and grabbed it with both hands. His indulgent mother, vulnerable to persuasion by Zhong, lobbied her husband on her son's behalf. The only surprise to Yong was that the judgement of the magistrate, normally steady and reliable, could be thus swayed. Perhaps, as a hopeful parent, he was heartened by what looked like a desire in his wayward son to take on serious work, to be a man.

'Truth be told,' said Yong, 'I thought about the issue last night. I have always had you and Mr Zhou to guide me. I don't think I can operate there without both of you.'

'You are well capable of doing this. Just be sure you consider thrice before making any major move. I trust your judgement.'

Madam caught the attention of Zhong and, with the type of wordless communication between mother and son that involved almost imperceptible movements of eyes and brows, nudged him to speak up.

Right on cue, Zhong delivered a rehearsed line. 'Father, I will not let you down in this task. You can count on me.'

'This brings me to my next point,' said the magistrate, with his eyes still fixed on Yong. 'Zhong will go on one condition. On official matters, he—and Niu—will defer to Yong, whom I put in charge.'

Madam's face, which had settled into placidity, flared up. 'This cannot be! How can the young master be taking orders from his servant?'

'It has to be so. This is serious business, not child's play. Zhong, by his own choice I may add, has no experience at all in such work. He can either agree to the condition or stay home.'

Still bristling, Madam was preparing a comeback when Zhong intervened. 'It is all right, Mother. I accept the condition.' Another quick glance to his mother with a slight shake of the head convinced her to stand down, even if it was with great reluctance.

'You will move out as soon as you can,' said the magistrate. 'There are preparations to be made. I will draft a letter to the local magistrate for you to bring along. It will introduce Zhong as my son so there would be some courtesy extended. But you need to be shrewd and careful. Very careful.'

The magistrate paused to let the note of caution sink in. 'At the Centre, wolves in official's clothing prowl, eager to devour the naive. One wrong step and you could heap trouble upon yourself. Stay out of the way of the local authorities as much as possible. I do not know them and have no idea if they can be trusted. Only if you are sure any particular one is clean and you need his help, do you approach him with the letter. Do you understand so far?'

Both young men nodded while Madam shifted in her chair, now not so sure sending her precious son on this mission was such a good idea.

The magistrate stared at Yong. 'You are not to take unnecessary risks. While the objective is important, remember safety is paramount.'

'You'd better remember that,' said Madam.

'Yes, Madam. Yes, Sir.'

'Once there,' said the magistrate, 'check in at the Yunxiao Inn, north of the Bian River and just to the east of the main avenue. I will look for you there when I arrive. You may need some cover to poke your noses around. Mr Zhou will ask for a letter from

Young Master Ouyang to appoint you as representatives of the Ouyang merchant family. He should be open to help given his gratitude on the case of the fraudulent monks. The Ouyang family business has branches in other cities, so the letter will say you are from a city other than Renli, scouting for goods. This will lower the likelihood of our suspect linking you to the case at hand. Am I clear?'

Again, both Zhong and Yong nodded.

'There is much preparation to be done. Get to work, lads.'

There was one thing for Yong to work on, but it was not something he would mention in front of the Lius and Zhou.

Chapter Eighteen

'Are you sure you want to do this?' said Bing as he led Yong through the dark alley.

'For the fourth time tonight, yes,' said Yong, though he did not feel quite so sure. He had never met Big Dog, the leader of the Beggars' Sect in Renli. Conflicting accounts made it hard to ascertain whether he tended towards chivalry or lawlessness. Facing Big Dog before trust could be established was a risk, but one he felt he had to take.

'He does not like you people, that's for sure,' Bing said, by way of reminder. 'If Big Dog turns on you, there's not much anyone can do.'

Yong had heard much about Big Dog's inclination to violence, chiefly from Bing and his gang but also from various other quarters including the magistrate's constables. He reasoned that a street chief had to take care of himself and his people in a ruthless environment that suffered no weaklings. His followers might have padded some of these stories to thicken the aura of power around him. At least Yong hoped so.

'We need the help of your brothers in the Capital. Big Dog is probably the only person here who can help us make the connection. I'm just going to talk to him. Why would he turn on me?'

'I've seen him give someone a royal kicking for commenting on the way he walked. I'd watch my words if I were you.'

Progress was slow as the paths leading to the supposed headquarters of the Sect in Renli were back lanes shrouded in darkness. Yong had heard the place itself was an abandoned temple in an area that even law enforcement officials were not inclined to tread upon.

Unlike Bing's hideout, Yong could see Big Dog's den a fair distance away. Dancing rays of light told of a sizeable fire within the compound and a disregard for concealment. He heard loud voices as he neared. It was apparent Big Dog and his immediate circle of followers had little to fear from the outside world.

The chatter died down as soon as Yong and his friend walked through the opening of the ramshackle temple compound. Dozens of pairs of eyes locked on to the intruder.

'Wait here,' said Bing, who left Yong standing alone amidst the hostile crowd while he disappeared into the shell of what used to be a temple.

Yong tried his best to maintain a calm façade. With feet shoulder-width apart and hands behind his back, he took in slow breaths to try and suppress the trembling emanating from his belly. It was not working.

It did not take long for Bing to emerge from the building. 'The Boss said he won't see you. Let's go back.' Bing started to make his way to the compound exit.

Yong held on to his friend's elbow before he could walk past. 'What do you mean go back? Did you tell him about the case?'

'Of course, I did. It's no use. We'll go back and figure out what to do next.'

Yong let go of Bing and marched towards the temple's opening. This time, it was Bing who did the holding back. 'What are you doing? You crazy?'

'I have no time to waste. I'm going in to reason with him.'

'Reason? This is not the court. Don't be foolish!'

Out of the entrance to the temple came another beggar, middle-aged, long-haired, and black-bearded, holding a wooden staff. He planted the staff right in front of himself and rested both hands on the top end. 'You want to go in, young man? Go on,' he said as he stepped aside. 'Just be prepared to be stretchered out.'

Yong stared at the long-haired beggar for a while, then said to Bing in a low voice, 'Let me go.' Bing looked into the eyes of Yong and breathed a heavy sigh. He loosened his hold on the younger man and followed him into the temple building.

The interior, though spacious, looked like someone had strewn two cart-loads of rocks and dust all over. The positions of the beggars told him of the hierarchy in place. The half dozen who appeared to be elders of the Sect sat in an approximate concave arc facing the entrance while eating and drinking. Younger ones stood at the sides, most of them better built than the typical beggar, forming a protective hedge around the leadership. Two other youngsters, skinny and tall, seemed ill at ease amongst the gathering, standing subserviently to one side as the rest chattered and exchanged banter.

Right in the middle of the seated beggars was one, perhaps, in his mid-thirties who stood out from the elders. While lean, he was the most muscular of the lot. He had angled eyebrows that lent his eyes a fierce edge. A scar ran from the side of his right eye to near his cheekbone. Though he had never met the man, Yong was sure this was Big Dog, the leader of beggars in this city.

Big Dog was preoccupied with polishing off a chicken drumstick. When he was done, he flicked the bone on to the dusty ground before him, where a few more bones lay. Two other small piles of bones were neatly collected on broad lotus leaves laid on the ground.

'Look what we have here, brothers,' said Big Dog. 'We're made to believe this skinny lad is a law enforcement officer.

I suppose he feels his colleagues can come by at any time to rescue him. Forget about it, boy. I have not seen any officer of the law around these parts for a long time. For good reason too.'

Yong, trembling inside, steadied himself and forced his words out. 'My co-workers and superiors do not know I'm here. I came on my own accord.'

'You are either brave or foolhardy, and I reckon it's the latter. I've heard of you lending a hand to our brothers once in a while, but I've never asked for your help, so don't count on any favours.'

'Your men have helped me too. You don't owe me anything. I'm appealing to your sense of justice, and that of the Sect, to help the woman accused of killing her son. In my view, she has been wronged.'

'Why should I care? And why should I help you bunch of dog officials?' said Big Dog, jabbing his forefinger in Yong's direction to drive the point home.

'The Beggars' Sect has come to the aid of the defenceless before. You have done it yourself.'

'Not with dog officials. You people are only keen on your own dirty agenda.'

'Hear me out first before passing judgement.'

Big Dog curved up his lips to one side and sniggered. 'Amusing, this is. An unweaned pup from the almighty court interested in my judgement. Since you're here, you might as well regale us with your story. Perhaps we can get some much-needed entertainment tonight.' A ripple of chuckles broke out from the inner group and spread to the outer hedge.

'We are going to the Capital to investigate the case,' said Yong. 'There is evidence someone from there came with the intention of killing both mother and child. I'm asking for the help of the Sect in the Capital to find the perpetrator.'

'Why would a high and mighty magistrate need my help?'

'I've told you he does not know. He's not going with us.'

'Oh? How many of you going?'

'Three including myself.'

Big Dog burst into laughter. 'Three? I sure hope the other two are not kids like you. On what basis do you think you can find the person amongst hundreds of thousands? What do you have? Let me guess—you're going to bribe your way through. Or perhaps you plan to gather your corrupt chums there to frame an innocent man. Laughable.'

Yong felt anger bubbling up, a feeling he welcomed as it crowded out fear and calmed his nerves. Adrenaline was taking over. He stood staring at Big Dog, who did not seem pleased to be stared at.

'What?' said Big Dog. 'Got something to say, boy?'

'Nothing. I was thinking—if I can't secure your help tonight, at least I have solved the mystery of the missing temple offerings. It has not been a fruitless trip.'

Big Dog snarled at Yong, baring his crooked and yellow teeth. 'You have the nerve.'

Without being ordered, three of the henchmen shoved Bing aside and closed in on Yong at his sides and back. He felt the warm breath of the one behind him down his neck. Big Dog turned his attention to Bing. 'What did you tell him?'

'He did not tell me anything,' said Yong. 'You can see from Bing's expression he has no idea what I was talking about.' Bing was too busy shaking his head to say anything.

'Let me fill you in, Bing,' said Yong without diverting his gaze from Big Dog. 'In the past week, there has been a buzz around the town temple. The temple keepers reported some food offerings had been consumed by the patron deity. On a few nights, the chicken offerings have been stripped of meat, leaving bones behind. A miracle, they say, only I did not believe it and went to check it out.'

Yong made a show of glancing around and sniffing the air. 'The smell in here ... is of cheap rice wine, the type poured on temple food offerings like roast chicken.'

He pointed to the two tall and skinny beggars at the side. 'I was wondering what these two were doing here, for they look neither strong nor menacing enough to be on the guard detail. Until, that is, I noticed the patches of white on their clothes. You see, Bing, the temple is locked at night and the wall around it is rather high. And painted white, if I may add. With their height, these two are well capable of scaling the wall. The temple night watchman swore blind to not letting anyone through at night, as he would. I can tell you though, by the smell of alcohol on him, he would have slept through a whole troupe of men climbing in and out. You can also see the traces of oil on the clothes on these two. My guess is that they had wrapped the oily loot in the lotus leaves we see here on the ground and brought it all the way here.'

Big Dog was still staring at Yong, though now his eyes were narrowed and his forehead creased. Bing too was staring at Yong. His lips were moving without sound, mouthing words that begged Yong to stop talking for the sake of life and limb. Yong was not going to.

'The bones here would be collected and bundled in the leaves. Another stealthy break-in would allow your colleagues to arrange them on the altar in the shape of a chicken, to create the impression of meat magically stripped off. That is why your two tall brothers are waiting, their job unfinished. Amusing, and quite novel.'

Big Dog stood up, strode over to Yong and grabbed his collar with both hands, lifting the young man up and forcing him to stand on tiptoes. 'Tired of living, are you? What are you going to do? Arrest us?'

Despite his vicarious position and aware of how pathetic he appeared, Yong was somewhat surprised he felt more anger and contempt than fear. 'You would know I have extricated your men from far more serious trouble.'

'You're saying we owe you, is that it?' Big Dog jerked Yong towards himself. Yong could smell Big Dog's breath, and it was not at all pleasant.

Yong tried his best to keep his tone level. 'I'm saying this does not trouble me or the magistrate. The temple folks are telling anyone who bothers to listen that this is a miracle, a sign the deity is pleased with the city. Donations are flowing into the temple, which is not a bad thing. You might wish to consider how long you want to carry on this little scheme, though. The town people are getting a little too excited about this supposed miracle. It is a matter of time before someone stumbles on to the truth.'

Feeling Big Dog loosening his grip, Yong was emboldened to press on. 'You asked what we have. We don't pay bribes. My master hates to even talk to corrupt officials, let alone work with them. All we have are hard work, a sense of justice, and some ability in reasoning. In the case of the widow and her child, I fear these are not enough; hence my appeal to you for help.'

Big Dog let go of Yong but followed up with a shove on the chest. Not too forceful, but enough to cause him to stumble back two steps and to establish who was in charge. 'Entertainment was what I asked for, and entertainment was what we got. A nice story that changes nothing. Help is what you need, but you will leave here with none. As compensation for your amusing tale, you will be allowed to walk out of here in one piece. Now scram before I change my mind.'

Knowing he would share in whatever treatment dished out to Yong, Bing spared no effort in dragging his friend out. In spite of Yong's protest, Bing made sure he won the tussle this time.

Chapter Nineteen

Yong had slept little given the late preparations for the trip. First thing in the morning, Zhou passed him a carefully secured package containing the letters spoken about the previous day. Besides Magistrate Liu's formal note to the local magistrate, the other two were from Young Master Ouyang appointing Zhong and Yong as his representatives—one from the headquarters in Renli and another signed in the name of the Longtian branch. If necessary, they could use the Longtian version to mask their city of origin. About halfway between Renli and the Capital, Longtian was the location of the most far-flung Ouyang branch.

Magistrate Liu was right about the gratitude of Ouyang. The merchant was so keen to help that he had lent them an official seal to add credence to the cover.

'Take good care of it,' said Zhou as he bound up the ceramic block, with a tortoise figure sitting on top, in cloth. The name of the family firm was etched on the bottom face reddened with dried ink. 'This seal authorizes you to engage in transactions on their behalf. Don't lose it.'

Lian too had woken up earlier than usual to prepare a few fresh buns and plenty of dried food for the trip. 'Your first priority is to bring everyone back safely, you hear?' she had said. How could he miss the message, Yong thought, when the magistrate and Madam kept drumming it into him?

Zhong emerged from his room early by his standards, bright, excited, and raring to go. He had spent almost an hour with his parents, with his mother doing most of the talking. The magistrate decided that the sending-off party should proceed no further than the gates of the compound, to spare his wife from more tears.

As the Lius huddled a final time at the gate, Zhou took the opportunity to pull Yong to one side.

'You seem pensive,' said Zhou, 'not your normal self.'

'I'm all right. It's just that this is new for me. I should have listened to you, Mr Zhou. I'm not sure I'm up to it.'

'Old Master put you in charge. You remember that, and take charge.'

'I'm sure Young Master is fine with it.'

'I'm not talking about him. I'm talking about you.' Zhou had to hurry as the Liu family's farewell conference appeared to be reaching its conclusion. 'Old Master trusts your judgement, as do I, so you should too.'

'Don't worry, I won't let rashness overtake me. I'll play it safe.'

'You will do no such thing.'

'I don't under—'

'You did not become of use to the magistrate by playing safe. You are not journeying halfway across the land only to play it safe. Follow your heart, engage your head, and get the job done. Do you understand?'

Yong nodded.

Zhou's stern face hinted at a smile. 'Just remember to bring everyone back with body parts intact.' Zhou motioned with a wave of his hand for Yong to join up with Zhong, who had at last broken off from his parents.

Leaving the elders behind, the travelling trio were to link up with the pre-arranged horse-cart and driver at the main city gate. As it was still dark when they neared the rendezvous point, Yong did not recognize the figure loitering in the shadows of the row of shop houses until he came closer.

'Good morning, Bing. Nice of you to come see me off.'

'Not at all, my friend. After our little adventure last night, I would have been glad not to see you for a while. The boss, however, wants a word with you.'

They needed to set off early to make their next stop before sundown, and Yong was not sure what another meeting with Big Dog would achieve. However, this was a diversion he had to take. He told Zhong and Niu to go ahead of him to meet the horse-cart driver.

After four turns in a maze of narrow back alleys, Bing and Yong came to a clearing where Big Dog was standing on his own, leaning against a wall with his arms folded, his face expressionless.

'Here you are, young lad,' said Big Dog, beckoning Yong over with a wave of his hand. 'Must say it took guts to step into our lair with no backup. Who are you, really?'

'What you see—a servant boy assisting the magistrate.'

The Sect leader eyed Yong for a moment. 'Why are you going out of your way to help the woman? What are you getting out of it?'

'The opportunity to right an injustice.'

'Bull.'

'Magistrate Liu Ye arrived more than a year ago. You can see or at least hear about his works and actions.'

With his eyes locked on the young man, Big Dog reached inside his outer coat to fish out a small token that he handed to Yong. It was a rough wooden carving of what approximated a dog, painted black.

'They call the Sect chief there, Wild Wolf. Show him this wood carving and say I sent you. If you catch him in the right mood, he may help you.'

'How do we locate him?'

'His bunch hangs around a large, old house in the southwest part of the city. Ask any beggar for the way there. We go back some way, the both of us.'

'Thank you.'

'I'm not doing this for you or that master of yours. Remember to bring the carving back to me. If you lose it, be sure I will hunt you down and kill you.'

Without waiting for Yong's reaction, Big Dog turned around and walked away. Bing waved Yong a farewell and went after his leader, who had disappeared into the shadows of the alley.

Zhong, impatient to set off, was not too pleased when Yong joined up and chided his servant for time lost. First light had broken through. The horse-cart, pulled by a lone animal, got going without further fuss.

The three travellers sat cross-legged on the floor of the cart. They leaned back on the wooden boards making up the cart's sides, the wide Niu on one side and the two younger men sharing the other. Niu was decked out in his uniform with his sheathed sabre by his side.

'You look bright this morning, Young Master,' said Yong.

'I've told you before and I'll tell you again—the Capital will blow you away. There is none like it. Plenty of things to see and do.'

'Resourceful of you to manoeuvre your way out of confinement. Nevertheless, I should thank you. If not for your deft lobbying, I would not have this chance to go after the killer so soon.'

'Don't mention it, brother. Glad to help.'

'Speaking of help, would I be expecting some of it at the Capital, as Old Master alluded to?'

The answer came in the form of a wordless grin. Yong shook his head and smiled back. He traced the line of Niu's gaze to Renli, now illuminated by the early morning sun. A part of him worried about being away from the place he called home, where the magistrate and his teacher were always on hand to guide him and to bring him back on course when he strayed. For the next few weeks at least, not only would he need to fend for himself, he had to keep his young master out of trouble.

He could not afford to look back now. There was quite some catching up to do.

The sun had started to duck below the horizon when the horse-cart pulled into their first night's stop at an inn. After a long day of travelling, Zhong and Niu were only too glad to unload their cloth bags, settle down at a dining table to order refreshments, and ask for a room for the night. For Yong, the first order of business was to check for a trace of the suspect.

The inn assistant listened to Yong's description of the man and said, 'I remember him. He was here four nights ago. Checked in late, past midnight. Stayed one night and left first thing the next morning.'

Chapter Twenty

Four days.

Yong had held out some hope of shrinking the suspect's lead over them. He had set a relentless pace despite the protestations of first Zhong, then Niu, keeping the number of rest stops to a minimum.

Alas, their target also seemed intent to maximize distance covered every day, so the gap remained. Thus far, they had kept to the shortest route which were in parts rough and challenging, and had managed to stay on the same route as the suspect.

On the fifth day of pushing their limits, even the horse snorted its disapproval. Faced with the choice of going over or around a hill, Yong gambled on climbing. The horse and cart navigated the upward sloping terrain without too much difficulty at the onset, until it started to drizzle, rain, and then pour.

They found to their cost that the flimsy canopy of the cart could keep out a drizzle but not a downpour. Such was the ferocity of the wind that it felt like water pellets swept straight through the structure. Within minutes, they were drenched, cold, and miserable.

The driver and his horse had to battle the elements and terrain for half a day before they came to a small village near the foot of the hill, where the sprightly old keeper of the tiny village temple offered them shelter. After changing into drier clothes, they hung the wet ones up while waiting for the storm to pass.

But it never did pass until evening approached, by which time the driver reckoned there remained too little daylight time to make it to the next stop. Yong decided to camp at the temple overnight. In the cold and cramped confines of the temple, only Niu could get any sleep, but then he had earned an enviable reputation of being able to sleep anywhere, under any condition.

Next morning, as Yong went about serving his master and preparing for departure, he did not initiate any conversation as Zhong did not seem to be in the mood to talk. Zhong's unsmiling face and the dark circles around his eyes told Yong all he needed to know. After a hasty breakfast of dried biscuits, they thanked the host and loaded up wordlessly on to the horse-cart to continue with their journey.

The depressed mood lingered for the rest of the day. Though they were diligent in checking with proprietors of inns and rest stops along the route, they did not come across anybody who had seen the man with a limp. In all likelihood, Yong thought, he had taken the other route at the fork.

Unfortunately, after this stretch of the journey, there was more than one way to reach the Capital. That they lost track of the man at this stage was of concern to Yong. What if the man had been heading to another city all along? If so, there would be no hope of finding him.

After a long day, they checked into an inn late at night. The three of them were so tired that they retired right after stuffing some decent fare into their stomachs.

Next morning, like clockwork, Yong got up before dawn, shook Niu up, and prepared for the day's travelling. As he had done since they left Renli, Yong went about the preparations, packing up and getting ready his young master's breakfast, hoping to let Zhong catch a few more winks. When he was ready, he touched Zhong's right arm to rouse him.

Zhong had never been used to waking up early, and the routine in the past week had not been enough to shake him out of his morning habit. This time, though, he did not budge.

Yong touched Zhong's arm again, and then his forehead to confirm his fears. 'Niu, bad news. Fever, and a high one.'

The next hour or so was all about the two servants fussing over their master, who was feeling weak and in some discomfort. Yong made the sensible decision. 'Niu, go tell the innkeeper and our driver we're not moving out today.'

Four days.

The gap was irrelevant now. Any hope they had harboured of catching up with the man, already slim, was well and truly gone.

Chapter Twenty-One

'Awful. Downright awful,' said Zhong as he wrinkled his nose.

'That was a tiny sip, mind you,' said Yong. 'As they say, effective medicine is bitterness to the mouth. Stop being a baby and drink up.'

Pinching his nostrils, Zhong tilted the bowl of steaming herbal medicine in to his mouth until all the dark liquid was drained from it. 'Ai! The worst so far. By your reckoning, this must be elixir from the gods.'

'At least you're well enough to complain. Lie back down and rest. I'll wake you when Niu comes back with our evening meal.'

'Enough of that. I've been lying down for three days.' Zhong stood up from the bed and raised his arms above his head to stretch his back. He walked over to the window and looked out. 'We should go for a walk ourselves.'

The view was nothing to write home about, as nondescript as one would expect from the outskirts of an insignificant little town. Still, the relative quiet, coupled with the cool evening air, allowed the young men to stretch their legs and invigorate their spirits. For half an hour they strolled, Yong following a step behind his young master.

They slowed to watch a group of children chasing after a round rag ball stuffed with feathers. Oblivious to the dust kicked up by their scampering feet, the children ran and laughed with abandon, perhaps knowing that, all too soon, their mothers or siblings would be coming to summon them home.

At one point, the ball broke loose of the pack and two of the quickest boys rushed after it from opposite directions. Just as it seemed a head-on collision was inevitable; the two boys adjusted their body shapes and threw their arms around each other in a tight hug. They remained stuck as the ball bobbled off, laughing as the rest carried on with the game.

Zhong and Yong watched and smiled as they walked past the children, reminded of days gone by. Yong glanced at Zhong and spotted the smile on his master's face giving way to a more pensive countenance.

'Something on your mind, Young Master?'

'Any chance of us setting off again tomorrow morning? I feel much better.'

'Your fever has been on and off. I think we'd rest for another day to be sure.'

'We're falling behind.'

'Too far behind, I'm afraid. We won't be able to catch up with him on the road. We would have to find him the hard way, track him down amongst the teeming masses.'

'I feel bad for holding us back.'

'Not your fault.'

Still strolling, Zhong stared straight ahead at nothing in particular. 'Tell me—what's driving you? For this case, I mean.'

'Nothing different from other cases. I want to see justice done, to catch the animal who did this to a defenceless woman and child.'

'I see,' said Zhong, who thought for a while. 'I admire the sense of justice. And the tenacity.'

Yong knew his young master well enough to expect more, so he waited without saying anything.

Zhong obliged. 'I don't think I can do the same.'

'You don't think you can, or you don't want to?'

'All my life, I have been doing what my father wants me to do. What if this path is not for me? To be a magistrate or an official of any kind, I need to pass the Imperial examinations, right? But it is years upon years of gruelling memorization of classical texts, poetry, and stuff. I have buried myself in books and scrolls since I was five, and I've not taken the lowest level prefectural examinations. That is after twelve years of hard studying. Twelve years!'

'You will.'

'In three years, if I'm lucky. And if I pass, my reward is years of further studying for the metropolitan examinations. Then more studying for the Palace examinations. Do you know how many people make it every year?'

'That is how the best emerge.'

'Right, the best at memorizing useless stuff. I see what Father does and what you do for him. What has regurgitating classical texts got anything to do with your work? Do you remember how Father tried to get you to study with me? You gave up after a while.'

'Knowing how to read and write was enough for me. Classics? Waste of time.'

'There are horror stories of men still attempting the examinations in their seventies. I don't want my life to end up that way.'

'It won't. Look, you're different from me. You have the chance to be an officer of the court, to serve the Emperor and the people. Old Master always said we need upright and competent officials to address the problems we're facing.'

'Too many people, intelligent people mind you, see an official post as the pathway to riches and personal gain. Serving the country is just something that comes with the package. I hear of junior officials paying monetary tributes to their superiors to gain favour for promotion.'

'You don't have to play the game. Old Master doesn't.'

'And a fat lot of good that has done him.'

'How can you say that?'

'I'm not disparaging his ideals. Quite the opposite. The system is unkind to people like Father, and tragic for the people. If only we could get our act together, we would drive the barbarian tribes back to their caves in a matter of weeks.'

'Now you sound like your father.'

'Not at all.'

'Believe me, you do. Both of you should talk to each other more. Maybe what you want is not too different from what he wants for you.'

'That would be the day. I can tell you one thing for certain. Studying for the next twenty years or more is not my idea of a proper life. There are other ways to secure a nice position, you know. Donate money to the Imperial Court to snag a post. Set for life. Might even serve the people while one is there. What a concept, eh?'

'I bet your father would love the idea.'

'Yeah, right. If he hears it from my mouth, he will break my legs, I kid you not. Me? I don't think there's anything wrong with it.'

'You don't?'

'Yeah. These merchants, they have money. Their problem is society's dim view of them—crass, buying and selling goods they did not produce, profiting off the backs of others. At the same time, the country needs funds to sustain military campaigns at the borders, put down uprisings here and there, and feed the whole bureaucracy. So, a deal is struck. Merchants with heaps of gold and little societal standing buy that standing from the state, which distributes spare hierarchical privileges in exchange for much needed funds. At least, unlike the ruse on promotions, the loot goes to the Imperial coffers. Everybody's happy.'

'Everybody except the people who are supposed to be served by competent officials.'

'Well, at least they're good at making money. That is probably more relevant for public administration than memorizing books.'

'The ability to memorize at least suggests a functioning brain, and the Imperial examinations represent a competition of brains. It is also up to the individual himself, unlike a rich father using his wealth to buy a position for a son who cannot string a proper sentence together.'

'We can't stop people from buying influence, can we? We might as well make use of such a desire. The Ouyang family tried to do the same. The only difference is that they pursued standing in the afterlife. Pretty much the same thing.'

Yong had nothing to say about that. Money acquiring influence had always been a way of life and would continue, it seemed, in the afterlife too.

'Speaking of which,' said Zhong. 'This Ouyang is really going out of his way to help. The case you solved for him must have been quite something for them to be so grateful. Tell me about it.'

'It was nothing. Plenty of time for storytelling. We'd better get back. It's starting to get chilly.'

After they turned around, there was a period of silence before Zhong spoke up again. 'What do you plan to do now?'

'Now that we have lost our man, we would have to look for him and this Guo Wutian at the Capital. Guo could be the one who planned this.'

'How on earth are you going to find them?'

'We need to look for Guo in the sections of the Capital that Mdm Li pointed out. They are not small areas, though. There would be tens of thousands of people in those places. We would need help.'

'Beggars' Sect.'

Yong nodded. 'Either that or the local authorities. The locals could be territorial or worse, corrupt. I don't think I would want to risk getting them involved, at least not at the start. That leaves me with the Sect.'

'But you don't know them and what they are like.'

'I have a referral from Big Dog.'

'Whom you hardly know, by the way.'

'It is the best chance I've got. I will be careful. It should be fine.'

Zhong did not seem convinced. 'What about Mdm Li's husband, this ... what's his name?'

'Sun Jie. Mr Zhou had checked through past years' records of candidates who had passed the examinations and did not find his name. I'm hoping we can get to Guo and find out what had happened to Sun.'

'It sounds difficult, this case.'

'It is. You should watch what you say in the Capital. No more open talk of corruption and the like. The authorities, if they hear of it, will do more than breaking your legs, son of a magistrate or not.'

Chapter Twenty-Two

Once on the road again, the travelling party focused on preparing for their entry into the Capital. Their plan involved blending into the background, to be as inconspicuous as possible. Niu changed out of his uniform, which had been useful for protection on the road but would draw unwanted attention in a big city. His weapon could also invite scrutiny. After some discussion, Yong decided that the driver should drop them off right in front of the inn so that Niu could smuggle the weapon, wrapped in cloth, to their room.

As they came within two days of reaching their destination, the scenery started to change. The closer they got to the Capital, the more people they encountered and the more palpable the excitement that they were approaching the greatest city under the heavens. When they were about a day away, they experienced the bustle befitting a sizeable town. Local businesses thrived on the patronage of the numerous travellers and traders passing through. Eating places sprung up at every corner, signalling abundance at the centre of the Kingdom.

As Yong was going through his plan of approach for the final time and the cart rounded a corner, Zhong looked up and pointed to the front. 'There it is.'

In the distance, the imposing southern wall of the Capital cast a long afternoon shadow over a bank of low-rise buildings. There was a wall at Renli too, but this giant was at least twice the height.

From where they were, they saw the gate that allowed two-way traffic to flow with space to spare. Sitting on the wall, right above the opening, was a tower building so large it looked like it could house a hundred soldiers. It was beautifully constructed, two levels, each with its own emerald-green, four-sided tiled roof curving up into sharp tips at the corners.

The size of the gate tower hinted at the thickness of the wall, which Zhong said could accommodate two war chariots riding on top, side by side. Along the top of the wall stood other smaller towers, regular distances apart, nodes where soldiers could be stationed if needed.

City life was not confined to the space enclosed by the wall. Their horse-cart passed by rows of side streets lined with low-lying houses. There were street vendors shouting to attract attention, shopkeepers serving customers, children playing, workers engaged in various forms of manual work, and people just milling about in this city surrounding a city. Beast of labour like horses, mules, and camels were carrying goods or dragging wheeled wagons along.

'Impressed?' said Zhong to Yong, who watched the kaleidoscope of urban activities with eyes widened. 'Wait till we get inside.' Niu smiled. He had seen this before.

Zhong pulled out a map of the city from the inner pocket of his coat and spread it out. 'This is the Outer Wall. Once we go past it, we'd be in the Outer City. Near the middle of the Outer City is the Inner City with its own wall. The Imperial City sits at the heart of it all. See, a few rivers run through the city. Mr Zhou thinks the few sections Mdm Li was referring to are dotted around these rivers.'

Yong poked his head out at the front to look around. 'Constables and soldiers. I see quite a number of uniforms about, and we are not in the city yet.'

'Now that you mention it, I did not see so many of them the last time I was here.'

Their cart slowed down and halted behind a long queue of carts, sedans, and carriages. Zhong pulled up close to the driver. 'What's happening?'

'They're doing checks of some sort. There they are, soldiers checking incoming vehicles. Maybe they're tightening security for some important event.'

The last thing Yong wanted was for soldiers to sniff around the cart since Niu's weapon was too large to hide in the bare cart, even though it was wrapped up.

'What do we do?' Niu asked.

'Too late to bail out now. Young Master, keep the map.'

Zhong folded the map and stuffed it back into his pocket. 'Looks like our carefully laid-out plan did not survive its first contact with reality. What if they bring us to the authorities?'

'That could be a problem. We would have to own up to who we are.'

Before long, their cart reached the head of the line. While one soldier talked to the driver, another opened up the flap at the back and locked his eyes on the cloth bundles at the front of the cart. He moved to the left side of the cart, flipped up the cover and reached in to rifle through the bundles. It did not take long for him to point out the obvious.

'A weapon,' said the soldier, who sounded like the discovery was an imposition on his time rather than a security breach. He proceeded to peel off the cloth covering Niu's sheathed sabre. 'What's this about?'

'Officer,' said Yong, 'we're from the magistrate's office in Renli, about fifteen days' journey from here. Young Master Liu Zhong is the son of Magistrate Liu Ye, and Niu here is a constable tasked with protecting him.' There was no need for Yong to introduce himself. Zhong's dressing and appearance marked him out as someone from an elevated social class. Yong, with his rugged features and rough clothes, was assumed to be the accompanying servant.

The soldier said to Zhong, 'Are you here for official matters?'

'A private visit.'

'You have to alight. The cart and the driver need to stay outside the city while someone brings the three of you to the magistrate's office.'

When the three of them got down from the cart, the soldier took Niu's weapon and handed it to a constable he had waved over. On the soldier's order, the constable bade the trio to follow him.

As they started on the walk along the wide and busy main avenue, Yong exchanged glances with his companions. Zhong's face had lost a shade of colour while Niu seemed to shrink a little, his shoulders slumped.

'What's wrong with you?' the constable said to Niu. 'You don't look well.'

Yong intervened before Niu could open his mouth. 'It's nothing, officer. He's having some stomach problems, that's all. If you don't mind me asking, what's up with the tight security?'

The constable turned to face Yong. 'You're not aware?'

Yong shook his head, relieved that his effort to divert attention seemed to be working.

'I'll tell you since you're fellow officials. We uncovered plots of foreign spies trying to smuggle weapons into the city. Yesterday, three men, also on a horse-cart, had a stash of weapons hidden under the floor of the cart.'

'Where are they from?'

'That I can't say.'

'Why at this time?'

'Who knows? Last week, the Imperial Court appointed new magistrates and officials. Perhaps the barbarians smelled an opportunity to sow some fear and confusion.' The constable started to eye Niu again, who was looking down and wiping perspiration from his forehead with his sleeve.

'Er ... Mr Constable?' said Yong.

'What?' said the constable as he shifted his attention back to Yong.

'Bigger batch of new officials this time?'

'Not really. A number who passed the examinations, a few donation types. The usual. Mind you, it doesn't take much for these animals to come calling. We had some disturbances at the autumn festival last year too. We just tighten security every time.'

Yong silently cursed their unfortunate timing. Not only had the security tightening marred their entrance, it was also likely to hamper subsequent work.

It was late afternoon when they got to their destination in the Inner City. As the constable led them along a stone path, deeper into the compound, they saw a group of smiling men in fine clothing walking towards them. The men stopped and faced one amongst their group, whom they addressed as Mr Yan, to bid him farewell. This Mr Yan returned the courtesy with a wide grin on his face and watched while his visitors sauntered past Zhong's group.

Yan stood where he was, now watching the new visitors, sans the smile. A wafer-thin man who looked like he could be lifted off the ground by a strong gust of wind, Yan sported specks of silver on his hair and a well-coiffed moustache. Judging by the deferential manner by which the escorting constable approached him without being asked, head bowed, Yan obviously enjoyed some seniority in this set-up.

'Who are these young gentlemen?' asked Yan.

The constable bowed lower. 'A son of a magistrate from out of town, and his servants.'

Yan eyed Zhong from head to toe. 'Where from?'

Zhong stepped forward. 'My name is Liu Zhong, son of Liu Ye, magistrate of Renli.'

'Where is that?'

'It is fifteen days' journey on land from here, sir.'

'Bring them in,' Yan said as he strode back to where he came from, without waiting for his visitors to follow.

They tailed Yan to a courtyard surrounded by a few buildings. While their escorting constable led them into a small building on the right, Yan turned left to enter a room in a building on the opposite side of the courtyard. Both buildings were mirror images of each other, each with four sets of doors in front that were wide open, exposing what was within.

All smiles again, Yan greeted three men who stood up from their seats to receive him as they would an old friend. He then led the three men and their two servants out of the room, but not before the visitors' servants carefully lifted up two boxes wrapped in embroidered silk from a table. Yan and his three esteemed guests entered a larger building between the two reception buildings while the servants followed.

Zhong sat down on one of the cushioned chairs surrounding a rectangular table. A servant served him tea while Yong and Niu took their places standing behind their master. Yong had noticed differences from their Renli office. First, the furnishings. The sets of furniture back home were well-worn while the ones here projected high quality and prices. Exquisite paintings, sculptures, and other ornamental trophies adorned the walls. Second, the staff here dressed a notch or two above what he was used to. Perhaps this reflected the general prosperity of the Capital, or it could speak of different priorities. Yong bent towards Zhong and whispered his observations into his master's ear. They had to stay alert.

Less than half an hour later, the previous group came out with Yan, all appearing satisfied. Yong was not surprised to note that the visitors had relinquished the boxes. Following an exchange of farewell pleasantries, a servant ushered the guests out while Yan switched his attention to Zhong and company.

There was to be no warm and friendly welcome this time, only an icy look in their direction from a distance. He followed up with a nonchalant wave to the constable escorting the trio to move things along before he went back into the main building.

The constable nodded in the direction of Yan and turned towards his charges. 'Your turn. Follow me.'

Chapter Twenty-Three

The furnishings in the waiting room within the main building were yet another cut above those in the reception rooms outside. While Yong and Niu stood still, Zhong had plenty of time to browse and admire the expensive artworks decorating the walls. The wealth on display was not there for mere ornamental purposes. It projected a sense of authority, the type that got things done for a price.

Their host saw fit to make them wait for yet another quarter of an hour. When someone arrived, it was Yan, his strides slow and deliberate. He exchanged polite greetings with Zhong as he introduced himself as Yan Qingrui, adviser to the presiding official here, Magistrate Lei Jun. As the two of them sat down, an attendant came in to pour hot tea into fine porcelain cups.

Just as the room settled into a wordless silence, Yong picked up the soft bumps of sure and unhurried footsteps approaching. Like the main character of a Chinese opera making his entrance from the side of the stage, a squat gentleman appeared in front of the room, looked in, and paused.

Adviser Yan and Zhong stood up. Yan delivered a bow and a greeting that doubled up as an announcement. 'Magistrate Lei.'

The magistrate grunted and tilted up his head, which featured a high and prominent forehead. His face was oval and pale, not far in shade from the painted white one of an operatic character, adding to the sense of theatre. The fierce intensity of his eyes, however, proclaimed that this was a man not to be trifled with. While the attire of a black round cap and dark cotton robe was almost casual, his aura of seriousness, or perhaps it was self-importance, drifted into the room before he set foot in it.

Magistrate Lei gave up a smile and marched in with no small measure of pomp. 'Come, sit down.'

Lei took his seat next to Yan and picked up his tea cup.

'Young man,' said Lei, 'I heard you came all the way from Renli. What is the purpose of your trip?'

While Lei sipped his tea and spoke softly, the way he dispensed with small talk to cut to the chase indicated he was in a hurry. He might have kept his guests waiting, but his own time was not to be squandered on unprofitable engagements.

Introducing himself as the son of Magistrate Liu Ye, Zhong explained they were here on a private visit.

Putting his cup down, Lei eyed Zhong as he ran the back of his fingers across the patch of neatly-trimmed silvery bristles covering his chin.

'Purely a private visit?' said Lei.

'We may be taking a look at some goods for commercial purposes, but that is just a little something on the side.'

'It is true the Capital boasts of many fine products not seen in smaller cities. Just the three of you?'

'For now. My father will be coming in a week or so. He said he had not visited for years and would like to call on colleagues here.'

'I see. How long has your father been magistrate?'

'Almost eighteen years.'

'He is quite a few years my senior. It is understandable he would long to visit, being far away.' Lei paused to let the remarks, reminders of his superior career progression over Zhong's father, sink in. 'I would be honoured to host him for a meal, if he can find the time.'

'Very kind of you, Sir. I will be sure to let him know once he arrives.'

'And you, young man, do you need any help from us in the meantime?'

'There is no need to trouble you and your office. We will just be going around the city and trying to soak in as much as we can.'

'Please feel free to do so, but do be careful. As you can see, we have tightened security. There has been unease in and around the city the last few days. Any sign of disturbance, and we will come down on troublemakers with a swift and firm hand.'

'We will be careful.'

Lei looked Zhong in the eye. 'Let me put it in plain language so we understand each other. I am in charge of everything that goes on around here. I do not accept anyone else interfering with my work. Even if you just happen to come across anything that concerns law and order here, I expect you to keep us informed. Are we clear on that?'

'Yes, Sir.'

Lei nodded and smiled. 'Excellent. I will say the same to your father. The last thing I want is for any misunderstanding to come between us.'

His main agenda item dealt with, Lei spent the next few moments asking about Renli, though his wandering gaze made it clear he had little interest in the answers.

Mercifully, the conversation came to an end when the magistrate gave the tea table beside him a firm pat. 'Good. We are done here.'

Zhong stood and bowed. 'If there are no further instructions, we will take our leave.'

Lei and his adviser also stood up but did not return the bow.

'One more thing,' said Lei. 'Owing to the current situation, it would not do for your constable to carry his weapon around or to wear his uniform, if he has it with him. You have two choices. Either you leave him with us, and we will take good care of him, or you leave the weapon and uniform behind for our safekeeping until you depart.'

Zhong hesitated. He could protest but there would be little point to it. Until his father arrived, they were at the mercy of the locals. 'Then we would have to trouble your men to safekeep the weapon and uniform for us.'

'Excellent. Now, where would you be staying? One of my constables can bring you there.'

'Not necessary, Sir. We can find our way.'

'This I must insist. It is the least I can do for the son of a respected colleague.'

Again, there was no choice but to comply.

'Mr Yan, see the guests off,' said Lei and walked off.

Yan followed them only as far as the courtyard. After whispering some instructions to the constable who had been accompanying the visitors, he asked a servant to take away Niu's weapon and uniform. The now sullen constable escorted the trio to Yunxiao Inn without a word along the way. Clearly, he did not appreciate the additional work when he could be putting his feet up after a long day.

'Here we are,' said the constable when they arrived at their destination. The Yunxiao Inn was quite an imposing building, all three storeys of it overlooking the midgets in its vicinity, making a vain attempt at living up to its name as the inn amongst the clouds. Sunset was almost upon them and the ground level was teeming with guests. The constable did not bother to follow them in.

Yong approached the innkeeper at the counter by the entrance and asked for a room on the highest level, facing the road.

After being shown to their room, Zhong's first act was to walk around the room while Niu followed the inn assistant out to fetch a pot of tea. Yong went over to the side of the window, peeking out on to the street below and spotting the constable who had brought them here. He was sitting in a teahouse opposite the inn, not too bothered with concealing himself.

Zhong had completed his cursory inspection of the room and plonked down on the bed to remove his shoes. 'Not too shabby, I suppose. What a pompous dog official. The way he spoke, you'd think he owned this city.'

Holding his forefinger to his lips, Yong glided over to sit down on a bench to face Zhong. 'Careful of ears just beyond the walls.'

Zhong checked himself and said in a lower voice, 'Got it. What do you think of this magistrate?'

'You've said it—a dog official. So blatant he did not bother to hide his ill-gotten wealth.'

'The lecture he gave us on security and all that. What do you make of it?'

'His wealthy clients, like the few we bumped into at the compound, pay handsome sums for the magistrate to be in charge, to offer them protection. He has to demonstrate his authority and guard his turf.'

'Then he's going to love a magistrate from out of town and his little helpers hunting for a murderer in his territory.'

'It is beyond protocol. For someone like him, it is about control and the profits that come with it.'

'Do you think they will keep watch over us? Spy on us or something?'

Yong thought of the constable downstairs. 'Maybe.'

'That will be a spot of bother, no?'

'As long as they don't see us conducting court business, we'll be fine.'

'Then we won't be able to go on this investigation of yours, right?' said Zhong, rather hopefully. 'Don't you worry, brother. I'm not short of ideas on things to do in this fabulous city.'

Chapter Twenty-Four

When Zhong woke up the next morning, a basin of warm water, a plain bun, a cup of fragrant tea, and an accompanying teapot were already laid out on the table. Niu sat at the table, busy swatting a couple of persistent flies away from his master's breakfast. Yong was standing at the window, peering out and down.

Zhong wrung the water from a towel into the basin, wiped his face and said, 'Does not look like we can get much investigation done today.'

Yong did not answer. He did not even avert his eyes from the scene down on the street. The young master took a bite of the breakfast bun on the table, washed it down with some tea, and tried again.

'Yong,' Zhong called out.

'Sorry,' Yong said as he backed away from the window. 'Were you talking to me?'

'I was saying, what do we do, now that we can't engage in any investigative work?'

'What do you have in mind?'

'I was kind of thinking that since, you know, we can't get down to work, we might as well proceed with the ... um ... recreational programme. What do you think?'

'Where would you like to go? Show me on the map.'

Zhong's eyes opened wider. 'You mean ... sure.' Without hesitation, he pulled out the city map and laid it on the table.

'There are some excellent teahouses by the canal. Great places to watch the city come to life at the start of the day. After that, we can check out the Inner City.'

'Sounds good. Let's go with this plan.'

'Let's go with ... all right, of course,' Zhong said in a chirpy voice. 'Quick, Niu, get moving. No time to lose.' He wolfed down his breakfast and got dressed before Yong could change his mind. Niu too was unusually helpful in getting his master's clothes and shoes ready for the day ahead.

In no time, Zhong was all dressed up and ready to go. 'I'm done. Let's go.'

'All right, go ahead,' said Yong. 'Remember not to let the locals suspect you're conducting official business. Try not to come back too late.'

'What? Aren't you coming along?'

'Oh, no. You go ahead with Niu. If anybody asks, not that they would, tell them I'm not feeling well and need to rest.'

'Are you all right?'

'Yeah, fine.'

Zhong was not about to let some strange behaviour early in the morning deter him from a day of merriment. 'All right then. Stay out of trouble,' he said and skipped out of the room with Niu.

Yong returned to his inspection of the street. It did not take long for Zhong and Niu to emerge from the inn. Zhong was busy talking to Niu, probably giving a preview of the day to come. Both did not pay much heed to the constable, the same one from the previous day, stepping out of the diagonally-opposite teahouse thirty paces behind them, trailing them.

Yong was confident that Zhong and Niu would not be harassed as long as they stuck to their recreational programme, and he knew there was no danger whatsoever of any deviation on that front. The constable, decked out in full uniform, was more a warning and show of force than a concealed tail meant to cause harm. Zhong was after all the son of a magistrate.

Time to make his own move. At this hour, there was a hive of activities downstairs as guests, travellers, and service workers engaged in various forms of morning transactions at the inn. No one paid attention to a servant boy walking down the stairs and slipping out through the front exit. He turned right on to the street, walked about forty paces, and stopped at a roadside stall. Pretending to browse, he peeked back to scan for anyone tailing him. Satisfied he was not under surveillance, he joined the human flow on the busy street.

The first order of business was to touch base with the Beggars' Sect. Situated in the south-west quadrant of the Outer City, Wild Wolf's den could be reached on foot in about half an hour. As Yong neared the location, having checked with a few beggars along the way, he saw why the Sect chose this place as the gathering point for their leaders. It was a quiet and rundown part of the city within a labyrinth of alleys. Few people not residing in these parts would venture here.

As he was about to round yet another corner, he almost bumped into a middle-aged woman with her child in tow, heading in the opposite direction in a hurry.

'Quick, get out,' she said. 'Fight.' She did not even glance back as she dragged her child away.

Yong was about to double back when something told him to find out what was happening, the same 'something' that, at times, led him into trouble. Leaning against the wall, he inched his head out to take a peek.

There, in a small clearing about thirty paces away, stood seventeen beggars that Yong counted with a sweep of his eyes. They were all holding sticks of various lengths facing a small house, twelve of the beggars in an arc and another five a few steps behind. The front arc shifted back when three men, armed with sabres, took slow and deliberate steps out of the house.

The tall and lean beggar standing in the middle of the backline began to speak. 'Come out, all of you. There is no point dragging this out. Let's finish this, here and now.'

Another three men emerged from the house, this time brandishing swords. The one who came out last, tall with broad and solid shoulders, spoke first. 'Is this how you fight, many against the few? Where's the fairness you people of the Central Plains talk about?'

The tall beggar laughed. 'We're here to catch foreign dogs, not to show off in a martial arts contest.'

'This has got nothing to do with you. Turn around and walk away.'

'You plot in the dark to do our people harm and expect us to turn a blind eye? We are beggars, not cowards, and definitely not traitors.'

'See how the officials and the people treat you. Why risk your lives to protect what is not yours?'

'How we are treated is none of your business. Here are suggestions for you: lay down your weapons, hold out your hands, and accept capture.'

'I don't think you bunch of stray mongrels have what it takes.'

'Enough of worthless talk. We are not leaving here until we round you all up, dead or alive.'

With a wordless sneer, the main man from the house raised his sword in front of him and adopted a fighting stance, one foot in front and both knees bent. His men did the same.

The tall beggar started to beat the ground with his stick at a steady rhythm. His men mimicked the tapping, following the rhythm, amplifying the sound. As they tapped, the twelve beggars in the front arc shifted their individual positions, tweaking a symmetrical formation to adjust to the positions of the men opposing them.

When they appeared to be in position, the tall beggar struck the floor off the set rhythm, prompting his men to hit the ground with random timing. The chaotic tapping prompted the men from the house to shift their sights from side to side. A few of them glanced at their leader, who returned a passive expression.

'Go!' shouted the tall beggar.

The beggars at the front lunged at their opponents, two to a man, while the second line held back. The foreign men swung their weapons side to side, up and down, covering every angle of attack. They had to, for the pairs of street fighters were well coordinated.

The foreigners were no ordinary street hooligans. Every single one of them was solidly built, the strokes of their weapons fast and sure. With their backs to the house, they put up a stout defence of their front and flanks, closing ranks to shut any gap, displaying a level of discipline that spoke of elite military training. Their leader stood out with his technique, speed, and agility. Unlike his compatriots who had their hands full just defending, the leader fended off attacks without much difficulty and sometimes turned defence into attack in the blink of an eye.

In one such move, he chose to duck under a swing of a stick instead of parrying. He then spun around and landed a lightning reverse kick on his attacker's chest, sending the recipient flying back five paces. But no sooner had the beggar landed on the ground than one of those at the backline leapt in to fill the void.

Then it happened again. Another lightning sweep of the foreign leader's leg, this time lower, just above the ground. The powerful move caught not one but two of the attackers, who somersaulted and landed on their backs.

Before the replacement fighters could move in, the leader of the beggars lurched forward with a spine-tingling shout and aimed blow after blow with his stick in quick succession at the foreign chief, besting the work of two skilful attackers. The foreigner could barely keep pace with his sword and was forced to cede a few steps backwards. With that, a spell seemed to be broken. Apart from the crucial loosening of the defensive formation, the beggar leader's advance served to impart confidence to his men while draining the morale of their opponents. One by one, the men with swords and sabres were felled or otherwise momentarily disabled.

Their chief did not wait around to be captured. With a sudden burst of energy, born of desperation, he slashed the air in front of him with quick, strong, and clean strokes of his gleaming sword. Thus, buying precious space, he dived out of the formation and rolled forward as soon as he touched the ground. In one seamless motion, he sprang to his feet and ran for his life. The beggar leader and two of his men gave chase.

Unfortunately for Yong, they were heading in his direction and closing in fast. His instinctive response was to press his back against the wall to stay flat and, he hoped, go unnoticed by the men. But as he did so, he spotted a wooden pole the length of two arms lying on the ground amidst other debris. Without thinking, he picked it up and held it with both hands. There was no time for hesitation. When he heard the pounding of feet nearing, he swung the pole with all his might, at waist height, across the path of the onrushing men.

The foreigner saw it too late. His reactions were quick but he was still human. He tried to hurdle over the pole at the last moment, managing only to jump high enough for it to catch his shin. With an agonized howl, he fell. His momentum was such that the pole split into two, and Yong was sent spinning to the ground.

In a flash, the three chasing beggars closed in and subdued him. While his two sidekicks dragged their captive back to the front of the house, the beggar leader came up to Yong and said, 'Are you all right?'

'I'm fine, I guess,' said Yong as he got up, rubbing his right hip.

Just then, another beggar ran from the alley that Yong had come from, stopping to face his chief and heaving gulps of air into his lungs.

'Constables,' the beggar said. 'Four of them. Coming this way.'

'Right on time.' The beggar leader barked orders for his men to hurry in tying up the foreigners around the biggest tree in the vicinity. A few of his men had also gone into the house to bring out more sabres, swords, and daggers that they threw into a pile, ready to be collected by law enforcement officials.

'Where are you headed?' the beggar leader said to Yong. 'There might be more trouble soon. Quick, come with us.'

Yong could not imagine more trouble than what he had just waded into, but decided this was not an ideal situation for local constables to catch him in. He mixed in with the bunch of beggars as they made their swift exit from the scene.

No one spoke during the hasty retreat. It was not until the crew reached their base, a dilapidated house in a silent corner, that the back-slapping and banter broke out. The ones at the base welcomed back their comrades. As the beggars stood around and spoke to one another with much enthusiasm, their leader went around to check on the injured and to congratulate each team member on a successful mission.

Soon enough, he came to Yong. 'Well done, my brave brother. Thanks for your help. What's your name?'

'I'm Liu Yong from Renli.'

'Renli? I know some people there,' said the beggar leader as he smiled. 'I take care of this bunch of scallywags, and many besides. My real name is not important. They call me Wild Wolf.'

Chapter Twenty-Five

'Are those men the foreign spies the authorities were after?' said Yong.

Wild Wolf nodded. 'Yeah, Tanguts. Our men picked up suspicious movements a few days earlier and followed them to the house. We watched it for a few more days, hoping to net more of them, but we could not wait any longer. They looked to be on the move.'

'What were they planning to do?'

'We couldn't be sure though a few of them had been moving around the Inner City on the sly.'

'You work with the authorities here?'

'Not this bunch of incompetents. These spies have been operating right under their noses, and yet they were clueless. As you saw, we had to tie up the presents and get our men to create a ruckus at the marketplace to lure them in. Well, enough of these spies. What are you doing in this place, Brother Liu?'

'Call me Yong. I'm here for a few things, one of which is to get in touch with you.'

'Me? What for?'

'I need your help to find someone, or some people.' Yong told Wild Wolf about the case at hand. As he went through the story, Wild Wolf smile faded.

'Who are you?' asked Wild Wolf.

It was no use for Yong to hide his identity any longer. 'I … I'm an assistant to the magistrate at Renli.'

Yong had not raised his voice, but for the effect his words had, he might as well have been shouting. The beggars around him stopped talking and turned towards him, the joy and relief in their faces morphing into hostility.

'Be honest with me,' said Wild Wolf. 'Why are you here?'

'I've told you. I need your help to find the person or people who murdered the child. Look,' said Yong as he fished the black dog pendant out of his pocket and showed it to Wild Wolf, 'Big Dog gave this to me and told me I could come to you for help.'

Wild Wolf took the wooden pendant and rolled it with his fingers to inspect it. 'Big Dog gave this to you?'

'Yes. He said both of you go back a long way.'

'Of all people. What have you done for him?'

Yong had figured that this might be the most important speech he would be making on this trip. With all eyes on him, his pulse started to pick up pace. *Focus on the objective*, he told himself. Adrenaline left over from the fight and retreat got him over early nerves as he told them his story as a street kid and explained how he had worked with Sect members. He could see the glow in Wild Wolf's eyes soften as he spoke. Wild Wolf nodded when Yong cycled back to Yingxiu's plight and recounted his brushes with the local authorities, including the encounter with Magistrate Lei Jun.

'You spin a nice yarn,' said Wild Wolf when Yong finished, his voice calmer than a tense moment ago. 'How would I know whether you are using us to settle scores with people your master does not like?'

'I would be crazy or a fool to cook up a story like that, then admit I'm helping an official when you've made clear your view of them.'

'Fair point,' said Wild Wolf with a wry smile. He stared into Yong's eyes for a moment that lingered, as though he was searching for some truth. 'What do you need from us?'

'You were what!' said Zhong. 'Involved in a gang fight?'

'Not really,' said Yong. 'Just got caught up near the end, that's all.' He recounted taking down the foreigner.

'If you had missed, he could have cut you into two. Did you think about that?'

Yong had not, for he had no time to.

'My father put you in charge,' Zhong said. 'I don't have any problem with that. Using us to draw the constable away is fine with me too. But you going off to confront the Beggars' Sect without telling us is not right. If something had happened to you, what would I tell Father?'

'I had not thought about that. I'm sorry.'

Silence followed. Zhong was sitting down at the table in their room, facing outward, while Yong stood two steps away facing his master. Niu loitered close to the door, trying his level best not to be drawn into the discussion.

'Forget it,' Zhong said. 'I understand you're eager to help the widow. Remember safety is paramount. So, did you get what you wanted?'

'Yeah. This Wild Wolf agreed to help us search for Guo Wutian and the man with a limp. His men will check around in the areas indicated by Mdm Li. If these two men are there, we should get an indication of their whereabouts in a day or two.'

'What else did you find out?'

'I went to the sections west of the river to take a look and to ask around. It was a large area with lots of people. I got nowhere.'

'A busy day for you then.'

'Pretty much. And you?'

'Busy day too,' said Zhong as he flashed a broad smile and beckoned Yong to sit down on the bed, still facing him. 'So many things to see and do, and so much fun to be had. We can spend a lifetime here and still would not have enough time to take in everything. Isn't it true, Niu?' Zhong looked at Niu, who nodded with enthusiasm.

The twinkle in Zhong's eyes returned as he switched his attention back to Yong. 'So, what do we do tomorrow?'

'Tomorrow,' said Yong, 'we do the same.'

Chapter Twenty-Six

Same manoeuvre, same result. Yong had watched the uniformed constable, a different one from the day before, tailing Zhong and Niu. He wondered how long the locals would keep this up before concluding that Zhong was a harmless lad seeking nothing more than entertainment. Certainly, Zhong would be delivering a convincing performance, for he was not acting.

As Yong headed towards Wild Wolf's lair, he watched for tails on himself. There were none, the privilege of being a nobody. The moment he entered the city headquarters of the Sect, Wild Wolf greeted him with a broad smile. 'I was wondering when you would be coming by. I can see you're anxious for news.'

Without an invitation, Yong took a seat on a stone stool opposite Wild Wolf.

'I hope you are bringing good ones,' Yong said.

'Perhaps. Our men fanned out in the few sections you marked out and asked around. Took them the better part of a day to find traces of a man with a limp called Guo Wutian. This Guo used to live with a scholar on Xiushui Street. Nobody knows the name of the scholar.'

Hope and disappointment delivered in one line. 'Used to?'

'They lived in a house in one of the two rows facing each other that got swallowed up by a big fire four years ago. Four years to the month, in fact.'

A feeling of dread gripped Yong. 'What happened to them?'

'From what we hear, they moved out right after the fire. It was chaotic at the time. Nobody tracked where these two had gone to.'

'A fire,' muttered Yong to himself.

'It happens, given how close these houses are to one another.'

'At least I now know Guo Wutian and the man with a limp are one and the same, and that a scholar, probably Sun Jie, had lived with him. I would have to speak to the people who have some knowledge of them.'

'Our men found three people in the vicinity who knew Guo or at least knew of him. They did not tell us much. People don't like talking to beggars, you see. Still, there is something for you to work on.'

'Which is all I could ask for,' said Yong, nodding his head to emphasize his gratefulness. 'There's another thing. We heard of a plague.'

Wild Wolf nodded. 'Aye. Terrible time it was. Started in that part of the city, soon after the fire, and spread from there. People fell like flies in the weeks after. The undertakers could not keep up, and our men had to help with the burying. Nasty work but someone had to do it. We lost many men too.'

'That is awful.'

Wild Wolf sighed. 'We try to do some good. A beggar's life is always hard, that goes without saying, and more so in a prosperous city. Temptations abound, and we are no angels. In recent weeks, some of our men have been getting drunk and harassing the lady folk. This happens once in a while.'

'I understand. Such things happen in Renli too.'

'I tell you this though. Even for those of my men on the wrong side of the law, there is a line they do not cross. Targeting a poor widow and a helpless boy is cowardly and despicable. Some of my men told me they would love to get their hands on the man or men responsible.'

Yong nodded without saying anything. A part of him preferred the Sect's brand of what would be swift and brutal vigilante justice, but he knew Magistrate Liu would never allow it.

Wild Wolf smiled, as though aware of Yong's dilemma. 'One of my men will bring you to the place.'

Not only were people averse to talking to beggars, Yong had found out, they were not too keen to converse with anyone associated with beggars. Revealing his allegiance to a law enforcement agency was not an option, lest one of them ran to the locals to tell on him. As a result, the people he had talked to treated him with the disdain reserved for street people. The two he had approached refused to speak to him until after much coaxing that bordered on begging.

The first person only remembered Guo because of an altercation about a year before the fire. According to him, Guo had been drunk and had hurled insults at him, so the man, who would not be mistaken for a refined gentleman himself, exchanged blows with Guo.

The second interview was with an old man. Together with his wife, the man ran a provision shop frequented by Guo. The old man described him as a gruffy man with few words. He kept so much to himself that they knew next to nothing about him.

Of course, they did not know or care where he had gone to after the fire. They had not heard of Sun Jie, the scholar, either.

Now, the woman sitting in this cramped wine shop was the last person for Yong to approach. His last hope. A little boy who was scuttling around the woman reached for the assurance of his mother's lap when he saw the young stranger walk in. There was no other person in the confined space stacked with wine bottles large and small.

The woman stood to greet Yong with a smile. 'Can I help you?'

'Quite a range you've got here.' Yong made a show of going over the bottles close to him, fingering a few as he continued speaking. 'I'm here to ask about a man.'

The woman's smile vanished. She sat back down and put her left arm around her child. 'Are you the one the beggars said was asking around about this guy named Guo?'

Yong stepped closer to the woman and looked straight at her. 'Guo Wutian, yes. I'm looking for him.'

'Why? What is this about?'

'It's a simple personal matter.'

The woman eyed him with suspicion. 'Tell me what you want, young man. We're busy here.'

With no one else in the shop, she did not look all that busy.

'How often did he come here?' said Yong.

'I don't remember.'

'Was it often?'

'It has been a few years.'

'Tell me the best you can remember.'

'Liked a drink but too skint to afford a regular supply. He came by when he felt flushed enough.'

'What was his habit? For example, at what time of the day did he come by?'

'Always late afternoon. Or at least until he stopped coming a few months before the big fire.'

'How many months before the fire?'

'Five, six months maybe?'

'Did he switch to another wine shop?'

'Maybe. We're the only one in this neighbourhood though.'

'What would he buy?'

'He did not stick to a brand or type, if that's what you mean. But it was almost always the same quantity—one bottle each time. Sometimes, he'd hang around to check out the stuff he could not afford but, usually, he'd just pick up the bottle and leave.'

'You said "almost".'

'What?'

'You said he almost always bought one bottle.'

'Oh, now and then, he'd buy two bottles to share.'

'How did you know?'

'Of course I'd know how much he bought.'

'I mean, how did you know he was sharing with someone else?'

'Once, I asked him about it. He told me he was drinking with someone.'

'When did he start this sharing?'

'What do you mean? It's such a long time ago.'

'Let's put it this way—was it a year or so before the fire?'

'Oh, I'd say it was way before, a few years before.'

Then it could not be Sun Jie, thought Yong. 'Who did he drink with?'

'Hey, young man, you are asking too many questions for a simple personal matter.'

'To be honest with you, madam, Guo is a debtor to my master. I'm trying to find out where he had gone to.' This was not a lie, only that Guo owed Magistrate Liu neither gold nor silver but the truth. Yong tried again. 'Do you know who he drank with?'

'No.'

'Had he mentioned any name before?'

'He never mentioned any drinking buddy. Why should he?'

Just then, a customer walked in, putting the conversation on hold. Yong stood aside as the customer picked up a bottle of wine, paid for it, and walked out of the shop.

'Madam, not just a drinking buddy. Had he mentioned anyone at all?'

'Pesky young man, you are.'

Yong stood there without a word. He was not leaving until he got proper answers.

'Now that you mention it,' said the woman, 'he did say once, when he bought double, that I should be charging those to the account of Old Jiang.'

'Another of your customers?'

'Another one of those habitual drinkers. More hard-up than Guo. I think he does odd jobs and comes by when he has saved enough. Was here two weeks ago.'

'He's still around?' Yong asked, his hopes raised for the first time on a hitherto fruitless day. 'Where can I find him?'

Chapter Twenty-Seven

Following the woman's directions, Yong made his way to Old Jiang's dwelling, rounding two corners right and left, past rows of houses and craft shops.

The place, as expected, was not much. Narrow and windowless at the front, its door was shut. Yong walked up to the door and knocked a few times. No reply. He knocked harder. Still nothing. The next few bangs were so loud an old woman from the adjacent unit popped her head out to check out the commotion.

'Is Old Jiang in?' Yong asked the old lady. She shrugged her shoulders before disappearing back into her house.

Yong was about to land a few more blows on the wooden door when he heard someone coughing inside the house.

'Hello,' said Yong quite loudly, 'is anyone in? I'm looking for Old Jiang.'

The sound of shuffling feet was followed by the sliding of a wooden lock before the door opened up a crack. Part of a leathery and wrinkled face could be seen through the slit.

'What is it, boy?' The voice was hoarse but strong.

'You're Old Jiang, aren't you? My surname is Liu. I'm looking for information on Guo Wutian. Remember him?'

Before the last sentence could be completed, Jiang slammed the door shut and slid the wooden lock back in place.

Yong continued banging on the door. 'I need to speak to you, sir. It is important. I promise I will not take up much of your time.'

There was no response but Yong continued banging and pleading. The old lady next door stuck her head out again.

'Stop banging!' shouted Jiang from inside the house.

'I'm not going away until I talk to you.'

When the door opened a few inches, Yong leaned against it to prevent it from being slammed on him again.

'What do you want?' said Jiang.

'I've told you.' Yong glanced at the old lady and back at Jiang. 'Would you like to speak here or inside?'

Jiang hesitated for a moment before opening the door to let Yong in. The tiny space within was a basic room with a bed and not much else. Lighting was scarce and ventilation, poor. The whole place reeked of stale sweat and alcohol. Standing and toppled wine bottles were strewn all over the room. The old man closed the door, shuffled to his small bed and sat down.

Yong remained on his feet. 'The lady boss of the wine shop around the corner told me you used to drink with Guo. Is that correct?'

Jiang nodded. His hands, resting on his lap, were not only rough, but also marked with cuts and scratches, some fresh and others dried up, signs of hard labour.

'How long have you known Guo?' asked Yong.

'A number of years. We're not close by any means, you understand? We used to meet for drinks once in a while. I have nothing to do with him now. Haven't seen him for years.'

'Since the fire?'

'Yeah.'

'Where has he gone to?'

'Hey, hang on. Who are you, kid? Why do I need to answer your questions?'

'Guo owes my master a debt. I'm trying to find out where he is.'

'Nothing to do with me. Go bother someone else.' Jiang waved his arms as though swatting away a fly.

'You may be the only one around here who knows something about him.'

'Like I said, not my problem.'

Yong was not going to let this go. The old man in front of him represented the last known link to Guo and Sun. He decided he would use whatever means at his disposal to get the man to talk, taking some risk if necessary. 'I am representing the court, investigating an important matter involving Guo.'

The reaction was immediate though fleeting. For a moment, Yong saw fear in the old man's eyes. He reckoned Jiang had gone through harrowing brushes with the law enforcement machinery in town.

Jiang widened his eyes a tad to inspect Yong more closely and, just like that, the cloud of fear vanished. 'Bull. I have never seen you before. And you're a bit young to be running around conducting investigations, aren't you? Where is your backup, huh? Go on, boy, run home to your mum before it gets dark.'

'I represent the magistrate's office in Renli, investigating a crime that happened there.' Yong was by now not worried that Jiang would run to the locals to tell on him. Judging from the flicker of fear at the mention of the court, the magistrate's office would be the last place Jiang would approach.

'Renli? Never heard of it. Even if it's true, so what? I know the officials here. They are not going to let you run around on their turf playing your little games while they sit idly by.'

Yong must admit Jiang's points were valid. He stood frozen, thinking about how he could turn the situation around. He was searching for his next words but Jiang was not going to allow him more time.

'Run along, kid, and don't come back.'

Chapter Twenty-Eight

'What are you doing peeking out of the window again and mumbling to yourself?' asked Zhong.

Yong snapped back to present reality, taking his eyes off the busy morning street outside the inn. 'I was thinking.'

'Happy thoughts, by the looks of it. You had a grin on your face.'

'It's nothing.' Yong turned back to peer out of the window. 'I think I may have found the solution to my little problem.'

'I see. Last evening, you agonized over how to get this Old Jiang to talk. Now it is just a little problem, eh? So, what is your solution?'

'My solution, Young Master,' said Yong with a glint in his eye, 'has just arrived.'

Zhong and Niu were taking too long. Yong had sneaked up to Jiang's place to listen by the door and picked up the sound of shuffling feet within, confirmation that the old man was in. Presently, Yong hid behind a wall a hundred paces and one turn from Jiang's house, peering out towards a shop across the street, waiting for his companions to arrive.

And there they were, master and bodyguard, ambling down the street. Soon, they reached the designated shop, peddling various crafts and wares, and popped in. Hovering twenty paces behind was the tailing constable, his eyes trained on his targets.

Zhong picked up an item on display and held it up near the shop entrance to view it in better light and to allow himself to glance in Yong's direction. Visual contact thus established, Yong gave Zhong a thumbs-up and turned around to head for Jiang's house.

As in the day before, the shouting and banging on the door provoked no immediate response. Yong was well aware that timing was of the essence in this series of manoeuvres.

It was therefore of some relief when Jiang opened his door by half, though with a clenched jaw and fire in his eyes. 'I thought I told you not to come back. What are you, deaf?'

Without waiting for an invitation, Yong pushed open the door and forced his way into the house. 'I'm here to seek your cooperation again.'

'Why should I?'

'I thought you might say that. I did not want to trouble my colleagues here but your intransigence has left me with no choice.'

The fear returned to Jiang eyes. He steadied himself and stuck his head out of the door gingerly to look both ways. When he turned back to face Yong, the fire in his eyes had returned. 'What are you talking about, you little fool? There's no one else here.'

'There would soon be, I assure you. They wanted to come with me, but I told them not to. For now, I suggest you close the door so that our discussion can be more private. But it's up to you.'

Jiang stood there and thought about it for a moment. Decision made, he pushed the door to close it, sliding the wooden lock back in place for good measure.

Yong had to move things along without sounding rushed. 'Tell me about Guo Wutian.'

Jiang walked over to his bed and sat down. 'I don't know him that well and that is the honest truth.'

'How long have you known him for?'

'Told you we're not close, all right? Not at all.'

'You know what I mean. Answer the question.'

Jiang snorted his disapproval. 'I first met him more than eight years ago. We used to work on a few of the same odd jobs, but we did not talk much.'

'I thought both of you met up for wine.'

'That was later.'

'When?'

'About six or seven years ago, I think.'

'How often did you meet?'

'Not often. Every three months or so. Money was often tight, you understand?'

Just then, someone coughed right outside. It was Niu, a signal to Yong that both he and Zhong were passing by and about to turn at the corner ten paces away. As planned, they would walk past four houses, and Zhong would enter the fifth one, a wood craft workshop, to make a few enquiries. Niu would hang around the entrance to the workshop.

Yong carried on with the questioning. 'What sort of work did he do?'

'Like me, he had been doing odd jobs, carrying goods, moving stuff, that sort of thing. No fixed place. Six months before the fire, he landed a regular job. He seemed to be doing well too. Not long after securing the job, he started bringing back quality wine, not the cheap rubbish we used to drink.'

'This regular job, where was it?'

'Some merchant. I don't know which one or in which line. He did not want to tell me.'

'Where did both of you meet for drinks?'

'Sometimes at the street corner, sometimes his place. Never here.'

'Was there anyone else staying with him?'

'Who are you talking about?'

'A scholar, one who was taking the Imperial examinations.'

'Scholar? I thought it was Guo who owed your master the debt. What has it got to do with anyone else?'

'Let me worry about that. You focus on answering my questions.'

'Nope. Don't know of any scholar.'

Just like that, Jiang reached the limit of his willingness to cooperate. Yong knew that Sun had stayed with Guo. If Jiang had gone to Guo's place, it was not plausible that he had not heard of Sun. Jiang was hiding something, and Yong had to find out what it was.

Yong strained his ears to listen out for further footsteps and thought he heard some. 'I see. If that's the way you want to play it, I suggest you take a careful peek outside and come back to me again.'

Jiang curved up a corner of his mouth in a smirk dripping with scorn. Still, he got up, slid back the lock and eased open his door to peer out, expecting to confirm there was no one there. Instead, what he saw made him recoil from the opening and close the door with as much stealth as he could muster with shaking hands. The face that turned back to Yong had little colour left.

Yong did not have to look to know Jiang had seen a uniformed constable standing close to a wall less than ten steps from his door, back facing him. The constable would have been observing Niu behind cover and from a safe distance. To the old man, though, this constable was someone waiting for the call to either barge in to rough him up or, worse, drag him back to the courts to squeeze out a confession on some trumped-up charges.

'Now,' said Yong, 'do you want me to invite Mr Constable in for a three-way conversation, or would you rather just talk to me? Your call.'

'I … I think … How do I know he's here for me?' Jiang was mounting a last stand when it was clear his defence had crumbled.

'All right,' said Yong as he turned towards the door, 'let's ask him.'

Jiang grabbed Yong by the sleeve of his outer coat before he could advance further. 'No need,' he said in a voice at once hushed and urgent. 'What do you want to know?'

Grabbing Jiang's wrist, Yong freed his sleeve from the old man's grip. 'Come, sit down. You were going to tell me about the scholar.'

Like a puppet on strings, Jiang sat down on his bed as instructed while Yong remained standing. 'I did not know him well, much less than what I knew of Guo. I had only seen him a few times. I can't remember what he looked or sounded like.'

'What was his name?'

'He and Guo did not tell me his full name, and I never asked. His surname was, if I remember correctly, Sun. Yeah, *sun* as in grandchild, that's how I remembered. Guo used to belittle him behind his back, calling Sun his filial grandson.'

'I gather the two did not get along.'

'Guo told me they got into heated arguments sometimes.'

'Did the arguments turn … violent?'

'Not sure. I did not ask for details. I wouldn't be surprised, though. This Guo was quite a brute.'

'What did they argue about?'

'Money, I suppose. Guo likened the scholar to a money tree. Shook it a bit and money dropped down. That's what Guo used to say.'

'What else can you tell me about this Sun?'

'Nothing much. If he was in the house when I got there, he would soon step out with scrolls and books in his hands. He looked down on people like us. Thought he was superior and all. Even when he got a job, he behaved the same way.'

'A job?'

'Guo told me he had made the introduction for Sun to work at the same place as he did. He started from the bottom, and Guo said he was embarrassed by it at first. But he did well. Got promoted less than a month into the job. In no time, his nose was up in the air again.'

'When did he start working?'

Jiang squinted his eyes as he tried to recall. 'It was a couple of months after Guo started working at the place. I remember it was about a month or two after those examinations he went for.'

'I ask again—where did Guo work?' The question had taken on greater significance now that he knew Sun worked at the same place.

'I swear I don't know. I asked. I really did. I thought Guo could recommend me for a job, but he'd have none of it. He did not want me to look for him at his workplace, the dog.'

It was frustrating but Yong could tell Jiang was not lying. Since the constable might not stick around for long, he decided to go for the jugular. 'What happened to them after the fire? Where did they go?'

Jiang shook his head. 'I don't know.'

'Don't lie to me.'

'I'm not lying. It was a mess at the time. Many people had died or gone missing. As if that was not enough, the plague hit, bringing more deaths and chaos. Those who had survived soon dispersed. Guo moved out without telling me.'

'Besides you, was there anyone else Guo associated with?'

'He's a loner. I don't remember him having any friends.'

The trail was as cold as it had been before the day started. Yong still had no clue where Guo was, not even if he was still in the Capital.

Yong still had a bit of time. 'There was a piece of jade.'

The reaction was, again, instant and fleeting. For a brief moment, the right side of Jiang's face cringed a tad. Yong now knew why he was reluctant to talk about Sun.

'What jade?' said Jiang.

'You know what I'm talking about.'

'No idea.'

'I don't believe you.'

'That's up to you. I don't recall anything about any jade.'

'Perhaps we should make a trip to the courthouse to try out their new instruments. Bet those would jog your memory.' Yong, who had started to turn towards the door, was surprised by Jiang's speed in grabbing hold of his arm.

'Please, no,' said Jiang, his hands shaking.

Yong looked into Jiang's eyes and at his scarred hands. He got the impression the poor man had first-hand knowledge of the court instruments and felt sorry for him. 'I am not here to cause you trouble, only to search for answers, nothing else.'

Now, Jiang's whole body was trembling. Yong held his arm and sat him back down on the bed.

The old man shook his head. 'He told me never to tell anyone.'

'Guo?'

Jiang nodded.

'He is not here any more to bother you,' said Yong.

'He said he would kill me if I told.'

'An idle threat, I'm sure.'

'You don't know him. He meant it, I'm telling you. He told me he had killed a man before.'

'When?'

'Some years ago, before he moved here. He was on a job in another town. One of his co-workers owed him some gambling money. So, one night, he went into this fella's quarters when no one else was around, stabbed him, and took his money.

Nobody knew he did it. He was not kidding when he said he'd kill me.'

'I will not tell. He will never know.'

Jiang heaved a long sigh. The immediate threat was that of being hauled to the court for questioning. Dangers further out would have to be set aside for now.

'Once, when he was quite drunk, he asked me how he could sell a large piece of jade without anyone knowing. You see, he knew I … I had some knowledge of where stuff like that could be exchanged for money without fuss.'

'What else did he say about this piece of jade?'

'Stupid of me, but I was curious and asked him where it was from. He glanced in the direction of the scholar's room and sniggered. The scholar was out of the house, so he felt free to talk.'

'Wait. When did he tell you this?'

'A couple of months before the fire, I think it was.'

'You think the piece of jade he was talking about belonged to Sun, and Guo intended to take it from him?'

'The way he sniggered, I'm sure of it.'

'Maybe he was asking on behalf of Sun?'

Jiang sneered. 'Fat chance. In fact, just before the fire, he had started to boast about money.'

'What did he say?'

'He was careful not to spill specifics but said he was going to rake it in and settle down into a comfortable life. If the scholar had wanted to sell the piece of jade himself, all he had to do was to take it to one of many dealers and merchants around. He would have snagged a better price than those outlets that dealt in illicit stuff.' Jiang checked himself, having blurted out too much.

'So, you told him where to offload the piece.'

Jiang nodded, more slowly this time.

'Give me the name of the merchant and place,' said Yong.

'I can tell you but ...'

Having dealt with similar dealers before, Yong knew how this business worked. 'The problem is they won't talk to me without a referral, and you don't want your name mentioned.'

'Something like that. If they found out I divulged this information to officials, I'm as good as dead.'

'I'm just a civilian searching for information. I promised you wouldn't get into trouble talking to me, and I will keep the promise. Give me the name and place.'

There was no consolation or relief on Jiang's face, for how much was this young man's promise worth? Still, he had no choice. He had gone too far. The only things of relevance now were the tentacles of the law lurking on the other side of the door, eager to ensnare him.

'It is owned by the Chen family, northern tip of the main avenue. Legitimate traders with a side business.'

'Have you told anyone else of this information?'

Jiang shook his head. 'Not a soul.'

The questioning was done. There was nothing else Yong could extract from the old man.

The next port of call would be the Chen merchants, though he was not confident he would get anything of use from them. Merchants of such ilk had a side to them that asked no questions and retained no records. Tracks that led to them had the tendency to reach dead ends. Yong could not help but feel his search for Guo and the truth was hanging by a thread that was getting thinner as he dug deeper.

Chapter Twenty-Nine

The grey-haired gentleman who had introduced himself as Mr Chen did not conform to Zhong's image of a crook. Well-dressed and groomed, he appeared every bit the refined merchant, a front necessary to camouflage a side line of illicit trading.

Not that it mattered to Zhong, who was far from keen on this excursion to the storefront and then the backroom of the Chen merchants. Sitting down with shady traders by posing as merchants was not what he had in mind when he convinced his parents to let him come on this trip.

'Come, sit down,' Mr Chen said in a velvety smooth voice without rising from his seat.

Zhong claimed the seat opposite the man while his two servants took their usual places standing behind him.

After brief pleasantries, Chen got down to business. 'My staff told me you have an interesting proposition for us.'

'I do,' said Zhong. 'We are looking for a unique piece of jade and are offering a handsome commission on a successful purchase. It is of the highest quality and about three to four inches long. Exquisite carving of a dragon on one side and of a phoenix on the other. You would remember it if you have seen it.'

Yong was relieved. Zhong had been nervous and stumbled over his words at the front desk. Here, in the back room, he was once more his collected self.

'I remember hearing of the piece. It is possible for us to trace its whereabouts and facilitate the purchase, if that is what you desire.'

'We are serious about buying the piece and do not wish to be sent on fruitless expeditions. It is not enough for you to say you have heard of it, for a few dealers have claimed the same. We want to deal with someone who had handled the actual sale. The commission goes to only one dealer.'

Yong watched Chen as Zhong delivered the well-rehearsed spiel. While the merchant's face betrayed nothing, Yong could imagine the calculations going on in his head. It was clear the Chens had bought and sold Sun's jade piece. If not, Chen's staff would not have brought them here for this conversation. However, Chen's biggest concern would be law enforcement officials posing as buyers in a sting.

'How can we be sure,' Chen said, 'if your interest is genuine?'

'You can see the letter from Master Ouyang is authentic. What have you got to lose? The piece need not pass through your hands. Lead us to it and if we manage to buy it, the commission is yours.'

Chen leaned forward. 'What do we need to do to convince you we are the ones you should deal with?'

'We need to verify a few details. First, when was the piece sold?'

'If I'm not wrong, it was about four years ago.'

'Which month? It would help if you were more precise.'

Chen rubbed his chin. 'This was a month after the Spring Festival. I remember it well. There was some disruption to the festival that year due to the big fire at Xiushui Street and the plague after that.'

'So, it was about a month after the fire.'

'Correct.'

'Second question. Who was the seller?'

'Do we need to drill down into such details?'

'We know whose hands our piece was in. If you tell us who the seller was, we can match the names.'

Chen took his time to lean back and cross his legs. 'He declined to tell us his name. I remember him though, as he walked with a limp.'

'How did I do?' asked Zhong when they were a safe distance from the Chen premises.

'Very well. Calm and composed.' Yong stole a glance behind them to confirm no constable was tailing them. He was being extra careful, for he had already checked this morning when they set off for their mission.

The little operation near Old Jiang's house the previous day had taken the locals off their backs. Zhong's stopover at the craft workshop had not just been for placing the tailing constable in Jiang's line of sight. Inside the craft workshop, Zhong had also made enquiries on how he, representing the Ouyang merchants, could buy some wares in bulk. Yong was certain the tailing constable would duck into the workshop later to collect intelligence, leading the locals to conclude these young men from Renli were indeed here only to further commercial interests.

'We've got what we were looking for, right?' said Zhong.

'Right.'

'You don't seem pleased.'

'It's hard to feel happy when you've reached a dead end. We have now confirmed it was Guo Wutian who sold Sun's jade piece. Chen did not tell us the seller's name but it doesn't matter. Guo would not have used his real name anyway. Chen's description of his physical features fits what we know of him.'

'Where does that leave us?'

'It leaves us with some information on what happened to Sun. Let's start with the time he got here and stayed with

Guo, which was almost five years ago. We know the big fire happened four years ago. Six months before the fire, Guo found a regular job. Two months after that, Sun took on a job at the same place as Guo. Sometime after, about two months before the fire, Guo spoke to Old Jiang about selling Sun's jade piece. You follow so far?'

Both Zhong and Niu nodded.

'With the fire, the pair moved out. A plague swept over parts of the city, Guo sold the jade piece to the Chens and Mdm Li received Sun's ashes. These few events occurred so close together, it's hard to believe they are not linked.'

'You're saying Guo killed Sun for the lump of jade as Old Jiang said.'

'Men have committed murder for far less. There is also the timing. Guo told Old Jiang about selling the jade a few months before Sun's death. Either Guo possessed the gift of prophecy or a criminal mind planning to murder and steal.'

'And you do not think he's much of a seer.'

'The confusion caused by the fire gave him an ideal opportunity to execute his plan. It is possible Sun had succumbed to the plague and Guo simply pocketed the piece, though I think that would be too coincidental. In any case, what we do know is that Guo later sent Sun's ashes back to Renli. From Guo's point of view, it represented a neat closure. Then there was the last letter written by Guo.'

'The one that was burned up?'

'Yes. Why didn't the letter mention the fire or Guo moving? These were important events before the plague that claimed Sun Jie's life.'

'Perhaps the letter did contain the details but Mdm Li forgot about them.'

'We asked her specifically. She would remember such important facts.'

'Maybe Guo did not see the point of talking about these things. The only thing that mattered to Mdm Li was that her husband had died.'

'Possible. Or maybe Guo did not want Mdm Li to know too much. And by the way, Mr Zhou had this theory that the last letter from Sun Jie was in fact not written by him.'

'Another fake from Guo?'

'Another neat closure for Guo.'

'So, what's next?'

'We are stuck, I'm afraid. Nobody knows where Guo and Sun had gone after the fire. There are no more useful leads to follow. I could go from door to door in the area where they used to live, but since the Beggars' Sect had done that, it'd be a waste of time. Guo may not even be in this city any more.'

The trio walked the length of a street before Zhong spoke up. 'You've done what you can. I'll tell you what's a crime—you being here five days without a proper outing. Take some time to enjoy the city while we wait for Father to arrive. In fact, there is a busy street not far from here. Come with us, take a look.'

Chapter Thirty

The reputation of Bianjing as the greatest city under the heavens was not a hollow one. In his fourth day of exploring the city with Zhong and Niu, that much was clear to Yong.

The first thing that had struck him was food, more specifically its abundance and spellbinding variety. Everywhere he turned, there was food and lots of it. The street markets were a wonder to behold. All manner of produce was on display along roads, major and subsidiary, even on bridges. Indeed, there was a wooden bridge that arched like a rainbow over a river. In any other city, it would be a proud landmark, an impressive fusion of art and engineering to be treasured. Here, it was overrun daily by hawkers and buyers, turned into a rambunctious marketplace where one struggled to be heard amidst shouting and haggling.

Bianjing's status as a city of culture was also evident. Where people gathered, craftsmen and performing artistes were on hand to hawk their wares and demonstrate their skills. Scholars and men of learning could be spotted all over the city. It did not matter if they were rich or poor. With their refined and bookish demeanour, they stood out from commoners at street corners, gardens, tea houses, and other community spaces as they dissected the classics and discussed poetry.

After a day or two of soaking in the sights, sounds, and odours, Yong started to think that perhaps the half-million population Zhong and Zhou had been talking about was not such an exaggeration. They bumped into crowds everywhere.

Yong often felt overwhelmed in the major marketplaces just standing amidst the human tides sweeping by.

With no tailing constable in sight, the three of them were free to explore the city. Yong's mind too had been roaming—examining every issue, every angle, and every lead in the case. He often drew back in quiet contemplation behind Zhong and Niu as the two drank in everything the city had to offer. It was to no avail. The trail, as it stood, was stone-cold.

'Hey, Yong,' Zhong called out to him as he was again caught up in his thoughts. 'Looks like a street acrobat performance up in front is drawing quite a crowd. Let's check it out.'

'Why don't you two go ahead. I'll wait here at the corner.'

The street performers gave a few deafening whacks on a gong to gather people, generating more noise and justifying Yong's decision to seek some peace and quiet.

Zhong said to Niu, 'You go on. Give me a moment to talk to our friend here.'

Niu thought for a moment and decided to do as his master instructed.

'I'm fine,' said Yong. 'A bit tired, that's all. This city is full of people.'

As if to confirm Yong's assertion, another small crowd gathered at a public board next to them, raising their voices to discuss notices of the latest major happenings such as parades, religious ceremonies, appointments of officials, and even public executions. Some in the crowd were jabbing their fingers at portraits, presumably of the recent batch of appointed officials rather than condemned criminals. Yong could feel his head throbbing from the incessant noise and movement around him.

'Seems like you can't take a break from the case,' said Zhong.

'It's not that. It is just that ... You're right. I cannot get it out of my head.'

'I don't think anyone else could have done more or better. Let it go.'

'There is this question in my mind.'

'Here we go again,' said Zhong as he walked over to a stone bench just vacated by a few kids rushing over to the street performance, and plonked himself down. 'Tell me, what is this big question swirling around in that overly active head of yours.'

Yong sat down beside Zhong. 'The question is why. Why did Guo go all the way to Renli to kill off a poor widow and her helpless son?'

'Easy. To get rid of all connections to him.'

'Maybe, but as Mdm Li said, the trip is impossible for her given her difficulties.'

'Has it occurred to you that he, this Guo, might not know about her difficulties? There was no reason for poor Sun to tell him. These facts about his family would have been embarrassing for Sun.'

'True. But what Guo did carried risks. He could have been caught red-handed. He did indeed leave traces behind.'

'We, or you, were only able to make sense of those clues because Heaven spared Mdm Li. If she had died with her son, there would have been no one to tell us about Guo, and the clues would have led nowhere.'

'It still bothers me. If he had weighed the risks and benefits, he would have realized it was nigh impossible for Mdm Li to find him even if she had made her way here. He had moved out of the old address and nobody from there knows where he had gone to. The chances of a random search succeeding in this great city are negligible.'

'Maybe he wanted to make sure he would never be found. To tie up the loose end. And you're assuming Guo had acted after careful consideration. Perhaps it was an impulsive move, driven by fear.'

'Why now?'

'I thought you said you had only one question.'

'If Guo had wanted to silence mother and child, he could and should have done it years ago, when the need to bury things underground was the highest.'

'Who knows? Perhaps after a few years, the worries and fears caught up with him, and he felt he had to do something.'

'Possible, I suppose.'

'And yet you are not satisfied.'

'I need to do more thinking.'

Chapter Thirty-One

Well past sundown, the wheels of commerce in the Capital continued to spin with considerable energy, though the complexion of activities changed. Fewer edible items on sale and more entertainment.

This typical night, the common folk, having partaken of their evening meals, came out in search of leisure. There was something to suit every taste. Singing voices from teahouses, an *erhu* player sitting at the side of the street drawing melancholic melodies from his thin string instrument and accompanying bow, jugglers tossing a variety of objects in the air, and a fire-breather staking out the middle of a stone arch bridge. These were just a few attractions Zhong and his servants wandered by on their way back to the inn. Bellies satisfied after a hearty meal, they had sat at the restaurant to watch streams of passersby while sipping quality wine for almost two hours before deciding to call it a day.

After days of sight-seeing and feasting, the novelty of Bianjing had long worn off for Yong. In contrast, Zhong and Niu were still brimming with energy, like they were just getting started.

'I hope you enjoyed dinner, Yong,' said Zhong, his laid-back tone of voice matching their leisurely pace.

'Not bad.'

'You did not say much, mind. At least Niu was chattier after a few cups of wine. Did you hear him talking about the cases you guys worked on?'

'He was exaggerating, quite liberal with the facts.'

'No, I wasn't,' said Niu.

'I would add,' said Yong, 'especially on his own contributions to the cases.'

'Hey, the thanks I receive for helping you out.'

Zhong laughed. 'I'm sure Yong appreciates your help. Why else would he call on you every time?'

'Pick on me, you mean.'

'Though you seem to have quite a bit of fun yourself.'

His cheeks still pink from the effects of alcohol, Niu smiled and did not dispute the point.

They walked past a teahouse. A sweet female singing voice wafted out of the place, accompanied by shouts of 'Good!' and 'Great voice!' and enthusiastic applause. The sound of merriment dominated and the mood was light. Yong managed a smile.

'So, Yong,' said Zhong, catching the upturn in Yong's spirits, 'why don't you tell us about the case of the monks? You said you would tell me but never got down to it. This is the one Niu had no part to play in.'

'I dragged the monks to their cell, didn't I?'

This time, both Zhong and Yong laughed, prompting Niu's face to redden further.

'It was nothing,' said Yong. 'We did not do much. The monks tripped over themselves, really.' Yong proceeded to give Zhong a summary of how he exposed the fraudulent monks.

'Well, that explains why Ouyang was so grateful.'

'That he is.'

'Funny that. I mean, respect for the dead and all that. But it is another case of the rich using money to buy privileges in life, isn't it?'

'Oh, Young Master,' said Yong, 'not again.'

'Well, it's true. We ought to be grateful for Ouyang's generosity in helping us, but his father started the whole episode in the first place. Don't you agree?'

'I suppose so.'

'The old man should have totted up more charitable deeds when he was alive to secure a better position in the afterlife. And the son is no better, crying foul when the deal did not work out for him. To be blunt, they're all using gold and silver to ... What's wrong, Yong?'

Yong's smile had melted away, his face dead serious. He slowed down, then came to a complete halt.

'What's wrong?' Zhong said again.

'I need to check something out. Back at the city centre.'

'What, now?'

'Yes, now.' Yong turned around and started to jog off.

'You want us to come with you?'

'Go back to the inn,' shouted Yong, only half turning back. 'Don't wait up.' He turned the corner and was gone.

Chapter Thirty-Two

Zhong sat up on his bed, eyes still bleary and adjusting to the morning glare from the window. Tea and breakfast were laid out on the table.

'Where's Yong?' said Zhong.

'He has gone out to fetch water,' answered Niu, sitting at the table.

'Did you see him come in last night?'

Before Niu could answer, Yong had returned with a basin of warm water in his hands. 'Morning, Young Master.'

'Someone's bright and cheery. You got back late last night.'

Yong put the basin down on the table. 'Well past midnight. You two were out cold.'

Putting on his shoes, Zhong went over to sit at the table and picked up the wet towel that Niu had handed to him. 'Looks like you enjoyed a fruitful little escapade last night. Solved the case?'

'Not yet, but it has at least risen from the grave. Hurry up, will you? We have work to do.'

'Well, well. Just yesterday, you were all gloom, sapped of energy. Now, we're up and running again. Would you care to explain?'

Yong sat at the table facing Zhong and waited until Zhong was done wiping his face. 'Are you listening?'

'Yeah, yeah. Go on.'

'Do you remember I told you I was bothered by the question of why Guo would take the risk to silence Mdm Li and Xiaodong? When you talked about the case of Ouyang and the monks, an idea came to me. But sorry, it is a big jump. Let me start from the beginning.'

'That'll be helpful.'

'As Mr Zhou has reminded me, when there are roadblocks, rather than butting our heads against them, sometimes we need to try another path. I was focusing too much on Guo. That's the roadblock. Since the path was not leading anywhere, I considered an alternative. I decided to focus on Sun.'

'Who has been dead for a few years.'

'What if he's still around?'

'Still around? Our discussion on the afterlife and spirits. Was that what got you going?'

'No, no. I mean, what if he's still alive? So far, the only person who said he died is Guo, who is at best unreliable. What if the death was faked?'

'You mean Guo staged the death?'

'Both Sun and Guo. Sun has to be in on it.'

'Of course. But the ashes.'

'Could have been anybody's. Even from an animal, for all we know.'

'Why? To keep Mdm Li from looking for her husband?'

'That's the only reason I could think of. We know Sun started working not long after he attempted the Imperial examinations. Maybe he was running out of money. Perhaps he had planned to stay on to retake the examinations and needed income. The only thing we are certain of is that he never passed.'

'Wait. You're saying Guo and Sun were in cahoots. But the piece of jade. Old Jiang said Guo stole it from Sun.'

'That's not what he said. He said he *thought* Guo would steal it based on how Guo asked him about selling it. Guo could have been asking on behalf of Sun.'

'I thought Mdm Li said her husband would never sell his family heirloom.'

'Let's think of why he would do that.'

'He needed the money.'

'A possible reason, but there could be others. Strained family relations, perhaps. Or maybe—'

'He wanted to sever links to his family, his background.'

Yong tapped his young master's knee. 'Now you're getting my drift. Let's say he wanted to get rid of the piece. But given its worth, he's not going to chuck it in the rubbish heap, right? The best way would be to sell it to a dealer who asks no pesky questions and keeps no records.'

'So, the two moving out, Guo selling the jade piece, and sending the ashes back were indeed linked but not in the way we had thought—that Guo had killed Sun and proceeded to cash in and clean up. Rather, it was both of them erasing their tracks.'

'Correct.'

'But why would Sun want to cut family ties and in so ruthless a fashion?'

'Ah,' said Yong, straightening his back, 'we come back to the big question of "why". Sun had come to the Capital with dreams of passing the examinations and bagging an official post, his only meaningful purpose in life since childhood. Alas, those dreams were left in tatters when he flunked. Then he started on a job. It would have been a source of shame for him, the son of a rich man and a scholar, to lower himself to work for a crass merchant. Perhaps he changed his name to mask his identity, thinking it would only be a temporary disgrace. When the time came, he could retake the examinations. Another shot at glory.'

'Sounds reasonable.'

'But something changed. He did well at work. Promoted early into his stint, and goodness knows how many times after that. An educated man bringing his smarts and a veneer of prestige to a merchant. He proved himself capable in business. They started grooming him for greater things and he began to get comfortable, very comfortable. You see that?'

'It's a plausible story. You're saying he and Guo tried to kill off his wife and son to keep his privileged life.'

'Not quite. To do that, it would be enough to fake his death, for Sun would know it was almost impossible for Mdm Li to come look for him here. And in fact, they did stage the death and stay quiet for a few years. A few years later, something else happened, a hastening event that, in Sun's mind, called for the removal of his wife and child. It was something that opened the door for his secret to be exposed. A public event, perhaps.'

'And you have figured out what this was,' said Zhong.

'It was right under my nose, and I did not see it. Talking about Ouyang and the monks reminded me of the rich using their wealth to buy social status.'

'You just mentioned that. A wealthy merchant family hired a scholarly gentleman to add some shine to their business.'

'Try a higher status.'

'What, a scholar who was successful? I thought you said Sun did not pass the examinations.'

'Perhaps he did not need to. Remember,' said Yong as he waggled his eyebrows, 'there is another way into officialdom.'

'Another way. You mean ...'

Yong smiled and nodded, sensing Zhong's realization.

'Donation official,' said Zhong. 'You think Sun's employer stumped up gold and silver to buy him an official post. Being a court official turns him into a public figure.'

'You've got it. As a scholar who had prepared almost his whole life to enter officialdom, he would be the perfect candidate to be pushed up as a donation official. In terms of bringing prestige to whichever family he was working for; it would be the ultimate prize.'

'But you were right to say "family". Why would they elevate an outsider to such a position? The investment would be considerable.'

'Very good question. If he had been an employee, an outsider, I agree the investment needed would be hard to justify. I think he has become part of the family, either adopted or married into. From Mdm Li's description, Sun was a handsome man with pleasant manners. With his learning, he would have been an attractive package.'

'And it would explain the big "why".'

'If he had been an employee, having a wife and child back home would not be an insurmountable problem. Committing murder would be a sizeable risk, too big a risk to remove a mere embarrassment. No, I think he has gone in too deep with the merchant family, like marrying into the family, such that abandoning a family back in Renli would be a scandal too far. At some point, somebody from Renli might recognize him and ruin everything, not just for him, but for the merchant family too. In his mind, he *had* to remove his wife and child.'

'Whoa, hold on. It is a plausible story, I admit, but you have jumped a few speculative steps to come to this conclusion.'

Yong flashed a wide grin. 'Not speculative. Imaginative.'

'From coming to the Capital for the examinations to murdering his own wife and child, that's quite a leap.'

'I understand. Hence my little late-night trip to test my theory. Remember we went past the town noticeboard yesterday, the one with notices on the officials appointed? I did not pay much attention to them before and had to go back for a closer examination. There are four donation officials among the lot. I was comparing the portraits with Mdm Li's description of Sun.'

'Looks could have changed in four years.'

'True, especially if one is trying to look different. However, certain features like the shape of the nose and size of the eyes can't be altered. I narrowed it down to two men. One is a Jing Mayun. Neither thin nor fat, clean-shaven. The other one, by the name of Duan Shiyu, is plump and has a bit too much facial hair—moustache, beard, the works. Both share the small eyes, sharp nose and pointed ears of Sun.'

'All right, but that's no proof. Those features you mentioned describe thousands of men in this city.'

'Yeah, I know. What the portraits have done is keep my theory alive. Our next step is to find out more about these two to ascertain, which one is our man. This morning, I found out which merchant families they're from. We can go to the areas around the merchants' premises to fish for information and hunt for a man with a limp. If we can confirm Guo is still working with him, we've got them both—Sun and Guo.'

'Doesn't sound too difficult.'

Chapter Thirty-Three

It turned out to be a lot more difficult than Zhong had anticipated. Piecing together a reasonably useful picture of Jing, whose family operated a rice trading business, had been easy enough. The local community around the household knew him well through his philanthropic contributions. Jing Mayun was the eldest son of the family patriarch and had thus far led a gilded, if unremarkable, life. Some old folks in the community remembered his younger days, including his childhood. He was therefore struck out as a person of interest. Jing Mayun was not Sun Jie, a relative newcomer to the city.

Public sources told them the other family, the Duans, bought rice wine from the surrounding region to sell to distributors and retailers in the Capital and cities nearby. This fitted in well with Old Jiang's recollection that Guo had supplied premium quality wine not long after he had started regular work.

Beyond such surface facts, the surrounding community knew little about the family. Workers and servants from the household refused to talk. Yong had approached a few wine retailers, many of whom had dealings with the Duans. However, all they knew was that they bought their goods from the Duans on favourable credit terms. In return, the tacit understanding was that they asked no questions about the family.

The one germane nugget of information they managed to gather was something that was impossible to hide. Duan Shiyu was not a Duan by birth. Although no one they spoke to knew how, he had appeared on the scene some years back and later married into the family, adopting the family name. Society considered the abandonment of a man's own family name a disgrace, though it was not unheard of in rich merchant families with no male heirs. This was indeed the case for the Duan family, whose patriarch had five daughters and no son.

Even then, such straightforward facts were whispered to Zhong by a couple of men at a teahouse, as though discussion of matters relating to the Duans was taboo. The Duan family wanted the outside world to know as little about them as possible.

After more than a day of trying, the trio decided to ease off. Suspicion was mounting amongst the natives. The last thing they wanted was to draw attention to themselves.

They were now milling about in a market. An afternoon of aimless strolling beckoned until Yong caught sight of two old ladies carrying baskets and scouring stalls for produce.

'These two old ladies look familiar,' said Yong, looking in the direction of the pair. 'Aren't they from the Duan household?'

'Oh yeah,' said Niu, 'we saw them entering the house yesterday.'

'Wild Wolf mentioned something useful. You have put on a bit more weight, but let's see what we can do.'

'Walk faster,' one of the old ladies reminded the other. The shorter one quickened the shuffling of her feet to keep up. This forced march had been their daily ritual for a month, since beggars started harassing women. While they tried to keep to busy streets, there was no way to avoid some quiet stretches no matter which route they chose.

'Those cursed beggars,' said the shorter old lady. 'Shouldn't they be spending what little they possess on food rather than alcohol?'

The taller one was too busy putting one foot in front of the other in quick succession to respond. Chatting would have to wait. The immediate priority was to navigate past this stretch without harassment from drunk beggars, a recent scourge.

The alley seemed clear. There was no one in sight, which was at once a relief and a source of concern. A few more steps later, this concern materialized into something more threatening. From the shadows of a side alley emerged a male figure, clothes somewhat rumpled but body shape a bit too plump for a beggar, staggering into the main passageway and towards them in an apparent drunken stupor. Alarmed, the ladies quickened their pace but the man, with surprising speed, dashed past and halted in front of them to cut off the escape route. Startled, they dropped their baskets.

Oddly, the man's shoes did not seem that ragged though his hair and clothes were dishevelled, and his face and hands marred with dirt. Clasped in one hand was a wine bottle. Unmistakable too was the smell of alcohol from a few feet away. By now, the ladies were cowering in fear. Between the two of them, a feeble stammer of 'What do you want?' was all they could muster.

The man groaned and let out an unintelligible series of grunts, which only frightened the ladies even more. They were summoning the strength to scream when a figure bolted past them from behind and stood between them and the drunken menace. They did not catch sight of the man's face and could only conclude from the view of his back that he was young, tall, and lean. They could not help but worry if this lad could stand up to the towering brute.

'What do you think you're doing?' they heard the young man ask.

In response, the drunkard reached forward in an attempt to grab hold of his inquisitor's collar. Before the aggressor's grubby paws could reach him, the young man executed strong outward swipes of his arms, knocking away the beggar's own hefty ones. Drawing his hands back to his chest, the young man anchored his right foot behind him and used his whole body to push out. The young man's palms connected with the fleshy chest of the drunkard, who fell backwards, hit the floor, and mumbled something vague about taking things too seriously.

The bigger man took some time to get up, all the while rubbing his buttocks. Before he could stand upright, the young man lurched forward, adding vigour to his shout of 'Get lost!' to the beggar's face.

And so Niu rose gingerly and staggered away.

Yong turned around to contrasting expressions—a smiling face from the taller lady and a sullen look from the other.

'Are you ladies all right?' Yong said.

'Fine, we're fine. What a brave young man, eh?' said Mdm Smiley to her companion. The smaller old lady mumbled a vague response as both of them loaded spilled produce back into their baskets.

'Don't mind her,' said Mdm Smiley. 'She is always like this in front of strangers, even nice ones.'

There was not much time left, for the Duan residence was less than five hundred paces away. Yong had to get down to business.

'Where are you ladies headed?'

'Just ahead, to the house at the corner of Yuewan Street,' said Mdm Smiley.

'I'm heading that way myself. Why don't I walk you there? Come, let me help with the baskets.'

Mdm Smiley made a short and polite show of resisting help before ceding. Mdm Grouch grunted once more but was nevertheless happy enough to hand over some of her load to Yong.

'Quite a lot of stuff you have here,' said Yong. 'You must be cooking for a sizeable household.'

'Yes, the Duan household,' said Mdm Smiley.

'Ah, Duan Wine Merchants. Famous in all of the Capital!' Yong figured a bit of flattery never hurt.

Right on cue, Mdm Smiley's grin spread wider. 'In the whole region, in fact. It has been around for more than a century. Myself, I've been in the household for more than forty years.'

'That's something. There has been quite a buzz around town about your master, him taking on a court appointment and all that.' Yong hoped he was not too quick in going for the kill. He had little time to potter about as the three of them started walking.

Nodding, Mdm Smiley flashed another grin.

Yong had to press on to keep the conversation going. 'Honourable of him to want to serve the court and the people. A kind boss, is he?'

The smile on the lady's face was now a tad cagey. 'He treats us well enough.'

Yong sensed an opening in the reticence. 'He must be a capable man. Rose through the ranks to be where he is today, I heard.'

'The education helped, I suppose.'

'You mean Master Duan is a man of books?'

'Yeah, one of them scholars.'

'Impressive. A scholar in business would be of great help, I'm sure.'

'I'd say. He has got a fair business head on him but I think Old Master already had that well covered. In fact, I can tell you from serving the family for three generations that they all have good business sense about them, including the women. Young Master was useful though in lending some respectability to the business.'

Mdm Smiley was now receiving daggered glances from Mdm Grouch, who evidently did not feel it was prudent to share household gossip with a stranger, even one who had just rescued them from a pest. Mdm Smiley rambled on about the happenings in the household. While some small talk was necessary to loosen the tongue, her tendency to veer off course was eating up precious time.

Yong picked a brief break in the monologue to interrupt. 'A useful catch for the family, I must say. Master Duan, I mean.'

'Well, he was a capable and learned young man whom Old Master wanted to keep for good. Also of marriageable age was Old Master's youngest and favourite daughter. Match made in heaven!' said Mdm Smiley, whose forearm copped a snappy tug from Mdm Grouch.

'How long has Master Duan been with the business?' asked Yong. They were now making the final turn before the last stretch of narrow alley leading to the back of the Duan residence no more than two hundred paces away.

Mdm Grouch finally spoke up. 'What has that got to do with you?'

'Come, now,' said Mdm Smiley, pacifying her companion. 'Why does it matter if this kind young man is taking some interest in the household? It's not like we're sharing deep family secrets here. Don't mind her, young man. You were saying ... ah, how long, you asked. Well, it must have been more than four years since he joined the business.'

Yong slowed down to delay the approach to the house and hoped Mdm Smiley would follow suit. She did.

Mdm Grouch shuffled on at first, then turned back in annoyance. 'I'm not going to wait for you,' she said and pushed ahead on her own.

'Suit yourself,' said Mdm Smiley, before turning back to Yong. 'Yes, almost four and a half years ago.'

'I see he has taken on the Duan family name.'

Walking forward again, the old lady shielded her mouth with her hand, speaking with a soft voice. 'Old Master has five daughters and no son. The first four daughters married into respectable families, and there was no way the husbands would take on the Duan family name. Young Master Duan was different. He had no family ties and was more than willing to take on the name. And why not? From a poor background, he now stands to partake in the Duan inheritance. Not a bad exchange, if you ask me.'

'You said he had no family ties.'

'Yes. He came from a border town. Rampaging barbarians killed his parents years ago while he was away. Horrible.'

Rather convenient too, thought Yong. 'What was his family name before?'

'It was ... Yang. Yes, Yang. Oh my, I'm getting old.'

No surprise there. Yong did not expect Sun to use his real family name. 'What about friends? Did he bring one or two along to the Duan business? He must know quite a few scholars.' The back door of the Duan residence was now just a few steps ahead.

'Aye, he did have a companion but it was the other way round. This fellow started work first, then introduced Young Master to Old Master. You see, at the time, Old Master needed help, and this fellow sensed an opportunity to curry some favour with the boss. He has done well out of it, I must say. Scholar? Don't make me laugh. Just blind luck to be in the right place at the right time.'

'This fellow is close to the bosses?'

'Oh, yes, very close, but just with one. The ingrate would not even listen to Old Master any more. He is always following his master around like a little lap dog. Nice talking to you, young lad.'

'What is the name of this gentleman?' said Yong as he laid the baskets on the ground outside the Duans' back door, drawing a quizzical look from the lady. Awkward it was, but he had no time to dress up his last shot. 'I just want to figure out who to contact in case my master would like to approach Master Duan.'

'I appreciate your help, young man,' said Mdm Smiley while she moved the baskets one by one into the house. 'Our masters do not like us talking about the household.' Her voice dropped to a whisper. 'I have said too much.'

Before Yong could say anything else, the wooden door swung on its hinges with a moan, then shut off his access to further clues with a final thud.

Chapter Thirty-Four

Zhong sat on the bench by the table, both palms pressed down and elbows locked to prop up his shoulders. 'I'm not sure about this.'

'We went through our plan in great detail last night,' Yong said while tidying up the bed, his back to his young master. 'I've sent Niu to his stake-out post. Once I'm done here, we're ready to go. Do we have to go through it again?'

Zhong relaxed his arms and let his shoulders sag. 'This smells like another one of your little schemes that lead to trouble.'

Yong stopped what he was doing and sat down on the bed to face Zhong. 'What's wrong? You were fine last night.'

Zhong shifted his gaze to the floor. 'I had a bad dream last night. It was a trap. They were waiting for us, including Magistrate Lei Jun.'

'I feel silly saying this, but it was just a dream.'

'Aren't you concerned we may be found out?'

'How? We are holding a legitimate letter from the Ouyang family with the stamp of the authentic family seal. We would be prospective business partners paying a visit to Duan Wine Merchants. We take a look around and chat to a few people. After that, we walk out, cool and calm. What could go wrong?'

'Plenty. Thrown in jail, beaten up. Maybe silenced if they wise up to what you're up to.'

'No, we won't be, at least not you. Remember, you're the son of a magistrate who's coming to town in a few days' time.'

'Come, Yong, think this through. Last night, you said yourself the facts fit. The old lady said Guo started working at Duan Merchants and introduced Sun to the Duans a few months before the fire.'

'She did not tell me the name of the fella who brought Duan Shiyu to the business. I can't be sure if he's Guo.'

'The timings fit. We know Guo sold the Sun family heirloom another few months later. As you surmised, having done well in the business, Sun married the daughter of the merchant without a male heir and took on the Duan family name. Duan or Sun's appointment as an official is a clear motive to wipe out his family in Renli. You've got your perpetrators, both of them.'

'We can't be sure. We need to be certain these two are indeed Guo and Sun.'

'You should be busy congratulating yourself while we sit tight and wait for Father to arrive. Tell him what we have unearthed and he will do the rest. Why are we still venturing into the tiger's lair?'

'To prize away the tiger cubs, as the saying goes,' Yong said with a grin, though he could see Zhong was not amused. 'Young Master, it's not that simple.'

'Why isn't it?'

'We have no proof. Old Master, when he arrives, cannot just walk into the Duan residence and arrest the criminals. He has no jurisdiction here to even demand to see them. All he has—all we have—is a theory. What's more, one of the suspects was recently appointed a court official. In the absence of solid proof, Duan Shiyu's wealth and influence can obstruct Old Master with ease.'

'They cannot hide from Father forever.'

'They won't need to. A bit of delay, and the locals will ride to their rescue. Magistrate Lei will not allow your father the time or opportunity to poke around and to verify Sun's identity. If we are to succeed in bringing them to justice, we would have to pretty much lay the proof on a plate for Old Master.'

'There must be some upright official here who can do something.'

'Remember, Old Master does not know anyone here. Whom can he trust and what proof can he bring to the table? And if I'm wrong, he would be charged with falsely accusing another official of a heinous crime. Looking like a fool would be the least of his problems.'

That dreadful thought gave Zhong some pause, but he was not done yet. 'What if you miscalculate? Father gave you clear instructions not to take risks.'

'What he meant was not to take unnecessary risks. We are going in to gather information, not to confront anyone.'

'I'm still not sure about this,' said Zhong, a hint of wavering in his voice.

'If we don't do this, they might well stay out of our reach. Either you go with me or I follow through by myself. I cannot let our efforts go down the drain when we have come so close. I'm not going back to tell Mdm Li that I let her son's murderers off the hook because the risks put me off. But I need your help. You talk like a learned man. You can draw attention away while I sniff around. With the two of us looking out for each other, we won't go wrong. How about it?'

There was nothing more for Yong to say. By the look in Zhong's eyes, Yong knew he had won him over. Zhong blew out a heavy breath and stood up. 'Remember what you promised my parents.'

Yong sprang up on his feet. 'Your mother, you mean.'

'Including her.' Zhong started walking towards the room entrance with Yong close behind.

As Zhong neared the entrance, he stopped and let out a soft chuckle.

'What?' asked Yong.

'Nothing. I was reminded of how you frightened two innocent old ladies to get what you want. Not scrupulous with your methods, are you? Not sure my father would approve.'

'They are fine and your father is not here to disapprove. Now, stop wasting time and act like my young master, will you?'

Chapter Thirty-Five

Thirty paces from the Duan residence front gate, Yong glanced to his left, where he expected Niu to be. There he was, settled on his seat at the teahouse without a front wall, presenting him with an unobstructed view across the busy street. They were ready to proceed.

From their surveillance the past few days, they had noted the Duans opened the wide front gate only two to three times a day to let goods in and out of the compound. Workers and visitors trickled through a wooden door carved out of the gate itself. Every person using the front door had to go through the ritual of knocking and verification before access was granted.

Once Zhong had taken his position in front of the door, he nodded to his servant to signal his readiness. Yong took hold of the thick iron ring on the door hanging by the mouth of a metallic head of a lion and knocked it a few times against the door. At the third and final knock, the rectangular plate at Zhong's eye level slid open, revealing a pair of eyes.

'What do you want?' the voice behind the eyes was laced with no small measure of hostility. The guardian of the portal had in an instant ascertained the visitor as neither familiar nor mature enough for business of much consequence.

Zhong cleared his throat. 'I am Liu Zhong from Longtian. My assistant and I are here, on behalf of the Ouyang Merchants, to enquire about a bulk purchase of wine.'

'Who are you supposed to see?'

'We did not arrange for an appointment. We have known of Master Duan's good repute for some time and would be honoured to speak to him if possible.'

'You wish to speak to Master Duan?' With the condescending tone penetrating the thick wooden door, Zhong tried his best not to shrink with embarrassment. 'Wait here.' The plate slid shut again.

After some time, the sound of a latch sliding on the inside was followed by the door swinging open.

'Come in,' said the guardian, a hulk of a man whose physique was more suitable for intimidating than welcoming visitors. 'Follow me.'

The courtyard they were being led through provided a clear view of the compound, or at least the frontage. The elegant buildings to their left looked every bit the tranquil residence of a wealthy household. Where they were heading towards, to the right, lay what seemed to be the business end of the estate. Here stood two buildings, a large one lording over its diminutive companion at its side. Since a few workers were moving goods out of the large building, Yong guessed it was a storehouse. The smaller structure could be an administrative wing.

The guardian of the gate led Zhong and Yong into the storehouse through the front entrance, stepping aside for busy workers streaming out. The smell of wine, which had been wafting out of the door as they approached, launched its full assault on their nostrils as they stepped inside. Like bees around a hive, workers buzzed around rows upon rows of shelves stacked with ceramic wine bottles. Instructions were shouted across the spacious interior.

They were led to a man standing next to the shelf nearest the entrance. He had a book in one hand and in the other a writing brush that he used to point at bottles on the shelf while mouthing inaudible numbers.

'Talk to him,' said the gate guardian before turning and walking away.

The stock-taker glanced at the visitors, then switched his gaze back to the shelf. 'What do you want?'

'We represent the Ouyang family in Longtian,' said Zhong. 'We are planning to import some wine from this region.'

The stock-taker had eyes only for the wine bottles in front of him. 'How much?'

'Pardon?'

'How many bottles?'

'If the initial batch of five hundred bottles work out, we intend to order a thousand bottles every two months.'

This caused the man to set aside his task and turn his head to stare at Zhong. 'Wait here,' he said as he closed his book and walked away.

Yong took two steps back for a better view of the storehouse. The administrative wing was now to his left. With the tall rows of shelves blocking his view, he could not tell if there was a connecting door between the two buildings.

The stock-taker walked past shelves and workers, towards a lady shuffling around at the centre of the storehouse. Yong had noticed her when they first walked in. In her late twenties by the looks of it, her shimmering, lily-white silk dress and matching jewellery around the neck and wrists were hard to miss and out of place in the bustling worksite. Still, activities seemed to revolve around her. Passing workers paused to greet her with slight bows. Some came to her for instructions. Once the stock-taker neared her, his sour demeanour gave way to respectful bowing.

After a brief conversation, he bowed again, turned around, and came back to the visitors, every inch the sour prune once more. 'Come with me.'

He led them past three rows of shelves to the right, then along an aisle, hundreds of wine bottles to the left and right of them. At the end of the aisle, on a lone wooden stool, sat a clean-shaven man with rough complexion and an oversized cloth cap pulled over his hair, covering his ears. Looking to be in his early fifties, he was barking at a hapless young man who was standing and bowing, taking it all in.

As the stock-taker and the visitors approached, the older man dismissed the young man with a flick of his hand and looked up. 'What?'

The stock-taker, half-bowing with every sentence, briefed the senior man on what the two young guests had asked for. The man examined Zhong with his droopy eyes and sighed, annoyed with the interruption to his day.

'Are you serious in buying?' he said to Zhong.

'Yes, we are,' said Zhong.

The man got up from his seat. He was well-built for his age though on the short side, a couple of inches above Yong's shoulders. 'Come with me,' he said as he turned around and walked off.

While the man was seated, Yong had noticed something about his shoes. The part of the left shoe close to the big toe, just above the sole, was worn out compared to the one on the right. The whispers of the left shoe as it brushed against the ground were therefore not something that surprised Yong.

Eyes widening, Zhong had by now also caught on to Yong's observation. The man was dragging his left foot, a slight limp apparent as he walked in front of them, leading the way.

Chapter Thirty-Six

Zhong introduced himself and Yong as he followed behind the man, who grunted in response.

'How may I address you, sir?' said Zhong.

'Around here, they call me Uncle Wu.'

Wu brought them on a tour of the facilities to inspect different products in stock. Zhong displayed admirable poise after recovering from the initial shock of coming face to face with a killer, engaging him in discussion.

'Sweet fragrance,' said Zhong in what was to be the last sampling. 'You saved the best for last.'

'You mentioned a sizeable order.'

One thing was for sure. No one could accuse Wu of beating about the bush.

Zhong straightened his back. 'Shall we sit down to talk?'

Good, thought Yong, *create excuses to explore the facility as much as possible*. There was no chair in sight and no sitting area along the tour route. They would have to go somewhere else for a proper business negotiation. Yong hoped this would be closer to the administrative wing where they would stand a better chance of bumping into Duan Shiyu.

Alas, the older man turned to walk towards the side of the warehouse opposite to the administrative wing. The two young men followed and came to a corridor near the corner of the warehouse to their right. They walked along this corridor, passing rooms on both sides. The rooms on their right lined the front wall of the warehouse, with windows to let light in.

Their destination was a room on the right, second from last. The grouchy host plonked himself down on a stool at a circular table and motioned for the young men to take up the two remaining stools at the table.

Light came in through a window right smack in the middle of the outward-facing wall. In keeping with the business line, wine bottles were everywhere. Most of them were packed in a small rack on one side of the room, different varieties on display. A few stood on the round table together with a capped mug while a few more were strewn on a desk at the other side of the room. Of more interest to Yong were the few piles of paper sitting on the desk, weighed down by bottles. This seemed to be Wu's workstation. It was not for nothing Yong picked the seat closest to the old desk.

The host lifted the cap on the mug and took a sip. As though reminded of the presence of the visitors, he glanced up at Zhong and said, 'Do you want some tea?' It was a perfunctory offer, made more out of embarrassment than a desire to take care of his guests.

Zhong was about to decline when Yong cut in. 'Some tea would be nice.'

The host looked at Yong then at Zhong, expecting him to keep the rude servant in line. To his disappointment, Zhong smiled and nodded.

As Wu stood up and made his way to the door, Zhong locked eyes with Yong, who tipped his head towards the working desk. With one glance in the same direction, Zhong understood. They had to lure the man out of the room so that they could start mining the desk.

Alas, it was not to be. Wu stopped in his tracks one step out of the door, with both young men poised to swing into action.

He shouted an order to someone to fetch two cups of hot tea. This someone turned up at the corridor right at that moment, ruining the opportunity for the young men.

Wu sat back down, all gruff again. 'How many bottles?' He seemed determined to end the discussion before tea arrived.

Zhong decided to avoid that topic for now. 'Is there a chance we could call on Master Duan?'

'What for?'

'We would like to congratulate him on his appointment to the court.'

'He's not here,' came the curt reply.

'You mean he is not in town?'

'Not in his building, didn't you see? Are you here for business or a social visit?'

'Sorry, it is just that—'

'How many bottles?' Wu locked his eyes on Zhong, not letting him dodge the question any further.

Zhong took a while before replying. 'It depends on the price.'

'Every bottle of wine you sampled, I've told you the price.'

'I like the last bottle. We can pay seven-tenth of what you quoted.'

Wu smirked. 'Are you kidding? Not worth our effort.'

'What if we buy eight hundred bottles for a start? We will pay for delivery.'

There was no immediate reply, so Zhong decided to push the point. 'We would be happy to discuss this with Master Duan.'

Wu straightened his back, folded his arms, and looked down at the tabletop. Everyone in the room knew people like him did not make the important decisions. Zhong had calibrated the numbers to bring the boss into the picture.

After what seemed like an extended moment of contemplation, the host finally spoke. 'Where did you say you're from?'

'Longtian,' answered Zhong, fishing the Ouyang letter from his pocket and spreading it out on the table.

Glancing at the piece of paper with his arms still folded, Wu nodded like he was satisfied with what he was reading. Yong knew it was an act to project a semblance of authority and salvage some pride. The man needed to remind them he was the gatekeeper who granted access to important figures in the Duan family. It was how people like him made a living.

'It's too early for you to talk to the boss,' said Wu. 'For now, you deal with me. Understood?'

'I understand.'

'Good. I'll discuss your offer with the boss.'

Wu rose and ambled out of the room. As soon as he left, Zhong shifted his stool to sit close to the door, in a position to peek to the end of the corridor. Once Wu stepped out of sight, he nodded at Yong, who got right to work.

Yong figured that their host would need to check with Duan, who Yong guessed was stationed at the smaller administrative building next to the storehouse, at the opposite end. Still, he dived straight into running through the few stacks of paper on the working desk. He did not come across anything of interest.

'Quick, go back!' said Zhong in an urgent but soft voice as he slotted back to his initial position at the round table. Yong slid back as quietly as he could.

A tubby young man appeared at the door with a tray on which sat two steaming cups. Without saying anything, he stepped into the room and took his time to place the two cups on the table. The server then took what seemed like forever to shuffle out of the room.

At the signal of Zhong, who had edged his head out to watch the server walk away, Yong resumed the search at the desk. He pulled out the leftmost drawer, wary that any sound out of the ordinary might echo all the way to the end of the corridor. It jerked and protested on its way out, which was not surprising given the rickety state of the aged desk. Still, it made Zhong cringe and steal quick glances in Yong's direction. Yong could feel his heart rate climbing.

Nothing useful was to be found in there, only orders from customers and suppliers. Yong pushed it back into place with his left hand while pulling open the one in the middle with his right hand. This one stored stationery and was useless to him. He repeated his left and right manoeuvre with the rightmost and last drawer.

'He's coming back!' said Zhong.

That was quick, thought Yong. Even with the time lost with the serving of tea, it was too quick. He scolded himself under his breath for losing track of time. In this third compartment, a book similar to the one held by the stock-taker outside sat on top of another pile of papers. There was no time to do anything other than to return the drawer back to its initial state. Taking great care to minimize noise, he gave it a nudge.

The drawer slid in halfway but refused to cede another inch despite Yong's urgent promptings. The need for stealth now irrelevant, Yong gave it a harder push but it remained stuck. Zhong stopped breathing as he watched. Yong needed a bit more time. It did not look like he would be allowed any.

Without thinking, Zhong sprang to his feet and darted through the door. He checked himself once outside and sauntered towards Wu with a smile, though his heart was almost leaping out of his chest.

'Er ... Favourable news, I hope,' Zhong said as the older man stopped, his path blocked a few steps away from the room door opening. Zhong tried to speak loud enough to mask any noise from the room. He had wanted to say more to buy time but his mind blanked out. Did he just imagine a few soft thuds coming out of the room?

The host eyed Zhong for a moment, then broke into a smile.

'Patience, my eager young friend. No need to rush. I tried my best to speak to the boss, to get you a good deal. Why don't we talk inside?'

Zhong tried to say something to keep the conversation going but Wu had breezed past him. He scuttled after his host, almost bumping into the older man as they reached the room entrance. At that instance, there was the sound of sliding wood, but it was Yong pushing back his stool from the round table and standing up. All three sat back down. Everything was back in its rightful place.

Wu was still smiling, his demeanour an about-face from before.

'Young man, I can understand why you are anxious to close the deal. Surely, you did not come all the way here only to return empty-handed. Need to prove yourself to the boss, right? Our products are the finest you can find in the whole of this city. I'm certain your boss will be pleased.'

Zhong nodded without a word.

'Let me see what we've got,' said Wu as he got up to walk over to the desk and pulled out the rightmost drawer, taking out the stock-keeping book.

Now that the obstacle had been removed, Yong craned his neck to peep at what else was in the open drawer. What he saw caused his heart to skip a beat. He had to tell his face not to reveal anything and to force himself to look away, back at Wu.

The host flipped through the book in his hands. 'We've got sufficient stock for your initial batch and the next three months. Interested?'

'Yes, we're interested,' said Zhong.

'Good to hear,' said the host, nodding and smiling. 'Now for the price. A tenth discount. That is all we can offer.'

Zhong got up, not wanting to appear being talked down to in a negotiation, and stepped closer to his host. *Perfect*, thought Yong, as he too stood up to mirror what his master was doing.

'Still too steep for us,' said Zhong.

'A pity, for the boss was quite firm. Are you sure you cannot move a little?'

'Quite. Our budget is tight.'

'Right.' Wu flipped through the pages of the stock-keeping book, as if the key to unlocking the impasse lay within. 'I would hate to see you go home with nothing. Perhaps we can work something out. How about this? For a tiny fraction of the purchase price, I can try to secure another one-tenth discount for you. It would be like a … commission. Think of the money you're going to save for your boss.'

Zhong hesitated and stole glances at Yong, who nodded ever so slightly.

'That,' said Zhong, 'we can discuss.'

The smile reappeared on Wu's face. 'Very good. Now for the logistics. Longtian, did you say? I now remember where it is. As I was checking on the deal, the boss reminded me we've been there before. Three years ago, when we travelled around the region.'

Zhong just smiled and nodded. Yong could offer no help here. Both of them had never been to Longtian and knew nothing of the place. Their only hope was that Wu would not delve deeper into the subject.

However, Wu seemed to turn chatty now that a fat bribe was on the table. 'Yes, three years ago it was. We met a few merchants there. Which part of town are you from?'

'East,' answered Zhong without hesitation. 'We are from the eastern part of town.'

'Oh, right, we visited the Lin Merchants there. Do you know them?'

'We ... I mean, they—'

The shattering of a bottle of wine, tipped over from the top of the desk by Yong as he stepped forward, interrupted the conversation in the nick of time. The bottle landed right in front of Wu, splashing fragrant wine all over his shoes. He did skip back a step, but it was too late. With both shoes soaked, his mouth let loose a torrent of unsavoury phrases that, amongst other things, questioned Yong's ancestry.

'Oh no. I'm sorry,' said Yong. Rushing two steps towards Wu, he stumbled and had to press his right palm on the desk to steady himself, his body wedged between the fuming host and the open drawer. 'I did not mean to create this mess.' A mess it was indeed. The bottle was in a dozen or so pieces and the wine puddle fanned out in the shape of a dark flower with spiky petals contrasted against the dry, light-coloured flooring.

'Idiot! What on earth were you thinking?' shouted Wu, who stamped his feet in a vain bid to shake off the wine.

'I was going over to my master's side. I'm so sorry.' With one hand behind his back, Yong hoped the rustling whisper of paper being folded would not be picked up amidst the ruckus.

Zhong too apologized but Wu's anger was not to be assuaged. 'Darn it, my shoes! Soaked!'

While the older man focused on his shoes, Yong took the opportunity to slide his hand from his back, into his coat pocket and out again.

'This is terrible,' said Zhong. 'I think we should go. We will come back to you on the order.'

'What! You should have told me you had no authority to decide.'

'It's not that. Given the cost, we need some time to think it over.'

'You are not serious at all!' The thought of losing his commission only served to drive Wu's rage up another notch or two. 'Go, both of you, and consider my offer rescinded!'

The young pair scrambled out of the storehouse, then towards the outer gate. Their host, not done with his cursing, did not follow them. They made their own way out, along the corridor and across the storehouse. The lady boss, her position unchanged, trained her eyes on them with a quizzical look on her face. Zhong and Yong marched at pace to the exit, hoping they would not be pulled back. When the gate guardian saw them approaching, he let them through by routine, no questions asked.

Zhong breathed a sigh of relief when the gates slammed shut. 'A bit messy, but good move there. The questioning was getting a bit too close for comfort.'

Yong was looking right in front of him, lost in thought. 'Strange.'

'It was not too bad, was it?'

'Not good,' said Yong as he shifted his gaze to the teahouse where Niu was supposed to be.

'Where's Niu?' asked Zhong. Niu had vacated his seat.

Regardless, they did not dare slow down. They would have to trust that Niu would meet them back at the inn. 'This is not good,' whispered Yong, and Zhong started to worry.

Chapter Thirty-Seven

There was some time for Zhong and Yong to settle down in their room with cups of tea before Niu walked in.

'There you are,' said Zhong. 'We were getting worried.'

'There's a problem,' said Niu 'You were followed by one of the locals, the one who tailed us on the third day. He was in plain clothes but I recognized him.'

'Are you sure?' said Yong.

'Yes. I tailed him. He appeared right after you had gone into the Duan compound, hid in a shop, and waited for you to come out. I had to hide too in case he saw me.'

'He must have tracked us from the inn this morning,' said Yong. 'I thought they had given up on us. My mistake for letting down my guard. Did he follow us back here?'

'All the way.' Niu walked to the window and peered out. 'There he is, in the teahouse across the street.'

Yong slid next to Niu to peer out of the window. He too spotted the tail. 'Is he the only one following us?'

'I think so. I checked and saw nobody else.' Yong and Niu joined Zhong at the table. The young master and his bodyguard locked their eyes on Yong who stared at the tabletop in front of him, buried in thought.

After a while, Yong looked up. 'Got to give it to him. This Magistrate Lei is better than I thought. He's on to us, the wily old fox.'

'Why didn't they arrest us or something?' asked Zhong.

'I guess they have not found the reason to, but they will.'

'What do you mean?'

'Before we paid our little visit to the Duans, we were just bored youngsters indulging in little adventures. Thankfully, our friend downstairs is still sticking to his post. When he reports back, someone will infer that we hold some special interest in the Duans. For sure, Magistrate Lei will check in with Duan Shiyu and talk about these two boys from Renli. Duan would put two and two together. Then be sure they will come for us.'

'We've got to get out of the city.'

'It won't be so simple. I bet the constable out there is under strict orders to follow you wherever you go.'

'They can't stop us from leaving the city. We can pack up and go.'

'We told them we are waiting for Old Master. With their snooping around, I'm sure they would also know we have paid for this room another week in advance. If we leave all of a sudden, they would realize that something is amiss and bring us back for a chat.'

'We'd slip away at night.'

'They might well be watching. Too risky.'

'We can find a way to shake him off and head out of the city, can't we?'

'We won't make it.'

'You're right,' Zhong said with a sigh. 'The alarm would be raised, and the city gates watched. We're stuck.'

'This is what we'll do. You and Niu take a slow walk around the central marketplace. After an hour or so, you head towards the warren of alleys near Wild Wolf's den and circle around there. I can ask a friend or two from the Sect and find a way to ambush the constable.'

'Ridiculous. Attacking a constable will land us and Father in deep trouble. It is me they're after. I can lure them away while both of you leave the city.'

'The servants leaving their master behind while they slink away? No.'

'Why not? We can't call for help if they nab all three of us.'

'True.' Yong paused to ponder the options. 'I'm coming with you.'

'What for?'

'I'm the one with all the facts of this case at my fingertips. If it comes to it, I can confront them.'

'And me?' Niu asked.

'You need to escape while the two of us lure the constable away. Leave the city, and go along the main route so you can join up with Old Master.'

'I can't abandon Young Master. What will Magistrate Liu and Madam say? I'm not a coward.'

'Of course, you're not. This task I'm giving you is risky and of the utmost importance. If you fail, our mission here will go up in smoke, and we would be at the mercy of the locals. Can we depend on you, Niu?'

Slowly, the big man nodded his head.

'You're a good man.' Yong got up to bring out one of their cloth bags.

Zhong looked on as his servant unpacked the writing materials they had brought along. 'What are you doing?'

'We still have some time before the constable reports back,' said Yong as he started rubbing the ink stick on a plate with some water. 'For now, Young Master, you and I will need to write, and write fast.'

Yong was quite sure their two whole hours of aimless strolling would give Niu enough time to slip out of the city.

He and Zhong did not dare glance back lest they spooked the tail. For the past half hour, Yong had been on the lookout in the busy city centre for an opportunity to shake off the constable.

The repeated clangs of a cymbal as they walked down a busy street hinted at such an opportunity. From about thirty paces straight ahead came the familiar din of street performers gathering a crowd for their show, some sort of martial arts performance involving a spear and gleaming sword. The circle of onlookers surrounding the performers grew at a steady rate.

What was more interesting to Yong lay about ten paces beyond. It was an opening to what appeared to be a narrow alleyway.

'Let's join in,' said Yong. He jogged forward as if anxious not to miss any part of the show. Zhong followed.

Not satisfied with standing behind the crowd on the near side, Yong pushed and shoved his way to the front, drawing flak from those who had to step aside to let him through.

Zhong was hanging on to Yong's coattails. 'What are you doing? We should be getting out, not in.'

'Just follow me.'

By unspoken social convention, the first few rows were reserved for children and those too short to get a proper view of the show. Since Yong and Zhong did not belong to either category, heckles started to ring out from behind. 'You're blocking!' a few of them shouted. 'Squat down!'

Once at the front, Yong was happy to comply with the angry requests. Bending down, he followed up with a bear crawl on all fours to the opposite side of the circle, hidden from the view of anyone outside this gathering crowd. With a mimicking Zhong behind him, he squirmed and crawled his way outwards, past rows of people. Rather undignified it was, but effective. Within seconds, the two were out of the circle at the far side. From there, they darted, crouching, into the alleyway. As soon as they got in, they straightened up and ran at full pelt, with the goal to disappear before their tail could cotton on to what was happening.

A few turns later, they came to another opening where they emerged and blended into the thick throng of passers-by, the local well and truly shaken off.

Chapter Thirty-Eight

Wild Wolf was not at his base when Yong and Zhong got there in the late afternoon, resulting in a long and uneasy wait. Yong was nervous they were now out in the open with the locals in all likelihood sniffing around for them. He was not sure whom he could trust.

The greeting Yong received from Wild Wolf, when he returned at dusk, was warm. Before Yong introduced Zhong, it was apparent the Sect leader had guessed who the young man was, for he almost sneered at the magistrate's son.

'A surprise, Brother Yong,' said Wild Wolf as he led the visitors indoors. 'What brings you and the young master here?'

'Trouble.'

Wild Wolf arrested his smile and ordered all his men, other than the two most senior of them, out of his inner sanctum. As his men filed out, he seated his two guests down in front of him. 'What sort of trouble?'

With his head lowered, Wild Wolf listened without saying anything as Yong recounted what had happened the last few days. When Yong was done, Wild Wolf glanced at Zhong before facing Yong.

'You made the right decision to come here. They probably secured the city gates once you bolted and will now be searching for you. What do you need from us, Brother Yong?'

'Our best bet is to link up with Magistrate Liu, who is due to arrive any day now. If you can offer us shelter to wait it out for a few days, we'd be grateful.'

Wild Wolf nodded. 'You can stay here for now. That is, if the young master does not mind this rundown shack.'

Zhong said nothing as Yong expressed his gratitude.

'I'll ask my men to watch for a visiting official who fits your master's description. As soon as he arrives, we will inform you.'

'There's another person—Niu, the constable who came with us. We told him to head back to Renli. He is a big fella. If he falls into the hands of the authorities, your men may hear about it.'

Wild Wolf summoned one of his men to bring the guests to a room at the back of the compound, a place that appeared to have been free from human intervention for years. The two young men cleared the low-lying cobwebs and gathered straw to sit on. The place was still filthy, but at least they were safe for now. Exhausted, both of them could finally sit down to rest.

'Are you all right, Young Master? You have been quiet.'

'I'm fine. It is just strange. The roles are reversed in this place. Here, the beggars view me with disdain.'

'It's not personal. They don't hate you; they just hate people like you.'

'That's a relief.' Zhong smiled. Then another thought took the smile away. 'Do you think we can trust the Sect? In a twisted sort of way, Wild Wolf's open disdain towards me is comforting, free of duplicity. But, like you said, the Sect is made up of all sorts of people.'

'I trust Wild Wolf but there was a reason why he cleared the hall, leaving just two elders behind. This is for now the safest place for us, one of the last places the locals would probe. For how long, I don't know. Our priority is to rest. There is some way to go before we can call an end to this.'

Chapter Thirty-Nine

Despite his reassurances to Zhong, Yong could not settle down to proper rest. He had too much on his mind. Next morning, the dark circles around Zhong's eyes told him that the anxieties had been shared.

The same man brought all their meals to them—rough and simple fare. The furthest they had ventured out was the backyard to stretch their legs, and in short spurts. They spent plenty of time on the beds of straw cushioning them from the cold, hard ground.

'You know,' said Zhong, 'You sometimes have a creepy look on you when you talk to yourself.'

'Oh, sorry. I was thinking about them.'

'Duan and Guo?'

'And Magistrate Lei. Chances are, this brood of vipers are in cahoots. I have underestimated Lei.'

'That doesn't sound good for us.'

'Not necessarily. Sometimes, it is easier to deal with a clever crook than a stupid one. A dumb criminal can be unpredictable and therefore more dangerous. As for a smart crook, one can make intelligent guesses of what he would do, if we understand his motives.'

'So, what are they thinking, you reckon?'

'For Duan and his lapdog Uncle Wu, or Guo, the biggest question on their minds would be why we are tracking them.'

'I see. They would be wondering whether it is just about uncovering Duan's identity or murder.'

'That might come into it, though in a way, it does not matter.'

'What do you mean? Surely, murder would be much more serious than covering up one's identity.'

'Yes, but remember that people like them have no conscience. What matters to them is the outcome, that is, whether they can get away with it. And a large part of that is tied to our motives.'

'*Our* motives?'

'That's right. To these people, it would make little sense for us to conduct an onerous investigation a long way from home, at the risk of wading into a bureaucratic mess, to help a penniless widow and her disabled child. Even an upright magistrate would have just passed the information along to his colleague here. If Mr Zhou had had his way, we would have done that. Unless ...'

Zhong smiled. 'Unless there is something to be gained. By us, that is.'

'Yep. Duan could be thinking we are just looking to extract our pot of gold from this affair. They are merchants, the Duans. Dealing with extortioners and corrupt officials comes with the territory. Murder would be more troublesome to deal with, certainly, but that just means a bigger pot of gold to settle the issue.'

'Then there's Magistrate Lei.'

'This old fox presents an interesting problem. I've been wondering whether he knows about the false identity and the murder. If I were Duan, I would never tell Lei unless I had no choice. Possession of such knowledge would give Lei great leverage over Duan. I bet Lei is in the dark about Duan's past.'

'So, Duan needs to bring us in, find out what we know, and strike an agreement with Father.'

'That is how he can wrestle back control of the situation. But it won't be easy for him, for he does not command the men and networks Lei does as magistrate. He needs to secure Lei's help without letting Lei in on his secret.'

'What if he can't or doesn't want to play this delicate game? The alternative method of keeping us from spilling his secrets may not be so civilized.'

'Well, for the sake of our general health, we would just have to keep him away from such wayward thoughts.'

'And Lei? What would he be thinking?'

'Lei would want to find out why Duan is worried about two lads from Renli, and he'd smell profit. Lei's motivation to take advantage of the situation may be something we can exploit.'

'How?'

'I'm working on it.'

Just then, the man who brought their meals came to them. 'Wild Wolf wants to see you. Now.'

Within a minute, they were standing in front of the Sect leader. Besides their escort, there was only one other person in the place, an elderly beggar with a weather-beaten face, who stood to the side of Wild Wolf and wore a worried frown. 'We must move you both out of here.'

'What's wrong?' said Yong.

'Early this morning, the magistrate's office put up notices offering a rich reward for your capture, at almost triple the going rate. I did not know you were so valuable.'

'Sponsored by the Duans, I'm sure. They are moving fast.'

'They have just put up the notice, but it won't be long before news of your whereabouts reaches the authorities.'

Yong understood what Wild Wolf was trying to say. The Sect leader was too embarrassed to add that the leaks would likely be from his men. The Beggars' Sect had always been a large and mixed bag of individuals—most good, some bad, and many desperate for food in their bellies.

'Hope we won't land you in trouble,' Yong said.

'Don't worry about us. We boast numbers that even the authorities accord three measures of respect. There is little time. Old Xie here will bring you to your next hideout. He's an old dog but I trust him with my life. Go now.'

With no time for extended words of thanks, the duo followed Xie out of the compound. Though the leading legs were not young, they were strong and fast, and the young men struggled to keep up. By the time they reached their destination, yet another dilapidated house, this one sitting on a site with multiple escape routes, the young men were huffing and puffing.

'Stay inside,' said Xie. 'Don't come out. People will keep watch, bring you food.'

Chapter Forty

The evening meal was a wordless affair until Yong broke the silence. 'Sorry about this. You came as a tourist and wound up a fugitive.'

'With a hefty price on my head. At least I can now assure Father I'm not worthless.'

'I should not have insisted on going in to the Duan compound.'

'What's done is done. I understand why you had to do it.'

Yong nodded, appreciating his young master's show of support.

'So,' said Zhong, 'how long do you think we'd last out here?'

Yong shook his head. 'Hard to tell. Running from place to place might help us evade capture for a while. But once someone talks, I reckon it won't take long for them to search through the usual Sect hideouts.'

'You look worried.'

Yong sighed. 'I knew they were looking for us, of course. It's just that the mad dash from the Sect headquarters to this place brought the point home. We really could be caught.'

'What's going to happen if we fall into their hands?'

'We'd be all right if the locals hold on to us. Though corrupt, Lei is still a magistrate who has to follow some rules. What I'm worried about is the locals handing us over quietly to the Duans. After all, the Duans are paying for this hunt.'

'And the Duans are desperate to keep us from talking.'

'That they are.'

Zhong stared at the ground in front of him. 'I am concerned about Father. Hope he's all right.'

'I'm sure he is. Don't worry, he'll be here any day now.' Despite his words, Yong had himself worried about Magistrate Liu's delayed arrival. They had been in the Capital for almost fifteen days. Factoring in Justice Hou's likely short stay in Renli, Magistrate Liu should have been here by now. Without his old master, Yong felt like a little fishing boat caught in a squall at sea.

Yong put down his half-eaten mantou bun. 'Young Master, I want you to remember one thing.'

'What?'

'As the son of a magistrate, you enjoy some protection. Whatever happens, your first priority is to take care of yourself.'

'What do you mean by "take care of yourself"?'

'I'm saying that if they do something to me, you—'

'Stop there. You are asking me to be dishonourable. What would my father think of me?'

'This is not about what your father thinks of you. They may use me to get to you. Don't allow them any leverage over you. I'm your father's assistant. They won't do much to me.'

The argument was not convincing to Zhong who averted his eyes from Yong.

From there, a lull descended. The uncomfortable state of affairs continued into the night, after both of them laid down to rest. Yong could feel the ache at the sides and front of his head, brought on by relentless tension and lack of sleep. He was sure Zhong was also tired, but with anxiety swirling in their heads and insects buzzing around their ears, there was little chance of either of them drifting off to sleep any time soon.

'You know, you're good at this,' said Zhong, flat on his back and staring straight up while swatting insects away. Moonlight seeped through the holes in the ceiling, illuminating cobwebs that stirred with the light breeze.

Yong opened his eyes and tilted his head towards Zhong. 'Doing my job.'

'Just doing your job, eh?' said Zhong, also tilting his head to face his servant. 'If you were keeping within your station in life, you would be cleaning my father's desk this time of the night.'

'I'm fortunate Old Master lets me run around, I suppose. Beats washing spittoon pots.'

'You're nuts, that's what you are.' Both chuckled and went back to examining the cobwebs above.

After a while, Zhong spoke again. 'What do you want to do? In life, I mean.'

'What do you mean? This is what I do.'

'I mean, are you going to do this for the rest of your life?'

'Why not? I'm serving Old Master, helping people, and getting a kick out of it.'

'But what would you do when my father retires?'

'Then, my Young Master, I serve you.'

Zhong glanced at his servant before returning to the inspection of the ceiling. 'What if I'm not going to be a magistrate? What would you do?'

'Well, what would you be doing if not following in your father's footsteps?'

'I don't know. Set up a business, be a merchant or something.'

'That would be a problem. I'm not much use with an abacus, I can tell you.'

'Like I said, you're good at this. You should be working for a higher-ranking official.'

'Now you sound like your father.'

'He said this to you?'

'Well, yeah. In fact, he wanted me to meet this Justice Hou from the Censorate. Not interested.'

'Why not? With him, you would be doing important stuff, big things. You should think about it. Think for yourself. Be somebody in life.'

'And your father?'

'What about him? You know your old master well. He would volunteer to slice off his right arm if he thought it was beneficial to the country.'

'Have you ever thought that, quite beside the fact that your father saved my life, I like serving him?'

'What? For his sense of duty and loyalty? I have news for you, my good brother. I am not like that, so you'd better reconsider your plans to work for me when my father is done.'

Rolling on to his side and resting on his elbow, Yong looked at Zhong. 'You may not admit it but I see something there.'

'Nonsense. Now you sound like my mother.'

'I think you're developing a taste for this type of work.'

'That'll be the day.'

'Admit it. You've been having fun. In fact, you've done well in our little adventures so far with the Chens, the Duans. We'd make an official out of you yet.'

'Yeah? Don't hold your breath. Now,' said Zhong as he rolled to his side to face away from Yong, 'I'm exhausted. Let's try to get some sleep.'

Chapter Forty-One

'Quick, get up!'

Both young men awoke with a start and sat up. Yong's heart was pounding and his brain still adjusting from the abrupt end to his slumber. He scanned the three shuffling figures before him, silhouetted against the pale moonlight. One of the men was Old Xie.

'No time,' said Xie. 'Explain on the way.'

Yong sprang up on his feet, and Zhong did the same. Without another word, Xie and his companions turned and ran out. Yong and Zhong followed closely behind as they shook the grogginess from their heads.

From the level of darkness in the sky and the chilliness in the air, Yong guessed it was a couple of hours before dawn. He had spent most of the night fending off insects and had taken a long time to drift off to sleep. It felt like he had shut his eyes only a few moments ago.

'Constables coming,' Xie said in his economical way without turning his head, his full focus on racing forward, away from danger. Their whereabouts had been betrayed. They were now exposed, out in the open.

Rounding a corner, they almost bumped into another three beggars cloaked in the shadows, the chief of whom was Wild Wolf. The unsmiling face of the leader of beggars told Yong there was no time for greetings.

'Let's move,' said Wild Wolf.

As the contingent set off, two of the Sect's men went ahead of the group, acting as front scouts.

Yong pulled up to the side of Wild Wolf. 'What happened?'

'One of ours approached the officials early this morning. News got to us that constables were heading your way. We had to pull you out and move you somewhere else.'

Yong nodded. Having Wild Wolf lead this evacuation underlined the gravity of the situation. 'Many of them involved?'

'Quite a manhunt. Duan must be paying a fortune for this show.'

'Where are we headed?'

'They are still watching the gates of the Outer City, so you're stuck here. We are getting you to a quieter corner of the Outer City. You should be safe there for a couple of days at least.'

The group was able to make smooth progress in the quiet and dark alleyways. Indeed, the pace was nothing short of punishing. Yong had to hold on to the upper arm of Zhong, who was panting hard and grimacing, to offer some support and encouragement.

After less than half an hour, the front scouts came back with another beggar, concern written all over their faces.

'Constables,' said one of them. 'They're there.'

'The hideout?' said Wild Wolf. 'Not good.' He took a moment to evaluate the options. 'We head to the woods,' he said to his scouts. 'Lead the way.'

They took another half an hour to reach their destination, which was really a patch of high ground with thick and untamed vegetation. Wild Wolf issued quick instructions to the two eager scouts, who nodded and at once scampered off. After checking that they were free from prying eyes, Wild Wolf beckoned the rest of the group into the woods.

The ground was sheer and slippery, wet with morning dew. Light, already scant, struggled to drip through the dense greenery. The climbing men slipped and slid every few steps, and had to grab hold of branches and trunks to haul themselves upwards. All the while, stray dogs hiding in the depth of the woods, on top of the hill, barked their annoyance at the intruders. Still, these canines had little choice but to run off to make way for the new occupants.

Once at the summit, the group quietened down, listening for any other signs of movement in the stillness of dawn. Yong attended to his young master, who was drawing in deep breaths, his tongue almost hanging out.

Wild Wolf, satisfied with the long silence around them, signalled for the group to settle down.

No one spoke as the sun emerged from the horizon, sending golden rays through the foliage. A light breeze wafted through, bringing welcome relief and sweeping away the stench left behind by the dogs. Zhong, exhausted and seated with his back against a tree and knees up to his chin, had his eyes closed and head bobbing. Everyone else was on high alert, watching and listening.

A long time passed until, from the foot of the hill, came a whistle as that of a song bird. Wild Wolf cupped his hands to his mouth and replied in like manner. Soon, the figures of his two scouts, illuminated by the early morning light, emerged from the trees below. The group watched as the two reached the top, drenched in sweat.

Wild Wolf did not allow time for them to catch their breath. 'How is it?'

'It does not look good,' one of the scouts said, breathing hard. 'We sent out the brothers to sniff around. They reported back that officials are circling possible hideouts in the Outer City, including those we don't normally use.'

'All of them?'

'Not yet, but we reckon it is a matter of time.'

'Too risky. We can't use those.' Everyone waited as Wild Wolf paused to consider the options. 'Time to call in a favour. You two go check with Huang the ironsmith if he can house our two friends. Go now.'

'Wait,' said Yong as the scouts were about to turn around.

'What is it?' said Wild Wolf.

'The routes into the Inner City. Are they being watched?'

The two scouts looked at each other, then back at Yong. 'Seemed clear,' said the one who spoke up earlier. 'They have committed most of their men to the search in the Outer City.'

'Makes sense. They'd expect us to run outwards.' Yong turned to Wild Wolf. 'I say we head into the Inner City.'

'Why on earth would you do that?' said Wild Wolf.

Yong shared his idea with the group.

'That is crazy,' said Wild Wolf. The rest seemed to concur, including Zhong who was wide awake and nodding with vigour.

After looking at Yong for a while, the Beggars' Sect leader shook his head. 'It's downright crazy,' he said, following up with a grin, 'but it just might work. Let's do it.'

Chapter Forty-Two

Yong and Zhong sat on the ground, leaning against a wall in a back alley. Wild Wolf was resting on a block of stone, placed there by two of his men who were now watching the inlets to this quiet spot. Further out, more of his men kept a lookout.

Old Xie appeared from around a corner and approached Wild Wolf deferentially. 'Everything in place,' Xie said. 'Crowd inside.'

The young men and Wild Wolf stood up.

'I appreciate your help,' Yong said to Wild Wolf.

Wild Wolf nodded. 'Are you sure about this? Not too late to change your mind.'

'I'm not sure,' said Yong, 'but we have to give it a try.'

'All right, my friends. Take care. Both of you.'

After checking there were no constables lurking just outside, the two young men emerged from their hiding place, turned right, and headed straight for their destination, no more than a hundred paces away.

As they neared the gate of the magistrate's compound, they saw two beggars shouting and gesticulating at each other. The heated argument drew a small group of onlookers, but this was not the crowd Xie had referred to. The constable at the gate, perhaps thinking commoners were allowed access to the compound anyway, saw fit to leave his post to mediate the squabble, allowing Yong and Zhong to walk in unmolested.

They headed to the court, which was in session. As reported by Xie, a crowd had gathered outside the entrance. Since onlookers there were used to giving way to court participants, Yong and Zhong could wriggle their way through the crowd with little difficulty.

Their timing could not have been better. Magistrate Lei Jun, perched on an elevated platform in his judgement seat, had just slammed down his wooden block to conclude a case. The plaintiffs, defendants, and witnesses of the case began filing out of the courtroom.

Zhong cleared his throat. 'Your Honour,' he said in a raised voice so that everyone in and around the room could hear him, 'I heard you have been looking for us. Do you remember me? I am Liu Zhong, son of Magistrate Liu Ye of Renli.'

The ensuing murmur of the watching crowd was familiar and reassuring to Yong. Lei and his adviser Yan stared at the intruders with eyes widened.

It did not take long for the magistrate to recover his composure. 'Young Master Liu,' he said, 'where have you been?' The young duo had by design stood near the entrance so that Lei had to raise his voice to address them.

'I informed you, Sir, that I was waiting for my father to arrive, did I not? Then I heard about this reward for my capture. Rather unnecessary.'

'Oh dear, I apologize if we caused you alarm. You see, we had some trouble finding you.'

'All you had to do was to ask, and I would have been happy to call on you. I hope this is not how you treat the children of colleagues from afar.'

Lei forced a weak smile. Still, the tone of his reply was even and calm. 'I was worried about you, that is all. Now that I know you are safe and well, I feel much relieved.'

'Many thanks for your kind concern. So, am I a prisoner of this court or your guest?'

With Yan still stone-faced, the magistrate broke into laughter. 'You jest. Of course, you will be my honoured guest while we await your father's arrival. Goodness, this is no way to welcome our guest. Mr Yan.'

'Yes, Sir.'

'Show Young Master Liu to his room. I will catch up with him at the end of this busy day.'

Zhong cupped his hands in front of him as a gesture of gratitude. 'My sincerest apologies for intruding.'

'Not at all,' said Lei as he stroked his stubbled chin with the back of his hand. 'Not at all.'

The young men bowed in the direction of the magistrate and followed Yan and a constable out of the courtroom. They were led to the back of the compound where the guest house was. None of the four rooms in the house were occupied as far as Yong could see. Yan, who seemed incapable of altering his hardened facial expression, showed Zhong to his room. He was issuing orders to the constable to lead Yong to the servants' quarters when Zhong intervened, insisting his servant should stay with him.

'Up to you,' said Yan as he and the constable left the room and closed the door. Yong peered through the window and watched as Yan strode off, leaving the constable behind in the courtyard, ten paces away. The constable turned around and stared at Yong, who smiled and waved before ducking his head back in.

'That was nerve-racking,' said Zhong.

Yong sat close to Zhong at the round table in the middle of the room. 'Brilliant show there. Now that so many people have witnessed our entry, the old fox would not be able to hand us over to Duan without a good reason.'

'Hope so.'

'It has to be so. You're the son of a magistrate. Be sure that word will spread about the scene you worked up just now. You, Liu Zhong, son of Magistrate Liu Ye from Renli.'

'Funny. Your idea, remember that.'

'You saw the surprise on the faces of Lei and Yan. But once the dust settles, Lei will start planing his next move. Now that one path to a plump kickback is blocked, he will come up with another. The new path would demand more patience, but it could be more profitable for him, a lot more.'

'I've got a feeling you would make quite a successful criminal if you had not landed in law enforcement.'

Yong grinned but got straight back to serious discussion. 'Soon, Lei will figure out that if Duan is prepared to cough up such a fat sum for us, he would also be willing to pay big money for whatever we hold in our hands or heads. Remember, he is probably thinking that Old Master is scheming to dip his hand into the pot of gold and would want to muscle in on the act too. What's more, if he had handed us over to the Duans, the payment would be a one-off. If he knows what we know, he will have such a hold on the Duans, he could milk them whenever he desires.'

'Duan Shiyu would not allow that.'

'He has little choice. Sure, he would love to have us in his claws, but we're out of his reach now. As long as we play it cool, we'd be safe here.'

'How should we play it?'

'We keep our mouths sealed for as long as we can. While the knowledge is still in our heads, we remain valuable to Lei. That would buy us time until your father arrives. But there's a catch. In his mind, if Old Master deals directly with Duan, Lei would be out of the loop, rendered irrelevant. He has to do one of two things: extract what we know before Old Master arrives, or make sure Old Master includes him in any negotiation with Duan.'

'I'm not sure I like sound of the part on extraction.'

'It's not so bad. We just need to sing along with him.'

'I definitely do not like the sound of that.'

Chapter Forty-Three

Magistrate Lei's next move came soon enough. Near evening, two servants came by with a basin of warm water, towels, and a fresh change of clothes, informing Zhong that the magistrate had invited him to dinner.

Not long after, the constable on duty escorted Zhong to the residence building with Yong tagging along. They arrived at the dining room to find the magistrate and Yan sitting there, waiting. Plates of steaming food covered half the table, and servants were still introducing more.

Yan stared at Zhong's uninvited servant. 'You are to consume your dinner in your room, or in the servants' quarters if you so prefer.'

'It is fine, Mr Yan,' said Lei, who turned to Zhong. 'You and your servant must be weary from your little adventures these past few days. Come join us, both of you. The food is getting cold. Please do not mind the humble fare.'

The spread before them was anything but humble. Bereft of decent food for three days and not having had anything to eat for the whole day, the young men had to restrain themselves from gorging.

The conversation started out with polite small talk. Wine flowed freely. An attendant was on hand to fill up the cups while the magistrate took every opportunity to encourage Zhong to empty his. Yong got away with little sips since he was not the target of Lei's attention.

As dinner wore on, Zhong's speech evolved from tentative to more expansive, and more disorganized. The few attempts by Yong to restrain his master's drinking were put down straight away by the magistrate and his adviser.

'Come, drink up!' Down went another cup and a round of laughter louder than the last.

'So,' said Lei, after Zhong had set his cup down, 'you seem to hold particular interest in Master Duan's household. Something your father is working on?'

'Interest? Oh, yeah.' Zhong chuckled like he had delivered the punchline of an amusing tale.

'Young Master,' said Yong, putting his hand on his master's forearm, 'perhaps we should not—'

'Hold your tongue!' said Yan, his face turning pink. The authority and intensity in the command was so strong that Yong immediately withdrew his hand. Lei stared at his adviser, concerned that the sudden raising of voices might startle his young guest, but he did not need to have worried. His head drooping and eyes half-closed, Zhong was the picture of drunken serenity, untouched by surrounding disturbances.

'Young man,' said Lei, his hand resting on Zhong's shoulder, 'is there anything I can do to help your father?'

'Help?' Zhong lifted his head and looked at Yong. 'Didn't Father mention something about that, Yong?'

Lei tugged him back to keep him on track. 'Tell me what your father said.'

Zhong winked and smiled at his host. 'Well, he said we could ask for help if we needed it, but ...'

'But what?'

'Father told me he did not know anybody in the Capital, and ... I'll be honest here.'

Yong tried to reach out his hand towards Zhong, but Yan stared him down.

'He told me he did not know if you could be trusted,' said Zhong with a chuckle.

Lei laughed along. 'I understand. I understand perfectly well. The people here are unknown to him and the ground unfamiliar, is that not so? Connections and resources in this place are what I have in abundance. With my help, your father would be able to accomplish double of what he planned for with half the effort.' The magistrate paused and swirled the wine around in his cup. 'Do you think your father would be open to working with me?'

Yan continued boring his eyes into Yong to make sure he did not attempt any move to disturb the moment.

'It depends,' Zhong said with a smile.

'On?'

'On whether you treat me well.'

'I will, dear lad,' said Lei while patting Zhong's shoulder. 'Of course, I will. Excellent. Come now, empty cups!'

Zhong, unsteady on his feet, had to be propped up by Yong as the pair stumbled back to their room, supervised by a constable who closed the door and walked off as Yong unloaded Zhong on to the bed. A basin of warm water was sitting on the table and a thin straw mat strewn on the floor for Yong's use. While Zhong continued to moan and mumble, Yong took a wet towel from the basin, wrung water out of it, and sat on the bed.

Zhong, still lying down, opened his eyes. 'How did I do?'

Yong stuck out his right thumb. 'Superb performance.'

'I don't know. Was it too subtle?'

'Not at all. It was perfect. You gave him enough to make him think Old Master would be open to work with him. He won't stop at this. Be sure he will come at you again. Next time, you can afford to be more upfront about it because you have, on the face of it, revealed your hand.'

Sitting up, Zhong took the wet towel from Yong to wipe his face. 'All that drinking has given me a bit of a headache. Hard work, this.'

Yong craned his neck to peek out of the window. 'Our value has shot up. There are two constables now, making doubly sure we do not escape. They need not have bothered. This is for now the safest place for us. We are going nowhere.'

That night, the young master and his servant had their most restful slumber in days.

Chapter Forty-Four

As expected, Magistrate Lei took the opportunity at dinner the following night to confirm Magistrate Liu would include him in any deal to be made with Duan. This time, with much less drinking involved, Zhong said his father would be happy to work through Lei, although he politely declined to reveal more.

After that, it was as though nothing had ever happened. The days that followed were tranquil, almost boring. Zhong and Yong were only allowed strolls in the garden outside their room and visit the latrine under escort. They never saw Lei again.

'Not a word from Lei after the second dinner,' said Yong. 'We have been here five days.'

'Maybe he was satisfied with what I told him,' said Zhong. 'Or maybe he's got something else up his sleeve.'

'Another deal with Duan?'

'I don't think so. Lei will feel he now has the upper hand over Duan and would not want to lose his leverage. I don't know what he's up to, and it bothers me.'

'I'll tell you what bothers me. Every day that passes, I get more worried about Father. He should have been here days ago.'

'I'm sure he's all right. He is late but he will be here.'

'Hope Niu is all right too.'

'I won't worry too much about him. That ox can take care of himself. And if he follows the route I told him to, he has a good chance of running into Old Master.'

By evening, the mood had not brightened. As the sunlight was signalling the departure of its source with a lazy orange hue, the door flung open. An attendant and the two constables on guard duty stood at the entrance.

'Good evening, sir,' the attendant said to Zhong. 'Magistrate Lei would like to see you, both of you. Right now.'

Escorted by the constables, Zhong and Yong followed the attendant to the residence building. The compound was still and light was dimming. Yong felt something was different this evening. There was a palpable tension in the air. He caught a whiff of smoke from the gentle breeze drifting across the grounds, though he saw no fires around. As the little delegation walked along the path closest to the street outside, he heard faint voices laced with animosity.

'Let them go,' one of the voices said. This was followed by a softer exchange Yong could not make out. He slowed his steps to try to gather up the conversation.

'Move along,' said the constable behind them, supplementing his instruction with a shove to Yong's back. They walked a short distance further and arrived at the residence building.

The entrance to the building was shielded by a panelled silk screen, on which was painted a lively scene of storks standing in a splashing stream, hunting fish. *A signpost on the road to success,* thought Yong, *or portent of imminent trouble?*

As they rounded the screen, he saw four people in the plush and spacious reception area. They sat on dark solid wood chairs arranged in a rectangular formation surrounding two low and square tea tables. The four were in the midst of a conversation while servants and constables, armed with poles, stood behind. As expected, Lei and Yan were there, seated on the side facing the entrance. Clad in a light silk robe, with Yan to his right, the magistrate was talking to two visitors, a man and a woman, on the adjacent side of the rectangle, seated to his left.

What caught Yong's eye was the servant standing behind the pair of guests. He was none other than the man Guo Wutian, whom he had known as Uncle Wu. Guo was looking down and did not seem to notice Zhong and Yong coming in.

The seated woman was the same lady they had seen at the Duan storehouse. At the storehouse, her garments were by no means shabby. Here, they were a few notches more luxurious, augmented with eye-catching jewellery around her neck and wrists, her privileged background in full display. Her attention was on Lei as he spoke.

The lady obscured Yong's view of the well-dressed man seated next to her as he walked in. Even then, it was clear who he was. Yong felt his pulse racing as the angle shifted and the left side of the gentleman came into view. This man's considerable paunch spilled forward as he leaned in to listen to the magistrate. The copious facial hair—moustache and beard—did a passable job of obscuring his thin lips and angled jaws, yet the smallish eyes, sharp nose, and pointed ears could not be masked.

As the ones seated stopped their conversation to eye the fresh entrants, Yong could not help but stare at the plump man's face. This was the person whom they had spent weeks searching for, the supposedly deceased husband of Mdm Li Yingxiu, the rich merchant who had bought official power through the backdoor and murdered his own flesh and blood. Now known as the Honourable Duan Shiyu, here sitting in front of them, was the man formerly known as Sun Jie.

Chapter Forty-Five

'Here you are, Young Master Liu,' said Lei, the only person in the room who was smiling. 'Come, join us.'

On the two square tables surrounded by the chairs, tea cups were arranged on three sides, making it obvious that Zhong was to sit to the right of the magistrate and his adviser, on the side with the solitary cup. Zhong sat down with little ceremony while Yong took his place standing behind to his right. Both of them now faced Duan, the woman, and Guo. Even now, Guo declined to meet Yong's eyes.

Still smiling, the magistrate started the proceedings. 'Allow me to introduce Master Duan and his wife. I believe you know of them and have paid a visit to their residence. In spite of his busy schedule, Master Duan was quite happy to accept my invitation for a little chat to clear the air.'

The gloom on the faces of the Duan entourage told another story.

The hosting official widened his smile. 'Now that we are all here, why don't we bring all matters to the table?'

'Sir,' said Zhong, 'I thought we agreed to discuss this only when my father gets here.'

'Impatience can get the better of me at times. I am always anxious to get to the bottom of important issues brewing in my domain.'

'Magistrate Lei,' said Duan in a soft tone, 'hand them over to us. I will make sure they tell us everything.'

Lei sniggered. 'You see, young man? Master Duan here is most anxious to be granted exclusive access to you. I think a calm conversation in my residence would be more productive and, shall we say, better for your health.'

Duan leaned further towards Lei. 'Give them to me. There is no need to trouble you. Once the matter is settled, your reward will be well worth your while.'

'It is no trouble. In fact, your eagerness to host our young friends intrigues me.' The magistrate smiled at Zhong. 'So, what say you?'

Zhong shifted in his seat, uncomfortable with the thought of the desperate and the crafty competing to extract weighty information from him. 'I … I will wait. Wait for my father.'

'I see,' said Lei. 'I was hoping for a more collaborative stance. Then again, given the nature of your activities the past two weeks, perhaps I should not be surprised.'

'We have done nothing wrong.'

'That is not what my investigations have uncovered.'

'What are you talking about?'

'I think you have a good idea what I am talking about.' His smile fading away, Lei picked up his cup, uncapped it, brushed the cap three times against the rim, and sipped his tea. He left no one in doubt he was in full control of the proceedings and could take as much time as he wished. After two long-drawn sips, he reversed the process to set the cup down on the table.

'I must admit to a mistake,' said Lei. 'When we uncovered your attempt to smuggle a weapon into the city, I should have suspected something more nefarious.'

'A legitimate weapon belonging to our constable.'

'You would say that, would you not? The timing, though, was too convenient, coinciding with the enemy's efforts to infiltrate the city. We had constables tail you for a few days to let you know we meant business. At the end of the initial surveillance, we thought the message would sink in. Alas, a few days later, we received word from our network that you were spying on important merchants in our city.'

'I have told you—we are representing the Ouyang family.'

'Is it mere coincidence the two merchants you checked on were recently appointed as officers of the Imperial Court? What's more, you poked around the Jing household, asking lots of questions but never made the move to initiate contact with the household itself. I do not consider that to be the way business representatives operate. It is quite obvious to me you have malicious designs on the economic and political fabric of our society.'

'This is ridiculous.'

'Is it? Master Duan's servant here told me you claimed to be from Longtian, an outright lie. Three days ago, we had important sources come in to tell us you have been associating with criminal elements in the city.'

'I'm not going to dignify that with—'

'Don't deny it. Our informants are prepared to testify to you linking up with the Beggars' Sect, and say that you were right in the midst of a devious plot involving the Sect and foreign spies. While the beggars slipped away, we were able to nab the foreign spies. In fact, the criminal Sect is, right at this moment, congregating outside the compound, demanding your release. What other proof do we need?'

Yong was impressed with the amount of work the magistrate had put in over the past few days, and the cogent narrative he weaved despite the facts. The young servant almost nodded his appreciation.

'I reject all these baseless accusations,' said Zhong.

'Of course, you would. Do not think your father can protect you. Any matter concerning the security of the Capital and the Palace trumps everything else. In fact, I am not ready to rule out your father's involvement in all these. He may land in trouble yet.'

'Outrageous nonsense! My father is a loyal official and servant to the Emperor.'

'No need for outrage. I am just doing my job. Believe me, I wish our investigations had uncovered happier findings, but facts are facts.' The magistrate sighed with mock concern as he leaned forward. 'Let me help you. Work with me to clear this up. Tell me what you know, what your business here is about, so that we can reconcile the facts and sort out this regrettable situation.'

'Thank you for your concern. Only my father can speak on the matter at hand.'

Lei straightened up, slapping the arms of his chair. 'So, this is how you want to play it. You leave me with no choice.' He stood up and Yan followed suit. 'I suggest we reconvene in the backyard. The fresh air may remove the fog from our minds and allow us to make, shall we say, wiser choices.'

The magistrate looked at Duan who, with a pained expression, rose together with his wife. Two constables drew up on either side of Yong and right behind Zhong, leaving him with no other option but to get up from his seat.

Led by Lei and hemmed in by constables, the group made their way out of the building wordlessly. Only the crunching of gravel beneath their feet interrupted the silence as they skirted round the building to the backyard. Here, in a clearing overlaid with square stone slabs, six chairs were placed to form three sides of a rectangle, two on each side, with the open sector nearest to the residence building.

The evening glow, while faint, lingered. At the four corners of the rectangle stood poles on which were hung lit lanterns. Like pendulums, the pale-yellow lanterns swung in the light breeze, which now whispered evil omens into Yong's ears.

It was the items strewn around the centre of the backyard, surrounded by the chairs, that sent a chill into his heart. Instead of tables and tea cups, various pieces of equipment were on display, instruments used in court to induce pain and extract confessions. Yong recognized them: flax rope to tie up a suspect, a bundle of iron chains to kneel on, and thin metal rods strung together with sturdy strings designed to crush fingers, slowly.

Lei waved his palm over the chairs. 'Let us sit down.'

With some reluctance, the guests took their seats, reverting to the seating arrangement in the house. Yong and Guo resumed their standing positions behind their masters, with the constables a step further back.

'The air tonight is so crisp and soothing,' said Lei. 'It is a pity we may have to spoil the tranquillity with some ... noisy procedures. I decided we should do this outside. My wife was concerned, quite justifiably, we might leave a mess in the house. Now, Young Master Liu, would you like to reconsider your position? It would be easier for all of us if you just tell us what you know.'

'My father will be incensed. You have no right to do this.'

'You will find I have every right, in fact the duty, to uncover and neutralize any threat to the Palace.'

'Is this how you treat a son of a magistrate? I protest in the strongest terms!'

'Oh dear, did I frighten you? My sincere apologies,' said Lei with a chuckle. 'These are not meant for you. You are too precious for that. No, Young Master Liu, these are meant for the person standing behind you—your servant.'

Chapter Forty-Six

Knowing the tools were for Yong frightened Zhong even more, for it meant they were not merely for intimidation.

'Yong is my father's assistant,' said Zhong. 'You are not to lay a hand on him.'

Yong could almost hear his own heart thumping in his chest. He had anticipated Lei making offensive moves to further his position, but the old fox was moving ahead of him. He needed to calm down and find his footing. While his mind swirled with new calculations, he shifted his eyes to the Duan couple and Guo. Yong thought the worry on their faces was more apparent now that the odds of Zhong and Yong holding out had plummeted.

'So many demands from one with so few options,' said Lei. 'I am under no obligation to protect anyone in the investigation of a conspiracy against the Palace, certainly not a servant. We will perform the necessary procedures on him until you tell us everything we need to know. Men.'

The two constables on standby behind Yong grabbed his arms, one on each side, and dragged him forward.

Zhong sprang to his feet and blocked their way. 'Let him go!'

A third constable, burly and tough, grabbed hold of Zhong's forearm and yanked him aside. Before Yong could protest the manhandling of his master, he was pressed to the centre of proceedings.

The torture instruments came into sharper focus as Yong looked down, while, in the background, Zhong tried his level best to protest. The pile of iron chains was right at his feet. Any moment now, the two constables would drag him down with all their might. Even if his kneecaps could survive intact from meeting the chains in full force, he was sure the resultant pain would overwhelm his senses. He gritted his teeth, hoping to suppress a scream when the moment came, but what was the point? The screams would surely come when they got to work on his fingers, for that particular procedure knew no bounds.

Then he felt it, two warm paws on his shoulders. As he braced himself for the downward shove, Zhong's shout woke him from his near-trance. 'Stop it! Stop it now!'

'Well, have you come to your senses?' said Lei. 'Are you prepared to talk now?'

'We will talk,' Zhong said. 'But you may not like what you hear.'

'I shall be the judge of that. Let him go.'

The guards released their grip on Yong. With all eyes on him and the stakes high, he felt his pulse picking up speed from its already elevated state. He stared at the ground and patted his clothes, buying time to let the anxiety subside. He focused on his promise to Yingxiu to remind himself this was about avenging a defenceless boy and seeking justice for a widow who had lost everything.

'How long do we have to wait, Young Master Liu?' said Lei. 'My patience is wearing thin.'

'Your Honour,' said Yong 'I … I request for permission to speak.'

Lei eyed Yong with disdain. 'You?'

'Yong will speak on my behalf,' said Zhong.

'You let a servant speak for you? This had better not be a prank, or I will deal with you too for contempt, son of an official or not.'

Zhong returned to his seat, his hands shaking. 'Go ahead, Yong.'

Yong took two steps back and adjusted his position to face the magistrate. 'First, the … the background. More than two weeks ago, in Renli, there was a case of a widow whose son had died of poisoning. Testimonies and the confession of the widow herself in court pointed to her killing the boy, her own son. You see, the poor woman had been in hardship for years. Her son had been … had been mentally disabled from birth and—'

'Why do I get the feeling this stuttering dimwit is stalling for time?'

'Please hear me out, Sir. This woman's husband had left her five years back to sit the Imperial examinations. A year later, she received news that he had died in a plague. The name of this widow is Li Yingxiu.'

Yong scanned the faces of the Duan household members as he spoke the last sentence. Duan stared in the direction of Zhong, his hands balling into fists. Guo resumed his examination of the ground. Mdm Duan's eyes were boring into Yong.

'A tragic little story,' said Lei. 'I am still waiting to hear the relevance to the matter at hand. Perhaps proper interrogation of the young master and his tongue-tied servant is still required.'

'A moment, Sir,' said Yong as Lei was beginning to lift his hand to call his men into action. 'From the widow, we found out her husband Sun Jie had stayed with a relative here, whose name was Guo Wutian.' Facing Guo, Yong added, 'That is your name, isn't it, Uncle Wu?'

Guo did not answer, though his body started to tremble. His master, Duan, squirmed in his seat. Mdm Duan, sitting poised and ramrod straight, looked at Yong with fire in her eyes. The magistrate raised his eyebrows and folded his arms across his chest.

Yong waited for a response. His breathing and heart rate were even, now that his mind was focused on the mission.

It was Mdm Duan who broke the silence. 'You are not telling us anything new. We know about Uncle Wu's background. He had told us of this relative who, as you said, had died. Nothing to do with us.'

Duan nodded.

'But it has quite a bit to do with you, Mdm Duan.' Yong turned to Lei. 'Your Honour, things got a lot more interesting once we tracked down Uncle Wu. Turns out Uncle Wu, having worked with the Duan family for a while, brought a relative into the business. This relative, a distant cousin, rose through the ranks in the firm. So impressed was Old Master Duan that he took this man as a son-in-law, who adopted the family name.'

'That *is* rather interesting,' said Lei. 'Are you saying …'

'Yes,' said Yong, who observed Mdm Duan tugging at her husband's forearm, 'I'm saying the relative is—'

'Impudence!' said Duan. 'Stop right this moment if you know what's good for you. I will have you dragged before the court and flayed for throwing baseless accusations at a prominent family and an official of the Imperial Court.'

'Calm, Master Duan, calm,' said Lei, smiling at Duan, arms still folded. 'Let the lad continue. Any claim would have to be substantiated. I, for one, am rather curious.' He paused to rest his hands on arms of his chair. 'Go on, boy.'

'The relative whom Guo brought into the business is, as we could all guess by now, Master Duan Shiyu, previously known as Sun Jie, the poor scholar from Renli who left his wife and son behind to pursue fame and fortune.'

Duan slapped his hand on the arm rest of his chair. 'A vicious lie. I am not this Sun Jie. You are guessing and have no proof.'

Yong had figured Duan's defence would be based on lack of proof, that if he stood his ground and denied everything, the allegations would not stick.

'But I do.' Yong reached into his pocket to fish out two pieces of paper and held them out in front of the magistrate. 'Sir, in my right hand is an accounting note written and signed off by the treasurer of the Duan Merchants, Master Duan Shiyu himself. It is a bit crumpled but you can see the stamp of his official seal.'

'You stole our document,' said Duan.

'"Steal" is too strong a word, Master Duan. Uncle Wu left his drawer open and I thought I'd borrow it, that's all. Your Honour, the one in my left hand is a letter I borrowed from Mdm Li, the widow. It was written by her husband, Sun Jie. See, the writing styles are similar.'

Lei leaned forward and squinted his eyes. 'The curves, ticks, and lines—distinctive and, for all intents and purposes, identical. Clearly written by the same person.'

'Give me that!' said Duan as he jumped up and reached out to grab the note in Yong's right hand. However, the younger man was too quick for him, and he could only grasp thin air as Yong retracted his arms.

'Master Duan, watch yourself!' said Lei, betraying his disdain for the merchant who bought his way into officialdom. 'This is no way for an official to behave.'

Chastised, Duan sat back down. The thick layer of make-up powder on Mdm Duan's face covered up any change in the colour of her complexion, though her ears were glowing pink and the intensity in her eyes grew.

'A most fascinating piece of evidence,' Lei said as he nodded, betraying a smile. 'In my court, and in any other, this would qualify as proof of identity. You are saying this Sun Jie came here from Renli, pronounced himself dead, and took on a new name to work for the Duan family.'

'Well, it was later that he faked his death, around the time of his marriage to Mdm Duan,' said Yong, stuffing the letters back into his pocket.

'Yes, of course, this makes sense. This Sun had to cut ties with his wife and child back home. Excellent. Most intriguing.'

'How much?' said Duan.

'What are you saying?' said Zhong.

Lei chuckled. 'What Master Duan is saying, Young Master Liu, is that he is opening the doors to do business. There is much to admire about your style, Master Duan. Bold and direct. Excellent indeed.' Even Yan broke into a smile.

Duan said to Zhong, 'And you. Did your father not give you authority to name a price?'

'We are not here to do a deal with you,' said Zhong.

'Spare me the holier-than-thou front. Your father is like the rest of them—just one in the lot of gold-diggers.'

Yan shot Duan an angry look. 'Mind your words, Master Duan.'

'No, no, Mr Yan,' said Lei, his face placid. 'It is quite all right. What we see here is Master Duan attempting to claw back some pride and dignity. Herein lies a lesson for us. We should never allow our egos to stand in the way of achieving important objectives. Keep our eyes on the prize.' He did not have to say that offending the accusers might cost Duan more in bribes, for that was not his concern.

'He is not,' said Yong.

'What did you say, boy?' said Duan.

'You cannot buy off Magistrate Liu with your dirty money.'

Duan snorted. 'I do not believe you came all the way here only to go back empty-handed. What else would a magistrate from Renli be after? Not like he's on the path to greatness, is he?' He switched his attention back to Zhong. 'Come off it. How much?'

You scumbag, thought Yong as he stared at Duan. *Let's see your haughtiness when I get to the interesting parts.*

'Don't do it, Yong,' said Zhong, who seemed to read Yong's thoughts.

Mistaking Yong and Zhong's lack of response for a climbdown, Duan pressed on with his perceived advantage. 'Do not think I cannot find a way out of this. Once I start handing out benefits, the court would not want to turn everything upside down for a penniless widow. I am sure the Honourable Magistrate Liu Ye can discern the logic in this regrettable matter and act according to the circumstances. Everybody wins.'

'Xiaodong,' said Yong.

'What?'

'Your son, remember? Does he mean anything to you?'

Duan said nothing.

Lei, thus far enjoying the show before him, decided it was time to settle down to the business end of the discussion. 'What say you, Young Master Liu? Shall we work on an arrangement that satisfies all parties?'

'What if, Sir,' said Yong, 'what if there's more?'

'More?'

The pink on Duan's face started ebbing away.

'Stay calm, Yong,' said Zhong. 'Wait for Old Master.'

It was as if the servant could not hear what his young master was saying.

'Yes, Your Honour, there is more,' said Yong, letting the words hang in the air. 'A whole lot more.'

Chapter Forty-Seven

The magistrate locked his narrowed eyes on Yong. 'Go on.'

'You see,' said Yong, 'we found out the widow had not administered the poison that killed her son. There was someone else, someone who had left tell-tale signs of his presence at the crime scene. This person is standing here—Guo Wutian.'

'Lies!' said Duan.

Guo raised his head, eyes wide open. His hands were now gripping the top of the chair in front of him, the knuckles turning white.

Yong looked into Guo's eyes. 'You were there, weren't you, Uncle Wu? You searched the whole house for letters pointing to you, leaving behind finger marks all over the place amongst the layers of dust. Reaching up to the top of the cupboard, you found a letter wrapped in cloth under the urn that was supposed to hold Sun Jie's ashes. You deposited imprints of your shoes in the woods behind the house, telling us the man responsible for the murder of Sun Xiaodong had a limp and a deformed left foot. Still, you did not manage to find the last letter you wrote to Mdm Li informing her of Sun Jie's death. How am I doing so far?'

Guo's mouth hung open, yet no words emerged from it.

Yong pressed on. 'That day, when I broke the wine bottle at your feet, the treasurer's note was not the only piece of evidence I collected. Your feet were wet with wine and you stomped around, hollering. It was then that I saw your shoeprints matched those we had found in the woods in Renli. We have kept a sketch of your precious and distinct left shoeprint back home. What's more, the assistant at the Qianxi Inn in Renli, the one who recognized your northern accent, will finger you out in an instant. Admit it.'

Duan reacted before Guo could. 'I ... we know nothing of this.'

'You see that, Uncle Wu?' said Yong. 'This is how your master repays you, by denying and betraying you. Speak up now before they throw you to the dogs. Tell us what you know.'

'But ...' Guo said, 'isn't she—'

'Silence!' shouted Duan.

'Come now, Master Duan,' said Yong. 'He was about to ask a valid question about Mdm Li being found guilty and locked up. Right, Uncle Wu? That was an act put up by Magistrate Liu to buy us time to investigate. Mdm Li is in fact well taken care of, resting in our guest house. The game is up, I'm afraid. Tell us now. Did you administer the poison that killed Sun Xiaodong?'

'I was ordered to,' Guo blurted out.

Duan sprang up on his feet and turned around to face Guo. He reached out in an attempt to grab his servant but was thwarted by a combination of Guo backing off in time and the barrier of the chair between them. Duan could only shout, 'Be careful of what you say, you fool!'

At the instruction of Lei, the two constables behind Guo stepped up. Duan saw that the opportunity to get to Guo was lost and slumped back into his seat.

'Your master is right,' said Yong. 'What you say is important. Now that your guilt has been established, your helpfulness to us could determine the severity of your punishment. Tell me, what were you instructed to do?'

Guo returned his gaze to the floor as though he was searching for guidance there. 'To go back to Master's hometown,' he said.

Duan and his wife glared at their servant.

'Mind your words, ingrate,' said Mdm Duan through gritted teeth, as if to emphasize her husband's warning. 'Watch what you're saying.'

Yong had to keep the momentum going. 'How did you know the way to the house?'

Guo fixed his eyes on his masters, frozen with fear and indecision.

'Uncle Wu, look at me,' said Yong. 'We have irrefutable evidence you had been to the house. Nobody would believe you found your way there by yourself. Not telling us the truth will only add to your crime. Tell me, who told you how to get to the house?'

'Master. It was Master Duan.'

With that admission, the dynamics of the situation altered, a spell broken. Duan started to stand, but a stern glare from the constable behind his seat told him in no uncertain terms of the futility of the move. He settled back down.

'Go on, Guo,' said Lei with a grin. 'Say more.'

'Master Duan told me how to reach the house through the woods. I had to wait for the right time.'

'How?' said Yong.

'He told me the woman and boy would go to town every few days. I hung around at the edge of town, on the route that led to the village, looking out for them. With the description given to me and the condition of the boy, they were not hard to spot. On the third day, I saw them going into town, and got on with it.'

'Got on with what?'

Guo cringed. 'Master Duan had instructed me to search for the letters in the house. I got one of them but could not find the one I wrote, the one to report the death. Master had told me about the hidden compartment in the bed. From there, I fished out a notebook and tore off a page that mentioned my name and address.'

'The poison. How did you do it?'

'I ... I smeared it on the ladle as Master instructed.'

'What else did you do?'

'That's all, I swear. Then I left town.'

'Not right away, though. You stayed behind for a while, didn't you? You had to make sure the job was done. Where were you? Inside the magistrate's compound?'

'No, no, outside.' Guo hung his head upon realizing he had let slip a bit too much. 'It was just outside the compound. None of this was my idea. All I did was to follow the plan given to me. What do I get from it but a world of woe?'

'After you went back to the inn, you left town straight away.'

Guo nodded.

Duan reached out to touch Lei's forearm. 'We made a deal.' It was, for Duan, one battle lost and off to the next, in a desperate bid to save himself.

'The circumstances have changed, Master Duan.'

'And so, the price has gone up, that's all.'

'Considerably.'

'Hand these boys over to me. Name your price.'

Lei stroked his chin and squinted his eyes, the beads of a mental abacus dancing in his head, performing calculations in his favour.

'May I remind you, Your Honour,' said Yong, 'that a roomful of people had seen us enter your premises as your guests. One other thing. You would recall we had a constable with us. We sent him away, to head home.'

Yong took out another piece of paper. 'He had with him a number of copies of this letter. All of them carry the same content: an outline of our findings and conclusions pointing to the guilt of Duan and Guo. Our constable was to keep one copy and hand the others to separate travellers going to or passing by Renli, with the promise of a reward for each letter delivered to Magistrate Liu Ye's office. It has been days. I think there is a good chance of at least one of the letters finding its way to its destination, don't you agree?'

Lei apparently did, for his eyes, thus far in the evening bright with the gratifying thoughts of growing profits, now dimmed with the look of defeat. With extortion and a deal with Magistrate Liu dead, gold had morphed into worthless dust. If he did not play this with utmost caution, he could even be dragged into trouble, the type that threatened careers.

As for Duan, he could see the situation for himself fast deteriorating. 'You can claim you had produced a hundred copies of this note and we would be none the wiser.'

'Magistrate Lei knows we have had no access to writing materials since we got here,' said Yong. 'If we had written one copy of this letter before coming here, I'm sure you would agree we could have written a few more.'

Lei did not say anything, so Yong decided to press on. 'Our findings will soon be in the hands of my master. Be sure he will not rest until justice is done.'

Still, the old fox was thinking, calculating, working out his strategy, though now it was on how to make the best of a losing position.

'Your Honour,' said Yong, 'I can understand the position you're in. For a case of mixed-up identities, you could gather all parties involved to work out an amicable solution. You had no idea it was going to be as grave a situation as murder. Now that you know, it is time for us to do what is right.'

Adviser Yan broke his silence. 'You insolent rascal, speaking to an official in this—' He was stopped by a hand held up by the magistrate.

'The lad has a valid point,' said Lei. 'Based on the indisputable evidence before me, there can only be one conclusion.'

'We have an agreement.' Duan was growling, anxious to get through to the official.

'No, we do not, Master Duan. I have nothing to do with your despicable deeds that injure Heaven and conscience. I will deal with the matter according to the facts and the law.'

'You gave me your word.'

'Say no more. I have decided and will not waver. Hand the note to me, lad.'

As Yong was about to pass the piece of paper to Lei, he saw, from the corner of his eye, Duan pulling out something shiny that had been strapped to his thigh, under his robe. Duan was getting up when Yong realized the object in his hand was a knife the length of a palm. Startled, Yong dropped the piece of paper in his hand and executed a half-turn to face Duan, ready to defend himself since he was now the object of the merchant's ire.

But something was wrong. Duan did not even look at Yong. He just got up and charged straight ahead. In a flash, Yong recalculated. Duan was not heading his way because he was just in front of Lei, who was well protected by constables. Hence, Duan had picked the next obvious target, the one sitting right opposite—Young Master Liu Zhong.

Yong darted forward and flung himself at the merchant, letting out a desperate and full-throated roar. He might have intended to divert Duan's attention, but there was little chance of that. Duan, raising his right hand over his head with the gleaming knife, was zeroing in on Zhong like a man possessed.

However, the drawing back of the knife did slow Duan down a touch, allowing Yong to crash into Duan and wrap both arms around him. The combination of the various forces in Duan's lunge and Yong's barge caused the interlocking pair to spin off course, and not a moment too soon. As the two of them twirled and Duan plunged the knife downwards, the blade swept within an inch of Zhong's raised arms. Indeed, Duan was so near his intended prey that his leg tripped over Zhong's. And thus, Yong and Duan, already teetering on the edge of stability, lost their balance and spun to the ground.

On the way down, Yong's back struck the arm of the empty chair right next to Zhong, delivering a sharp pain to his lower back and causing him to loosen his grip on Duan. The full weight of Duan crashed down on Yong as both of them hit the floor. Duan, his eyes wide like those of a madman, arched back again and drove the knife down, towards the left side of Yong's chest. Yong managed to catch his assailant's wrist but, in pain and short of strength, he could only push outwards, hoping to divert the weapon away from himself.

It was not enough. The blade tore into Yong's garment and sliced across the top of his left shoulder. Yong let out a cry, his grip loosening further. Duan lifted up the knife and plunge it down again, searching for Yong's heart. This time, a hand, that of Zhong, grabbed Duan's wrist. In rushing over, Zhong's momentum had allowed him to drag Duan's hand and knife upwards, pulling his arm so far back it must have hurt. Yet, a growling Duan refused to let go of the weapon, jabbing and slashing in random directions even as Zhong, also fallen to the ground, held on with both hands and Yong punched at Duan's plump face and thick neck.

By this time, all in attendance were on their feet, staring at the chaotic scene in front of them in astonishment.

'Don't just stand there!' said Mdm Duan to Guo. 'Do something!'

Guo moved almost by instinct to the command, but do what exactly? Restrain his master? Or help him commit murder right in front of law enforcement officials? The two constables on his sides relieved him of the dilemma. Confused though they were, the constables also intuited that, in such a tense setting, nobody should be allowed sudden movements. They closed in on Guo, at once stopping him from moving forward.

For a moment, the two constables guarding Zhong remained stunned, unsure whether to come down on the merchant whom they had known as their master's ally, or their young captives. In the ensuing confusion, Lei's shouted order provided much-needed clarity. 'Remove the weapon!'

The objective as handed down by the magistrate was now clear, but the method by which to achieve it, much less so. The three bodies on the ground writhed and rolled about with the one to be disarmed wedged in between the two young men. As soon as any of the constables spotted an opening through which to strike with the poles in their hands, rapid movements in random directions would just as quickly close the gap. Hitting the wrong person would tilt the precarious balance towards the aggressor and send the blade into Yong.

As it was, Duan was getting closer. Zhong heaved with all his might but could not overcome the force of Duan's madness. As the sharp blade inched an erratic course downwards, Zhong had to take a chance. Steadying himself, he jerked his body up, ceding some tension on Duan's wrist. The knife dipped dangerously, penetrating cloth and skin on Yong's left chest. Grimacing in pain, the young man managed to push Duan's hand up by an inch or so, though a crimson flower the size of a large coin still seeped through Yong's garment.

Thereby creating some space between him and the assailant, Zhong tucked in his right knee and pressed it on the lower back of Duan, who hissed as if vitality accompanied the air squeezed out of him. His arm was dragged further back and his body arched at an awkward angle, exposing his right flank. At this point, with the knife released from Duan's grip and dropping to the floor with a clatter, it was evident the battle was over.

To bestow finality on the merchant's defeat, the more alert of the pair of constables standing by closed in, pulled his pole back, and jabbed it into Duan's unprotected side. The end of the pole connected with a thud, drawing an animalistic cry of anguish. Strength gushed out of Duan as water would from a smashed earthen tub. Yong felt his assailant's body go limp.

'What is going on here?' came a shout like thunder in an authoritative, unfamiliar voice. Even as Yong and Zhong, with a blend of push and drag, were flipping Duan over, Yong angled his head to face the direction of the voice.

It was from another official rounding the corner of the residence building, flanked by men in the distinctive maroon uniform of Imperial guards. The black formal cap and matching, smooth robe with stitched floral patterns announced the official's high rank. Heavy brows and steely eyes lent him a stern appearance accentuated by a long, flowing black beard. Imperious in bearing, he strode towards the gathering. Amidst the confusion, those in his path stepped aside to let him through.

Despite the stinging pain in his left shoulder, Yong's heart overflowed with joy the moment he eyed the next person emerging from around the corner, a few steps behind. In his official garments and with the distinct furrows of concern on his forehead was the one he and Zhong had been longing to see—his Old Master, Magistrate Liu Ye.

Chapter Forty-Eight

Lei and Yan were the first to react. 'Our respectful greetings to Justice Hou!' the magistrate and his adviser said in unison, holding up clasped hands and bowing. Mdm Duan and Guo stood in a daze.

Zhong helped Yong up, the latter clutching his left shoulder. It took three constables to pick up a groaning Duan off the floor.

'Father,' Zhong called out as Magistrate Liu nodded towards him and came over to examine Yong's shoulder.

'How is your injury?'

Yong smiled despite the pain. 'Just a surface wound, Sir.'

By then, three others had also rounded the corner of the building. The wife of Magistrate Liu and Constable Niu were propping up the frail figure of Yingxiu.

Madam left Yingxiu's side to scurry over to the young men, worry etched on her face. 'How are you, child?'

The words Madam uttered must have been meant for her son, Yong thought, but she was looking straight at him, not Zhong. For a moment, Yong was too stunned to speak.

'Are you all right?' Madam said, tenderness mixed with anxiety. 'Say something, Yong.'

'I ... I'm fine, Madam. It is only a scratch. Please do not let your heart be troubled.'

Out came a white silk handkerchief that Madam held out to Yong. 'Take this,' she said.

Yong hesitated, clasping Madam's pristine personal item in his hand. She had to guide his hand to press on the wound with the handkerchief before going to Zhong, holding both his hands with hers.

'What is this about, Magistrate Lei?' asked Justice Hou after he had ascertained that Yong's injury was not serious.

'Your Excellency, please forgive me for not receiving you personally. You have come at the right time,' said Lei as he picked up the written outline of Yong's investigation findings from the floor. 'I am pleased to report that we have interrogated the criminal Duan Shiyu and extracted a confession of murder.'

'Quite an elaborate set-up you have here. Who was dishing out the interrogation and who was on the receiving end, I wonder? This had better not be another one of your dastardly schemes.'

'No, Sir. I would not dream of it.'

Justice Hou smiled at Yong. 'You are Liu Yong? Your master has told me a great deal about you. I have read the letter you sent out through Constable Niu. Good work, young man.'

'Thank you, Sir. Young Master Liu Zhong, Constable Niu, and I—we did it together.'

'Good. Is it true Duan Shiyu has confessed?'

'His assistant—this man Guo Wutian—has confessed to being directed by his master to commit the murder of Sun Xiaodong. When we laid out the evidence on Duan, he attacked Young Master Liu in an act of pure desperation, confirming his guilt.'

Yingxiu approached the front, step by agonizing step, helped by Niu.

'Mdm Li,' said Magistrate Liu, 'do you recognize this man? Is he your husband Sun Jie?'

Yingxiu locked her tear-filled eyes on Duan, who turned his face away.

'Why?' said Yingxiu. 'He was your son, your own flesh and blood.' It looked like she wanted to say more but, overwhelmed by emotions, all she could do was wipe away her tears with her sleeves. Madam, pulling her son along by the hand, returned to Yingxiu's side to offer consolation.

Justice Hou jabbed his finger at Duan. 'Face of a man, heart of a beast. What more have you to say for yourself? Nothing? Men, take this beast in human clothing and his lap dog away. I will deal with both of you as you deserve.'

'Hold on, Sir,' said Yong.

'What is it?'

'There is still some unfinished business. Before we came here, I just had an inkling, so I did not write it in the letter. After our visit to the Duan compound, I realized I might have made a mistake. When an old lady working for the Duans told me earlier that Guo always followed his one master around, I had assumed the one master was Duan Shiyu. I was wrong.

'At the Duan storehouse, Young Master had manufactured an excuse to make Guo go to his boss to check on a deal. I thought he would walk across the big building, to the administrative wing, to confer with Master Duan. But, no, he came back too quickly. You see, he was not checking with Master Duan who was, as we can see from the note I borrowed from Guo, just the treasurer, the person who handled the finances. The one who made the real decisions, and who was then in the middle of the storehouse, was Mdm Duan. The one master the old lady mentioned was not Master Duan but Mdm Duan, the favourite daughter of the patriarch.

'This evening, as I started to talk about Master Duan abandoning his former family, Mdm Duan's comment was illuminating. Before her husband could speak out, her first reaction was to explain away the story. As a wife, she should at least be curious about what I had to say, shouldn't she?'

Justice Hou and Magistrate Liu nodded.

'She knew,' said Yong. 'She has known for some time. Neither was she an innocent bystander, it seems. When I was questioning Guo, she repeated a warning from her husband for Guo to watch his words, which appeared superfluous but was not. She was reminding Guo not to implicate *her*. Hence, I would like to ask Guo one more question that I have thus far not asked because I had committed the error of presumption. Guo Wutian, who ordered you to kill Mdm Li and Xiaodong?'

Guo, with a constable holding tightly to this left arm, stood with his jaw slack.

'Speak up, criminal!' said Justice Hou. 'Tell us the truth or face the double wrath of the law. Did Mdm Duan order you to murder Mdm Li and her son?'

Guo nodded twice and hung his head low.

'Ingrate!' said Mdm Duan, her voice shaking. 'Messing up the job and now pointing fingers at your masters. Useless fool you are.'

'A fool indeed,' said Guo with a choking voice. 'I should never have listened to both of you.'

'How dare you—'

'Quiet, woman,' said Duan. 'It's all over, can't you see? None of this would have happened if that sickly father of yours had not yearned for some silly respectability for the family.'

'You were slow to accept the nomination, were you? If I had not overheard you and this old ingrate talking about solving the problem, I would not have known about this woman and the degenerate seed you had left behind.'

'I did not order the murder.'

'Oh, no, you did not have the guts to. Being the indecisive weakling that you are, you just went along with it. Did anyone compel you to supply the details of your old house and this woman's habits?'

Duan said nothing.

'We have heard enough,' said Justice Hou. 'What an utterly vile household. Men, get these criminals out of here.'

Chapter Forty-Nine

The mood was sombre as Justice Hou's men marched the Duan household out of the yard.

Yong walked over to Yingxiu.

'You have kept your promise,' Yingxiu said, eyes glistening with tears.

'You need not have come.'

'I had to see my son's murderer face to face. When Constable Niu told us what you had found out, I could not believe my ears. His own flesh and blood!'

'Come,' said Madam to Yingxiu while still clinging to Zhong, 'let us take our leave. You need to rest.'

As the delegation prepared to depart, Lei cosied up to Justice Hou. 'Let me accompany you out, Your Excellency.'

'Save it. You are not off the hook yet. Be sure that if I find out you had been up to no good, I will come after you. Let us see how your benefactor, the mountain you lean on, is able to shield you then. Good night.'

Justice Hou turned and strode off, the rest of his retinue following. After issuing instructions to Zhong to take care of Madam, Magistrate Liu signalled for Yong to come with him as he kept just a step behind Justice Hou.

'How are you feeling?' asked Magistrate Liu with a warm smile.

'I'm fine, Sir. Good thing you came in time.'

Justice Hou laughed and slowed down to allow the magistrate and his assistant to close up to his right and left.

'It sure looked like you had it all sewn up,' said Justice Hou. 'More like we came in time to witness the last notes of your opus.'

Magistrate Liu nodded. 'When I told Justice Hou about the case, he realized the difficulties you would face here and suggested we set off for the Capital right away. We pressed on as quickly as possible but there was a limit to how hard we could push Mdm Li. Four days ago, Niu joined up with us. Once we entered the city, we came here straight away. Justice Hou reckoned that even if we did not find you here, he could at least restrain Magistrate Lei. When we arrived and saw the commotion outside the gates, we knew something was not right.'

As they emerged from the compound, Yong saw the cause of the commotion, and grinned. Wild Wolf smiled back. He was standing in the midst of sixteen of his men, some holding flaming torches, facing off a small band of constables. Yong went up to Wild Wolf while Justice Hou ordered Lei's men to stand down.

Wild Wolf placed his left hand on the young man's uninjured right shoulder. 'Glad to see you again. I see you managed to collect nice souvenirs from your stay with the dog official. I saw the merchant and his entourage being led out. Well done.'

'Thank you for what you have done for us.'

'Not at all. Now that our work here is completed, we ought to go. Till we meet again, Brother Yong.' Wild Wolf then faced Justice Hou and Magistrate Liu, held up clasped hands and said, 'Farewell, Justice Hou.' It was as much respect as he would accord an official, on account of the righteous reputation of the Chief Censor, who nodded his acknowledgement.

As Wild Wolf and his men trooped off, Yong went back to his master's side.

'Your methods are rather unconventional, young man,' said Justice Hou. 'But they seem to work.'

After instructing his men to bring the Lius and Yingxiu back to his residence, the Chief Censor made his way to his own sedan. Magistrate Liu followed to send him off and Yong tagged along, as was his wont when his old master was around.

'You know, Magistrate Liu,' said Justice Hou, 'I did not quite believe it when you told me how this young man with no proper education has been helping you. Now, I see it with my own eyes. Remarkable.'

'Your Excellency, have you thought about my proposal?'

'Proposal? Oh, that.'

'Yes, Sir. Yong is a capable young man who learns fast. He will be of good use to you. I am sure of it.'

'Old Master, I don't—'

'Hush, Yong. Do not speak out of turn.'

'Come, now,' said Justice Hou. 'Let the young man speak his mind. This is about his future, after all. Go on, Yong.'

Yong took a moment to compose his thoughts and the next few words. 'I am young, incompetent, and have much to learn. I fear the weighty matters in Your Excellency's august office will find me out.'

'Pray do not listen to him,' said Magistrate Liu. 'He will come to his senses after he thinks it over.' The magistrate turned to Yong. 'And you will come to the right conclusion. Any man would consider it a great honour to work for Justice Hou. There is no better way to serve the country and His Majesty, the Emperor.'

The Chief Censor burst into laughter, the heartiest of the evening. 'I suspect, Magistrate Liu, that young Liu Yong has not revealed the real reason why he prefers to stay where he is. It looks like my trip has been a most fruitful one. I have found two servants of the Kingdom, loyal and able. Fruitful indeed.' With that, Justice Hou prepared to enter his sedan, one of his men having pulled aside the ornate curtain that covered the entrance.

'Your Excellency,' said Magistrate Liu, 'you will consider the proposal, will you not?'

'I will, my good magistrate,' said Justice Hou, looking back at the magistrate and his assistant while stroking the full length of his long beard. 'I most certainly will.'